Margaritas at
The Beach House Hotel

Judith Keim

BOOKS BY JUDITH KEIM

THE HARTWELL WOMEN SERIES:
The Talking Tree – 1
Sweet Talk – 2
Straight Talk – 3
Baby Talk – 4
The Hartwell Women – Boxed Set

THE BEACH HOUSE HOTEL SERIES:
Breakfast at The Beach House Hotel – 1
Lunch at The Beach House Hotel – 2
Dinner at The Beach House Hotel – 3
Christmas at The Beach House Hotel – 4
Margaritas at The Beach House Hotel – 5
Dessert at The Beach House Hotel – 6
Coffee at The Beach House Hotel – 7 (2023)
High Tea at The Beach House Hotel – 8 (2024)

THE FAT FRIDAYS GROUP:
Fat Fridays – 1
Sassy Saturdays – 2
Secret Sundays – 3

THE SALTY KEY INN SERIES:
Finding Me – 1
Finding My Way – 2
Finding Love – 3
Finding Family – 4
The Salty Key Inn Series . Boxed Set

THE CHANDLER HILL INN SERIES:
Going Home – 1
Coming Home – 2
Home at Last – 3
The Chandler Hill Inn Series – Boxed Set

SEASHELL COTTAGE BOOKS:
A Christmas Star
Change of Heart
A Summer of Surprises
A Road Trip to Remember
The Beach Babes

THE DESERT SAGE INN SERIES:
The Desert Flowers – Rose – 1
The Desert Flowers – Lily – 2
The Desert Flowers – Willow – 3
The Desert Flowers – Mistletoe and Holly – 4

SOUL SISTERS AT CEDAR MOUNTAIN LODGE:
Christmas Sisters – Anthology
Christmas Kisses
Christmas Castles
Christmas Stories – Soul Sisters Anthology
Christmas Joy

THE SANDERLING COVE INN SERIES:
Waves of Hope – 1
Sandy Wishes – 2 (2023)
Salty Kisses – 3 (2023)

THE LILAC LAKE INN SERIES
Love by Design – (2023)
Love Between the Lines – (2023)
Love Under the Stars – (2024)

OTHER BOOKS:

The ABC's of Living With a Dachshund
Once Upon a Friendship – Anthology
Winning BIG – a little love story for all ages
Holiday Hopes
The Winning Tickets (2023)

For more information:
www.judithkeim.com

PRAISE FOR JUDITH KEIM'S NOVELS

THE BEACH HOUSE HOTEL SERIES

"Love the characters in this series. This series was my first introduction to Judith Keim. She is now one of my favorites. Looking forward to reading more of her books."

BREAKFAST AT THE BEACH HOUSE HOTEL is an easy, delightful read that offers romance, family relationships, and strong women learning to be stronger. Real life situations filter through the pages. Enjoy!"

LUNCH AT THE BEACH HOUSE HOTEL – "This series is such a joy to read. You feel you are actually living with them. Can't wait to read the latest one."

DINNER AT THE BEACH HOUSE HOTEL – "A Terrific Read! As usual, Judith Keim did it again. Enjoyed immensely. Continue writing such pleasantly reading books for all of us readers."

CHRISTMAS AT THE BEACH HOUSE HOTEL – "Not Just Another Christmas Novel. This is book number four in the series and my introduction to Judith Keim's writing. I wasn't disappointed. The characters are dimensional and engaging. The plot is well crafted and advances at a pleasing pace. The Florida location is interesting and warming. It was a delight to read a romance novel with mature female protagonists. Ann and Rhoda have life experiences that enrich the story. It's a clever book about friends and extended family. Buy copies for your book group pals and enjoy this seasonal read."

MARGARITAS AT THE BEACH HOUSE HOTEL – "What a wonderful series. I absolutely loved this book and can't wait for the next book to come out. There was even suspense in it. Thanks Judith for the great stories."

"Overall, Margaritas at the Beach House Hotel is another wonderful addition to the series. Judith Keim takes the reader on a journey told through the voices of these amazing characters we have all come to love through the years! I truly cannot stress enough how good this book is, and I hope you enjoy it as much as I have!"

THE HARTWELL WOMEN SERIES:

"This was an EXCELLENT series. When I discovered Judith Keim, I read all of her books back to back. I thoroughly enjoyed the women Keim has written about. They are believable and you want to just jump into their lives and be their friends! I can't wait for any upcoming books!"

"I fell into Judith Keim's Hartwell Women series and have read & enjoyed all of her books in every series. Each centers around a strong & interesting woman character and their family interaction. Good reads that leave you wanting more."

THE FAT FRIDAYS GROUP :

"Excellent story line for each character, and an insightful representation of situations which deal with some of the contemporary issues women are faced with today."

"I love this author's books. Her characters and their lives are realistic. The power of women's friendships is a common and beautiful theme that is threaded throughout this story."

THE SALTY KEY INN SERIES

FINDING ME – "I thoroughly enjoyed the first book in this series and cannot wait for the others! The characters are endearing with the same struggles we all encounter. The setting makes me feel like I am a guest at The Salty Key

Inn...relaxed, happy & light-hearted! The men are yummy and the women strong. You can't get better than that! Happy Reading!"

FINDING MY WAY- *"Loved the family dynamics as well as uncertain emotions of dating and falling in love. Appreciated the morals and strength of parenting throughout. Just couldn't put this book down."*

FINDING LOVE – *"I waited for this book because the first two was such good reads. This one didn't disappoint.... Judith Keim always puts substance into her books. This book was no different, I learned about PTSD, accepting oneself, there is always going to be problems but stick it out and make it work. Just the way life is. In some ways a lot like my life. Judith is right, it needs another book and I will definitely be reading it. Hope you choose to read this series, you will get so much out of it."*

FINDING FAMILY – *"Completing this series is like eating the last chip. Love Judith's writing, and her female characters are always smart, strong, vulnerable to life and love experiences."*

"This was a refreshing book. Bringing the heart and soul of the family to us."

THE CHANDLER HILL INN SERIES

GOING HOME – *"I absolutely could not put this book down. Started at night and read late into the middle of the night. As a child of the '60s, the Vietnam war was front and center so this resonated with me. All the characters in the book were so well developed that the reader felt like they were friends of the family."*

"I was completely immersed in this book, with the beautiful descriptive writing, and the authors' way of

bringing her characters to life. I felt like I was right inside her story."

COMING HOME – "Coming Home is a winner. The characters are well-developed, nuanced and likable. Enjoyed the vineyard setting, learning about wine growing and seeing the challenges Cami faces in running and growing a business. I look forward to the next book in this series!"

"Coming Home was such a wonderful story. The author has a gift for getting the reader right to the heart of things."

HOME AT LAST – "In this wonderful conclusion, to a heartfelt and emotional trilogy set in Oregon's stunning wine country, Judith Keim has tied up the Chandler Hill series with the perfect bow."

"Overall, this is truly a wonderful addition to the Chandler Hill Inn series. Judith Keim definitely knows how to perfectly weave together a beautiful and heartfelt story."

"The storyline has some beautiful scenes along with family drama. Judith Keim has created characters with interactions that are believable and some of the subjects the story deals with are poignant."

SEASHELL COTTAGE BOOKS

A CHRISTMAS STAR – "Love, laughter, sadness, great food, and hope for the future, all in one book. It doesn't get any better than this stunning read."

"A Christmas Star is a heartwarming Christmas story featuring endearing characters. So many Christmas books are set in snowbound places...it was a nice change to read a Christmas story that takes place on a warm sandy beach!" Susan Peterson

CHANGE OF HEART – *"CHANGE OF HEART is the summer read we've all been waiting for. Judith Keim is a master at creating fascinating characters that are simply irresistible. Her stories leave you with a big smile on your face and a heart bursting with love."*

Kellie Coates Gilbert, author of the popular Sun Valley Series

A SUMMER OF SURPRISES – *"The story is filled with a roller coaster of emotions and self-discovery. Finding love again and rebuilding family relationships."*

"Ms. Keim uses this book as an amazing platform to show that with hard emotional work, belief in yourself and love, the scars of abuse can be conquered. It in no way preaches, it's a lovely story with a happy ending."

"The character development was excellent. I felt I knew these people my whole life. The story development was very well thought out I was drawn [in] from the beginning."

THE DESERT SAGE INN SERIES:

THE DESERT FLOWERS – ROSE – *"The Desert Flowers - Rose, is the first book in the new series by Judith Keim. I always look forward to new books by Judith Keim, and this one is definitely a wonderful way to begin The Desert Sage Inn Series!"*

"In this first of a series, we see each woman come into her own and view new beginnings even as they must take this tearful journey as they slowly lose a dear friend. This is a very well written book with well-developed and likable main characters. It was interesting and enlightening as the first portion of this saga unfolded. I very much enjoyed this book and I do recommend it"

"Judith Keim is one of those authors that you can always depend on to give you a great story with fantastic

characters. I'm excited to know that she is writing a new series and after reading book 1 in the series, I can't wait to read the rest of the books."!

THE DESERT FLOWERS – LILY – *"The second book in the Desert Flowers series is just as wonderful as the first. Judith Keim is a brilliant storyteller. Her characters are truly lovely and people that you want to be friends with as soon as you start reading. Judith Keim is not afraid to weave real life conflict and loss into her stories. I loved reading Lily's story and can't wait for Willow's!*

"The Desert Flowers-Lily is the second book in The Desert Sage Inn Series by author Judith Keim. When I read the first book in the series, The Desert Flowers-Rose, I knew this series would exceed all of my expectations and then some. Judith Keim is an amazing author, and this series is a testament to her writing skills and her ability to completely draw a reader into the world of her characters."

THE DESERT FLOWERS – WILLOW – *"The feelings of love, joy, happiness, friendship, family and the pain of loss are deeply felt by Willow Sanchez and her two cohorts Rose and Lily. The Desert Flowers met because of their deep feelings for Alec Thurston, a man who touched their lives in different ways.*

Once again, Judith Keim has written the story of a strong, competent, confident and independent woman. Willow, like Rose and Lily can handle tough situations. All the characters are written so that the reader gets to know them but not all the characters will give the reader warm and fuzzy feelings.

The story is well written and from the start you will be pulled in. There is enough backstory that a reader can start here but I assure you, you'll want to learn more. There is an ocean of emotions that will make you smile, cringe, tear up or outright cry. I loved this book as I loved books one and two. I am thrilled that the Desert Flowers story will continue. I highly recommend this book to anyone who enjoys books with strong women."

Margaritas at The Beach House Hotel

The Beach House Hotel Series
Book 5

Judith Keim

Wild Quail Publishing

Margaritas at The Beach House Hotel is a work of fiction. Names, characters, places, public or private institutions, corporations, towns, and incidents are the product of the author's imagination or are used fictitiously. Any resemblance to actual events, locales, or persons, living or dead, is coincidental.

No part of *Margaritas at The Beach House Hotel* may be reproduced or transmitted in any form or by any electronic or mechanical means, including information storage and retrieval systems, without permission in writing from the author, except by a reviewer who may quote brief passages in a review. This book may not be resold or uploaded for distribution to others. For permissions contact the author directly via electronic mail:

wildquail.pub@gmail.com

www.judithkeim.com

Published in the United States of America by:

Wild Quail Publishing
PO Box 171332
Boise, ID 83717-1332

ISBN# 978-1-954325-04-3

Dedication

To my friends on my special Facebook Page – Women
with Heart! I appreciate you all so much!

CHAPTER ONE

R eady?" asked my business partner, Rhonda DelMonte Grayson, on this early April morning on the Gulf Coast of Florida.

I stopped typing on the computer and turned to her with a grin. "As ready as I ever will be."

Wearing a yellow caftan that went with her hair, Rhonda waved me up and out of my chair with a grin that lit her face and had her dark eyes sparkling. "Then let's get this show on the road! It's not every day a vice president visits The Beach House Hotel."

I rose and looped my arm through Rhonda's, and we headed out to the front lobby to greet the latest VIP to come to our upscale hotel.

As we stepped outside to wait for our guest, the spring day greeted us with a kiss of sunny warmth. A soft breeze bobbed the colorful blossoms on the hibiscus bushes that lined the front of the hotel, softening the edges of the pink-stucco, two-story building that stood like royalty at the water's sandy edge.

"Seems like old times, huh?" said Rhonda, grinning at me as we approached the entrance.

"I'll say." Five years ago, when we'd first opened the hotel, Rhonda and I had greeted our guests like this at the front steps of the hotel, welcoming them personally as much as possible. Hospitality, discretion, and service were the three things we still relied upon to maintain the hotel's fine reputation. A warm welcome to the property was a must.

I studied her. When I'd first met Rhonda, I'd thought the

large, colorful, bossy woman, who said exactly what was on her mind and had no sense of private space, was completely overwhelming. I'd thought I'd never make it through my first visit to her seaside estate—a visit made to please my daughter, Liz, who roomed at college with Rhonda's daughter, Angela.

Now, even though my strict upbringing with my grandmother in Boston sometimes made me shudder at what came out of Rhonda's mouth, I loved her like the sister I never had. And I'd learned her heart was as big as her irrepressible spirit. Rhonda nudged me. "Here she comes!"

I ran a hand through my shoulder-length dark hair, flicked a speck of dust off my bright-blue suit jacket that matched my eyes, and drew a deep breath.

We headed down the front stairs of the hotel as a black limousine followed a large, black SUV through the gates of the hotel and drew up to the front circle. As soon as the limousine came to a stop, three different people, two men and a woman, Secret Service agents, I presumed, jumped out of the SUV and assessed their surroundings before the woman went over to the limousine and stood outside the back door. One of the men faced out to the road while the other climbed the stairs to the hotel and stood guard there. Then a somber-looking man stepped out of the front of the limo and stood a moment, scanning the area. Satisfied, he stood by as the female agent outside the limo opened the back door, and Vice President Amelia Swanson prepared to climb out of the car.

A tall, striking woman in her late 40s with chestnut brown hair and blue eyes noted for missing nothing, Amelia Swanson stepped out of the limousine and smiled as she walked forward to meet us.

"Welcome to The Beach House Hotel, Madame Vice President," I said, holding out my hand. "I'm Ann Sanders, one of the hotel's owners."

Strong fingers gripped my hand. "Very glad to meet you and to be here." She turned to Rhonda. "And you must be Ms. Grayson."

"Yes. We're honored to have you stay with us," said Rhonda, looking as if she didn't know whether to curtsey or not.

"Let's go inside where we can talk privately," Amelia said.

"Please, come in." I took her elbow and led her up the steps. The security agent who'd stood by the door headed indoors while another followed at our heels.

Behind me, I noticed the female guard pacing outside the limousine and wondered who or what she was protecting.

We entered the hotel.

"Come this way," said Rhonda.

She led us to the small, private dining room we used for confidential gatherings. Sound-proofed, it had housed many private discussions that never left the room.

The vice president waited for one of the agents to finish his visual sweep of the interior, and then she motioned both men to stay back before closing the door, leaving the three of us alone in the room.

"Would you like a seat?" I asked, a little confused by all that was happening.

"No, thank you," she said, smiling. "I've been sitting for a while and need to stretch my legs." She studied Rhonda and turned to me. "What I'm about to tell you can go no further. Understand?"

Rhonda and I glanced at each other and spoke together. "Yes. We do."

"I won't be staying here but will instead be secretly traveling to Central America to try and rescue a woman from a revolutionary group that's been holding her prisoner. I made the reservation here at the hotel because you're known for being discreet. Tina Marks, that fabulous actress, credits the two of you with saving her life. So, if newspaper reporters ask about my staying here, it won't seem out of the ordinary for you to decline to give out any information. A woman running from domestic abuse will be using my reservation in my place."

"I see ..." I began, but she held up her hand to stop me.

"This woman is my sister and the wife of the president's brother."

I felt my breath leave me in a rush and gripped Rhonda's arm.

"Oh my God! I read about her in the newspaper," gasped Rhonda. "It's a terrible story of abuse."

"You understand how important it is that no one, not even other members of the family, know where she is or what I'm about to do on a secret mission for the government."

"Not even the president?" Rhonda asked, wide-eyed.

"Definitely not him, though he knows, of course, that I'm pretending to be here and where I'm going," Amelia explained. "The president thinks my sister's recuperating in total privacy at their home in Vermont while her husband is in a rehab program in California. See why this is so important?"

I nodded silently, wondering what would happen if we failed. Lives were being placed in our hands. I recalled that Amelia's sister had met her husband on the campaign trail a couple of years ago. Their wedding had been the romantic story of the year. What on earth had happened?

"We're gonna take good care of your sister. What happened to her shouldn't happen to any woman. Right, Annie?" said Rhonda, elbowing me.

"Absolutely. I understand what a difficult situation this must be for everyone, but we'll do everything you ask. We've seen many people come and go at the hotel, heard many stories, and helped many people in various positions. We routinely have VIPs here at the hotel who need discretion," I assured the vice president. "Our staff is trained to protect privacy."

Amelia let out a long breath. "Okay, then. I've announced I'm taking a private vacation. My sister, Lindsay Thaxton, and I look enough alike to be twins, which is why people might not question my 'supposed' presence here. You have her placed in the private home here, correct?" she asked, looking at me.

"Yes. She'll be staying in the guesthouse on the property as you requested."

"My trip shouldn't last more than a week. During that time, Lindsay will decide if she wants to continue staying here or find another place to hide until things calm down. The president isn't happy about the situation, but there's no way I could let Lindsay remain vulnerable to that brute of a husband of hers. Now that she's filed for divorce, she still needs protection."

Amelia Swanson's history was much like her sister's. Married to a wealthy man who'd mistreated her, Amelia made her escape and began a foundation for abused women. A reputation for speaking out and holding steady helped her build a political career. Nearing fifty and single, she was known as a formidable woman who didn't take bullshit from anyone, not even Edward Thaxton, the president of the United States.

"Is there anything special we should do for your sister ... you ... while she's here?" I asked.

"A young woman I trust from past Secret Service experience will be staying with Lindsay in the house. She can be a confidential source of communication for you. Both of you come with me, and I'll introduce you to them."

"Would it be better if we met them at the house to avoid drawing attention to your sister or her companion?" I asked.

The vice president settled her blue-eyed gaze on me. "Good idea. As you can imagine, Lindsay's a little skittish anyway."

"Don't worry, we'll see that she's well taken care of," said Rhonda. "I've read the stories about it all, and I promise no frickin' rat bastard will ever treat her like that again."

Amelia's eyes widened, and then she laughed. "I like you two as much as everyone said I would."

Rhonda and I accompanied Amelia back to the limousine. She and the agents smoothly disappeared inside, leaving us with two other guards—the man and woman we'd seen now walked beside the limo as it began to roll along the front circle and over to the guesthouse.

Originally a caretaker's cottage that I'd transformed into a small but comfortable home, the house had served as a private retreat for my husband, Vaughn, and me for a time before we moved off the hotel property. Then it was turned over to the hotel as a unique, private accommodation for VIP guests. Nestled and nearly hidden among the greenery in a corner of the property, it was the perfect place for Lindsay Thaxton to hide.

We met the limousine in the guesthouse driveway and waited while the Secret Service did a quick check around the area before signaling me to open the door to the house.

I unlocked the door and stood aside as one of the bodyguards checked the interior. At a thumbs-up sign from him, the vice president stepped out of the car and turned to help her sister.

Lindsay Thaxton emerged and stared at her surroundings. So thin that she seemed a fragile china doll, she looked like a much more vulnerable version of her older sister. They shared brown hair, blue eyes, and facial features, but there the similarity ended. Lindsay's hunched shoulders, the way she glanced around nervously, and the trembling of her lips presented a much different woman from her take-charge, confident sister. After they'd entered the house and surveyed each room, Lindsay gave a slight nod of approval. "This is lovely. I'll be comfortable here."

As Lindsay stepped out to the lanai with Rhonda, I caught hold of the vice president's arm. "We'll have to tell a few others on the hotel staff and in our families about Lindsay. Rhonda and I are slowly introducing our daughters, Liz Bowen and Angela Smythe, to our business in the hopes they will someday assume duties here. We want them to know what's going on, along with Bernhard Bruner, our general manager. And, both our husbands are trustworthy. It would be awkward if they didn't know. Especially because of the time we'll commit to keeping Lindsay safe."

The vice president's smile was a little sheepish. "Oh, yes. I should have told you. We've done background checks on your families and all the staff here. It will, however, be up to you and Rhonda to control the information and help keep my sister secure. Failure is unacceptable." Her steady gaze unnerved me, but I dutifully bobbed my head. Rhonda and I had had to deal with a lot of challenges. Indeed, we could meet this one. Couldn't we?

CHAPTER TWO

Later, after the vice president had bid her sister goodbye and Lindsay and the woman assigned to protect her had unpacked, Rhonda and I met with them to go over the protocol we should observe during their stay.

I was pleased to see a little more color had entered Lindsay's cheeks. In time, I hoped the lines of stress that marred her beauty would disappear. Studying her more closely, I could see the pale yellow of bruises on her cheeks and noticed the off-center position of her nose. The news stories had told of physical abuse, but I hadn't realized it was so severe. One arm was still in a cast. It was disturbing to see how her husband had brutalized her.

Debra McDonald, the woman assigned to protect her, was of medium height and clearly worked out. Now dressed in shorts and a T-shirt, the muscles in her arms and legs were well-defined. Dark-brown curly hair cut short surrounded a face with strong features and light-brown eyes that drilled into you, making her appear intimidating.

"We want you to know that you will be safe here, Lindsay," said Rhonda. "Only a few people will know you're staying with us, and we're ready to provide you with any service you need right here at the house."

"Bernhard Bruner, Bernie, is the general manager, and he's as trustworthy as they come," I said. "Ana, our head of housekeeping, will be the only one to see to the cleaning of the house unless she notifies you with the name of another staff member."

Debra nodded her agreement. "As few staff members as possible should be admitted into the house."

"Our daughters, Liz Bowen and Angela Smythe, will also know the details."

"Yes, I'm aware of that," said Debra. "I received a full report."

"Is there anything we can get you now?" I asked. "The refrigerator and cupboards have been stocked as Amelia requested."

Debra turned to Lindsay.

"No, thank you. You have been so kind." Her eyes filled. "I appreciate being here. You have no idea..." She stopped, drew a long, shaky breath, and rose. "Thank you. Please excuse me. I'm not feeling well. I'm going to lie down for a while."

"Well, then," said Rhonda, giving her an encouraging nod. "If you need anything else, just give us a call."

I rose and followed Rhonda out of the house, wondering what we'd gotten ourselves into. *A full report? What else had Debra learned about us?*

Outside, Rhonda faced me. "I'm tellin' ya, Annie, after seeing what he did to Lindsay, if that guy ever comes here, I'll take care of him in a hurry. He'll be sorry he was ever born with balls." I grinned and gave her a high five, not doubting her words for a minute. Rhonda had grown up in a tough neighborhood and had learned to protect herself early on. It still amused me how her whole life had changed by winning one hundred eighty-seven million dollars in the Florida lottery. Without it, she might still be in New Jersey, and I might still be alone in Boston, wondering what I was going to do to survive after a nasty divorce.

"Guess we'd better call the girls and tell them what's going on," I said. "We don't want them stumbling onto any surprises."

"Yeah," said Rhonda. "Think the day will ever come when we can leave them in charge?"

"With Angela having one baby and another on the way and Liz wanting to start a family, it's not going to be anytime soon."

Rhonda placed a hand on my shoulder. "All these babies. Annie, that was us not long ago."

I laughed. "Now that your Willow and Drew are four and almost three, and my Robbie is six, it's a little easier, but we need to carry on until our daughters are ready to take over. I don't mind. The idea of someone else handling the hotel is something that will be hard for me. Especially after our experience with Aubrey Lowell and the Sapphire Hotel Group."

"Yeah, those bastards almost ruined The Beach House Hotel." Rhonda let out a sigh that spoke volumes. "If we hadn't repurchased the hotel, it would've become a South Beach wannabe. Not how we want to run our business."

"Absolutely not. There's a niche for us and guests who want an upscale, quiet, private time." I shot a glance at Rhonda. "I'm glad we can help Lindsay. I wonder what will happen when the president and his family find out she's been staying here."

"I'd be proud to tell them," said Rhonda. "Just because someone is in a position of power, they don't have the right to abuse others. Edward Thaxton may have run a campaign on moral values and helpful social programs, but it seems neither has been a real part of his life. All talk."

"Yeah, his opponent was no better," I said, disgusted. "Women have made many strides, but much more is needed. This idea it's okay for a guy to go after the woman who wants to divorce him is just plain wrong. A woman isn't a piece of property."

We walked into the hotel, and seeing Bernie, waved him over.

"Can we meet with you right now?" I asked.

He frowned. "I saw the black limo and security out front. I didn't realize they'd already arrived. We did not expect them until later."

"That's what we want to discuss with you. We just found out the story behind the vice president's visit," I said.

"Yeah, it's a doozy. Wait until you hear," said Rhonda. She looked around carefully and lowered her voice. "It's all very hush-hush."

We led Bernie into the library and closed the door behind us. "First of all, Vice President Swanson is not staying with us," I began. "Her sister, Lindsay Thaxton, is staying in her place."

Bernie's eyebrows rose. "The president's sister-in-law? The one who got beat up by her husband?"

"The same," said Rhonda. "We've got to protect her here."

"As far as anyone else knows, the vice president is having a private vacation. If people find out it's here, her sister, who looks very much like her, will be seen only from a distance, making the public believe Amelia is here."

"In the meantime, she's taking a secret trip," said Rhonda, her eyes alight with intrigue.

"For now, that's all anyone needs to know. The purpose for Lindsay's stay here is to have privacy while she heals and is going through the divorce process."

"How long is she going to be here?" asked Bernie, his expression grave. "Do we need to add to our security team? Special meals? What?"

"She has a bodyguard staying in the house with her," I explained. "A young woman named Debra McDonald, who looks very capable of handling anything that might come along. But I think it's a good idea to keep communication between the guesthouse and the hotel to a minimum and very private. Debra can be the go-between."

"But, Annie, if she orders special meals, how do we tell Jean-Luc about it?" asked Rhonda.

"We'll just say the vice president is requesting this or that. How does that sound, Bernie?"

Bernhard Bruner was a very dignified man who'd only relented to our calling him Bernie because of Rhonda's insistence we treat our staff like family. Besides, she'd informed him in her inimitable way, if she wanted to call him Bernie, she would.

"I think everyone will accept that it's the vice president making such requests. Jean-Luc and the others don't need to know anything more," said Bernie. "Ana, as head housekeeper, should be the only one on the staff to be assigned to the house. That will keep security tight and make it easier on them. If needed, I can be in touch with her regarding any changes."

"Yes, that would work. We've been investigated and found to be safe and reliable."

Bernie's eyebrows shot up. "Investigated? By whom? The Secret Service?"

"Yes. Amelia can't trust the president," said Rhonda. "That's why everything is so secret."

Bernie studied each of us. "Okay. It's highly unusual but nothing we can't handle."

"Love ya, Bernie," said Rhonda, clapping him on the back.

I hadn't realized I'd been holding my breath until it came out in a puff of relief. "Thank you. I just hope it doesn't backfire and hurt our business in the long run. We're playing with a lot of powerful people."

"I trust our staff to be discreet. They know it could be cause for losing their job if they're not," said Bernie. "But it's up to us to keep everything quiet. I'll go over and introduce myself so Debra and Lindsay can meet the real me. They, apparently, already know who I am."

"Okay, how about the rest of our guests? We're fully booked, aren't we?"

Bernie's smile acknowledged it. "For the next four days. It seems New England is having a nasty spring."

"Nice," said Rhonda. "Love to hear news like that."

I laughed, remembering my first visit with Rhonda ...

We'd had a beautiful Thanksgiving together in Florida while it sleeted and snowed in Boston for my ex-husband, Robert, and his new love, Kandie, the voluptuous receptionist in the office of our business. Kandie with a K, she'd called herself, as she eagerly took my place before I officially left it. Who knew that after an automobile accident killed them both, Vaughn and I would be raising their son, Robbie? At the time of their death, Liz was given custody of him. But a college student herself, she'd finally agreed it made sense for Vaughn and me to adopt him. As Robbie's parents, we could give him a stable life. And we truly loved him ...

"Is that all?" Bernie asked, checking his watch, startling me from my thoughts.

"Oh, yes, sorry. I was thinking how unpredictable life could be. When Lindsay married Thomas Thaxton two years ago, it was considered the social event of the year. Who knew a man so charming had a whole different side to him?"

"Nobody but his family," grumped Rhonda. "They should've known."

"That's a side of the story that may never be told," I said. "For us, it's a matter of keeping Lindsay safe until she can decide where to go from here."

"It's a shame that this happened, but we'll do our best to

help her," said Bernie. "I'll make my way over there now, and if any new information comes out of the visit, I'll be sure to let you know."

"Thanks, Bernie." After watching him head out of the hotel, I turned to Rhonda. "How about a walk along the beach? I need fresh air after all this talk."

"Go ahead. I'm going to stay here for a while. Dorothy offered to help with the mailings, and I want to show her what she needs to do."

"Okay, thanks. Say hi to her and tell her I'll see her in a little bit." I left the library, went into the office to take off my suit jacket and change into sandals, and headed outside.

As I crossed the pool area, I observed our guests sprawled in lounge chairs, enjoying the sunny afternoon on this April day. Although I noticed some wearing headphones, there was no loud beat of rock music, only some spa music playing softly in the background so that all the guests were relaxing. It was a pleasure to hear it. Playing loud rock music in the hotel had been just one of many things we'd fought about with the company who'd once bought us out.

As I kicked off my sandals and stepped onto the beach, I drew a deep breath of salt air and wiggled my toes in the soft, warm sand. It was always a special moment for me to be near the water. I loved the sound of the waves as they kissed the beach and rushed back like shy lovers. I faced the Gulf and allowed my muscles to relax from the tension of the day. The vice president's reassurances hadn't fooled me. The responsibility that lay ahead for Rhonda and me was heavy. Politics could be a nasty business, and we'd landed in the middle of something that could turn ugly. Very ugly.

I moved along, forcing myself to think of better things. We'd recently implemented a custom-designed program for post-partum mothers and were hoping to attract guests who needed a break, a place to relax, a time to feel better about themselves. Vaughn's daughter, Nell, had recently had a baby and had asked if she could come to the hotel for such a retreat. Rhonda and I pounced on that idea and were now sending out notices to former guests to promote this new service. That's why Dorothy Stern was coming to the hotel to meet with Rhonda about the mailings.

Short and feisty with thick-lensed glasses, Dorothy sometimes fancifully reminded me of a grasshopper springing about with energy as she went from one project to another in her retirement. She loved best of all working with us at the hotel a couple of days a week. Rhonda and I adored her. She'd helped us from our very first year in business and still kept us informed of sneaky maneuvers by Brock Goodwin, the president of the Neighborhood Association.

I walked down to the water's edge and stuck my feet into the frothy lace of it. It was refreshingly chilly. By summer, the water would welcome me with warmth.

Staring out at the waves, I watched seagulls and terns whirl above me in the air, their raucous cries riding the wind above their wings. Beside me, little sandpipers scurried along the sand, leaving tiny imprints, reminders to the world that they were there.

After living most of my life in the northeast, I treasured moments like this. My thoughts flew to the first time Vaughn and I had stood at the water's edge holding hands. I'd fallen in love with him at that moment. It still seemed magical to me that we shared such a strong, steady love for one another. A beloved soap-opera star, he could have had his choice of many women. Lord knew, his fans all wished he was theirs.

I strolled down the beach and laughed at myself as I studied the shore for unusual shells like any new tourist. It had become a habit of mine. One never knew what hidden treasures they might find among the broken remains of other shells.

I felt a presence and looked up to find Brock Goodwin strolling toward me. I paused. It was too late for me to turn and pretend I hadn't seen him. My flesh chilled at the thought of talking to him. A handsome, trim man in his sixties, Brock was a smooth-talker and a liar. No friend of either the hotel or Rhonda and me.

Forcing myself to be civil, I waited for what would most likely end in a confrontation of sorts. Brock was still very angry with Rhonda and me for canceling an order from his company when the hotel changed hands back to us.

"Well, look what the wind brought ashore," he said, his smile as false as his foolish attempt to say something pleasant.

"Good afternoon, Brock," I replied. For our business's sake, I would do my best to be pleasant. Lord knew, Rhonda wouldn't. And as much as I detested the man, he was an influential person in our community.

"Say, I saw a black limousine and a big, black SUV glide out of the gates of the hotel. What famous person are you hosting now?"

"You know I don't talk about my guests, Brock. We provide them privacy."

His chest puffed out. "I understand you can't share such information with just anyone, but as the president of the Neighborhood Association, I have the right to know these things."

I shook my head. "Unfortunately, you don't."

"Well, no bother. I have my ways. I'll find out sooner or later." His blue eyes pierced mine. "By the way, you might be interested to know that the decorative items you and Rhonda refused to buy, honoring the commitment your former owners made with me, are now sitting in a hotel in Miami. You missed out on having some unusual pieces on display at The Beach House Hotel. But then, you two have never really understood what damage you did to me."

I couldn't help the sigh that rolled out of my mouth. "Brock, you know perfectly well that your deal with them was a payoff for your voting to allow them to make changes to the property—changes that would have destroyed what Rhonda and I built."

He shrugged and then lowered his voice as he leaned forward. "Some businesses understand the need to change with the times. Others don't and will suffer the consequences for it."

I backed up. "Are you threatening me?"

He glanced around to make sure no one was close. "A word of warning. Ours is a close-knit community. It would pay to be kind to everyone."

Trying to keep my cool, I said, "Bullying won't help your cause. Now, if you'll excuse me, I'll be on my way."

I stepped around him and continued walking, more briskly now, aware of the darts of anger he was shooting in my direction. In his own way, he was a dangerous man.

CHAPTER THREE

L ater, back at the hotel, Rhonda announced she was ready for a break. "How about a margarita? It's almost time to leave, but I need a breather after all that has happened today."

"Sounds good." Every once in a while, on a late afternoon, Rhonda and I grabbed one of the hotel's signature drinks and escaped to a balcony on the second floor reachable only through a storage room. Certain of privacy, it had become a favorite place for us to talk over things while overseeing the hotel's activity.

Sitting there, I told Rhonda about my confrontation with Brock.

"What a frickin' jerk," she said, raising a fist in the air. "Dorothy just told me he's holding a meeting about our request to put up a privacy gate between the beach and the walk leading to our pool patio on our property. I tried to explain the gate was on our property, not on the area marked as a public beach. But she told me Brock isn't presenting it that way to the board."

"It's a good thing Dorothy is on the board, or we'd never be able to win any battle against Brock and his cronies."

Rhonda's soft laugh tinged on the nasty. "With her help and your willingness to speak at the meetings, we've won every challenge."

"True." I met her high five with my hand. "But with Brock, there will always be another reason to be careful. He told me that no matter what, he'd find out who was staying at our hotel. It seems he saw the vice president's limo and escort pull out of the hotel. Thank goodness, both vehicles were unmarked."

"We'll have to make sure he never knows. He's the type of person who'd happily sell the information to a newspaper."

"Yeah, I think so too. What's on the schedule for tonight?"

"A private dinner for the opera star appearing at the theater in Sarasota. Annette is going to act as hostess."

"Perfect." Bernie's bride, Annette, had turned out to be a fantastic resource for us. An older, cultured woman accustomed to meeting interesting people, Annette was a warm, attentive hostess to the private parties we held from time to time. It also allowed her to be part of the business that kept Bernie so fully occupied.

"Any word from Angela about the baby?"

"No. I'm going to stop by and see her on my way home. She had a doctor's appointment today." Rhonda clasped her hands together. "I'm praying it's a girl. I adore Evan, but he needs a sister. Then Angela won't have to worry about trying for more."

Frowning, I said, "You haven't mentioned this to her, have you?"

"No, but the time may come when I can. She and Reggie didn't waste any time getting her pregnant with Evan, and now this one. I'd hate to see her have so many kids she could never step into the business here."

"Either way, it's her choice."

"Or not," said Rhonda. "It wasn't a choice for me to have Drew so quickly following Willow's birth." Her face softened with affection. "But I love those two so much it sometimes hurts. Ya know?"

I gave her a warm smile. "I do. I've enjoyed having Robbie in my life. With Liz, I was so worried about being a good mother I sometimes didn't enjoy her. I'm much more confident with him, and having Vaughn be such a big part of his life makes it wonderful. Robert was never into that with Liz. He always said he was too busy with work."

"With the business that was yours in the beginning?" Rhonda said with a snort.

"The very one. God! I was such a fool to let him take my ideas and turn them into his business." Even though Robert gave me the role of vice president of The Rutherford Company, he made sure everyone believed it was his alone, never publicly acknowledging it was my money that had initially funded it. Women like my daughter, Liz, were smarter today.

"Well, I'm on my way," said Rhonda. "I'll think of some way to keep Brock from ruining our promise to Amelia Swanson and her sister."

"Good luck with that," I said, grinning. As much as I disliked Brock, my feelings about him were not nearly as deep as Rhonda's. Any friend of hers knew how she detested liars and cheats, like her ex, Sal DelMonte. Her good heart, alone, had allowed him refuge in her home when he was dying of cancer.

I went downstairs to Bernie's office, knocked on the door, and waited for him to answer.

He startled me by opening the door and motioning me inside.

"What is it?" I asked, unsettled by his serious expression.

"We may have a problem. I just received a call from the White House. At least that's what the person on the other end of the line said. That person asked to speak to the vice president. I know it wasn't the president."

"What did you say?"

"I told him we had no such person registered here, that

even if we did, we never divulge information about any of guests."

My pulse raced at the implications. "And the voice didn't sound familiar?"

"No. I don't believe it was even a staff member. The ID number on my phone said 'Washington, D. C.,' but in today's world, anyone can spoof a phone number to manipulate that kind of information."

"You did the right thing, Bernie, because as far as I'm concerned, not even President Thaxton is going to get any information about our special guest. As far as he or anyone else is concerned, it's private."

"I agree," Bernie quickly said. "I'll speak once more to the people at the front desk and tell them no calls are to go through to the guesthouse, and any calls from Washington, D. C. are to be directed to one of the three of us. Anything else?"

"Nothing I can think of at the moment except to let you know that our standard policy of giving no information of any kind to Brock Goodwin remains in place."

Bernie made a face. "Can't stand the man."

"He's not a friend of this hotel. That's for sure." I checked my watch and rose. "I'm going to head home. Tim is covering for you?"

"Yes, and I'll fill him in on the situation." His cheeks colored. "I'm going to stick around for a bit. Annette is handling the private dinner, and I promised to say hello to the group."

"She does such a wonderful job," I said, smiling. "I'm so glad she agreed to work for us." We said goodnight, and I left him, anxious to get home. Vaughn was in town for a long weekend before returning to New York to shoot more scenes for the show. Even after so many years on television, *The Sins of the Children* was still a top-rated favorite.

Judith Keim

As I drove into the driveway of Vaughn's and my house, my spirits lifted. Sitting on the shore of a small inlet from the Gulf, it was one of only a few homes in this very private area.

I parked and climbed out of the car, anxious to see "my boys."

Trudy, our black-and-tan dachshund, burst out of the pet door and raced over to me, wagging her tail so hard her whole body shook.

Chuckling, I bent over to scratch her ears as she liked and then straightened as Robbie came running toward me.

I held out my arms and caught him in an embrace. Six, now, Robbie was as sweet as ever, still needing hugs from me. I promised myself I'd continue doing this for as long as he'd allow.

"Hi, Mom! Dad and I have packed a surprise picnic." His dark eyes sparkled with excitement.

Trudy barked for attention, and as Robbie bent to pet her, Vaughn appeared. Tall and trim, with dark, curly hair slightly gray at the temples, brown eyes that drew you in, and an air of confidence, he was my hero.

My body came alive at the sexy smile he gave me. It was the same smile I'd seen on his face on television, but I knew this one was especially for me. It had taken me a while to be able to distinguish between the two, and despite one-time rumors of a relationship with his co-star, I'd learned Vaughn would always be true to me. He was that kind of man.

He reached for me, and I nestled close to him before lifting my face for a kiss. When his lips met mine, my body hummed with anticipation. When Vaughn was at home, we made up for the lonely nights he was away by enjoying a loving relationship. For a man in his fifties, he was fit in every way.

Robbie came close, and I wrapped my arm around him, pulling him in for a group hug. We used to call it a "pig pile" sitting on the couch when he first came to us and needed to know we loved him.

He looked up at me, his eyes shining, and for a brief moment, I saw a bit of Robert in him. That used to bother me, but it no longer did. This beautiful boy already showed signs of being very different from his father.

"Guess where we're going on our picnic?" Robbie said with a teasing grin.

Playing along, I said, "Mars? The Moon?"

Giggling, he said, "No, Mom! We're going sailing!"

"Nice!" Vaughn had taught Robbie how to sail as soon as he could. Now, Robbie was becoming a proficient sailor who loved being out on the water, and we'd gone from a day sailer to a 34-foot Pearson, a beauty of a sailboat. It had taken Robbie, Liz, and Vaughn several days to name her. The name they chose, *Zephyr,* suited her because no matter how hot it was, being on her was as refreshing as a gentle breeze.

"Thought we'd head right out to the Gulf, sail for a bit, then anchor for dinner. Sound good?" Vaughn asked.

"Sounds perfect," I answered. "Let me get changed into comfortable clothes and make sure we have some white wine chilled. I've had an interesting day, which I can tell you about later." I glanced at Robbie and back to Vaughn.

Understanding, he said, "I've got some news too. But it can wait. I just want to enjoy my time with you right now."

At the sound of a car pulling up, I turned.

"I've invited Liz and Chad to join us," Vaughn said, smiling and waving to them as they walked up the driveway toward us.

"Lizzie!" cried Robbie, running to his sister.

Tears stung my eyes as I watched them hug. Though they

didn't share facial features, there was an easy grace to their bodies that was similar, a trait from their father. Liz's long blond hair and sparkling blue eyes were different from Robbie's dark-brown hair and brown eyes, but they both had a way of charming people that came naturally to them. I adored them both.

After releasing Robbie, Liz looked up at me.

"Hi, sweetie! How's it going?"

"Okay, Mom," she said, but I knew by the sheen of tears in her eyes that something was wrong.

"Come chat while I change my clothes," I said to her, after giving her a quick hug and doing the same to her husband, Chad.

We left the men talking and went inside the house directly to the bedroom I shared with Vaughn. With a sitting area that overlooked the back lawn and down to the water, the room was one of my favorite spots.

"Want to tell me about it?" I asked Liz as she sank onto the king-sized bed and gave me a glum look.

"I got my period this morning. I'm so disappointed." She sniffled. "I'm trying not to let Chad know I'm so upset. You know all those stories about couples splitting up after trying for a baby."

"Oh, honey," I said, sitting beside her and wrapping an arm around her. "You guys have been married for only a few months."

"I know, but we want children right away."

I took a moment and then said what was on my mind. "This doesn't have anything to do with Angela about to have baby number two, does it?"

She gave me a sheepish look. "Well, sorta. I mean, we've always talked about having our children grow up together. At this rate, her kids will be babysitters for mine."

I choked back a laugh and caressed her cheek. Gazing into her blue eyes full of misery, I said gently, "Having babies isn't about being in a competition. I thought Chad wanted to wait until his business became more secure."

"He did," Liz admitted, "but now he agrees with me that we should try right away."

"You know, I wanted more children. That didn't happen for me for a couple of health reasons. But your body is healthy and strong, Liz. It'll happen for you, but it's best not to think about it so much. That puts a lot of pressure on both of you."

Liz let out a long sigh. "You're right. I just have to let it go."

"Good. Now let's have a pleasant evening. I've missed seeing you. Rhonda and I are going to set up a meeting with you and Angela tomorrow, hopefully. There's something we need to tell you about one of our guests."

"Is it about the vice president?"

I stared at Liz in surprise. "What do you know about the vice president?"

"I heard someone in the store mention that the vice president was coming to town, and I assumed she might be staying at The Beach House Hotel."

My heart sank, then frustration took over. "Oh my God! What is it about this town? Everyone knows everyone else's business," I sputtered, uneasy about the situation. Before we knew it, the press would be hanging around the hotel. "I'll tell you the full story tomorrow in the conference call, but in the meantime, please keep all inferences to Amelia Swanson staying at the Beach House down to a minimum. She needs all the privacy she can get."

Liz tossed her long blond hair over one shoulder and gave me a steady look. "You and Rhonda aren't in any trouble with this, are you?"

"Not yet," I said, wondering how to keep the press at bay.

In the past, sometimes a small press conference would settle things down, but in this instance, there's no way something like that could happen.

CHAPTER FOUR

L iz left me to get dressed, and I immediately called Rhonda.

"Oh, hi, Annie!" she said. In the background, I could hear the sound of her children shrieking with laugher. "Excuse the noise. Will is playing 'monster' with the kids, trying to get them in the bathtub."

I laughed at the image of Will, a quiet man in his early 60s, acting like that. But he loved his kids and was proud to have had them at his age. Rhonda called him an aging rooster, preening about the fact that Willow and Drew were his.

"What's up?" Rhonda asked.

All laughter left me. "Liz just told me there's talk downtown about the vice president staying at the hotel. We're going to have to be very careful about keeping any such information to ourselves and keeping Lindsay out of sight. The press will soon be nosing around. I suggest we put up some natural-looking barriers to the road leading to the cottage and add extra security."

"Okay, I'll get hold of Tim. He's on duty tonight," said Rhonda. "I'll have him see that something is placed there right away. Manny and Paul can take care of it. Bernie told me he already called in more security guards in case they are needed."

"Oh, good. Thanks," I said. "Vaughn and Robbie have planned a surprise sail, and I don't want to disappoint them."

"No problem. By the way, I think Angela's baby is coming

sooner than we thought. Reggie's mother is already planning a trip to Sabal." Rhonda's voice shook with anger. "I just can't warm up to that woman. Not after the way she treated Angela."

"You have to find a way to do it. You share grandchildren," I said, understanding how she felt.

"I know, but you might have to help me practice being nice because she's one of the snobbiest women I know. If I weren't rich, she wouldn't even speak to me. But now that my daughter has married her son, she can't get away with pretending I don't exist."

"Reggie is one of the kindest, most honest people I know. He'll help keep things pleasant," I said, trying to encourage her. The truth was, his mother, Katherine Smythe, was a pain in the ass.

I hung up the phone, thinking of Angela and Reggie's wedding and how painful some aspects of it had been with tensions between the two families. Funny how babies could bring people together.

After I finished dressing, I hurried out to the boat, carrying sweaters for everyone. The evenings on the water could get cool in this spring weather.

Trudy jumped off the boat onto the dock and hurried toward me, her short legs pumping furiously as she tried to reach me. She wore a pink lifejacket around her body, making her look like a hibiscus blossom gone wild.

Amused by her antics, I encouraged her to trot beside me back to the boat. It had turned out that Trudy was a good sailing companion. On board, she usually propped herself between cushions atop the seats in the cockpit, where she could watch activities both above and below deck.

Vaughn picked up Trudy, handed her to Robbie, and then offered his hand to me.

"Welcome aboard," he said, smiling. "My co-captain is awaiting the chance to get you settled in the cockpit so he can hoist the mainsail."

I glanced at Robbie. Wearing a yellow lifejacket, he was standing behind the wheel of the boat with a big grin spread across his adorable face. "I'm going to help steer the boat out to the Gulf," he announced proudly. The breeze ruffled his dark-brown hair.

"I know you'll do a good job," I said, sitting and sliding into a lifejacket that had my name on it. Liz was sitting opposite me. Chad was standing on the dock, ready to toss the line to Vaughn and hop on board.

The sound of the engine as Vaughn and Robbie backed up the boat and turned it caused Trudy to bark with excitement. She loved sailing adventures as much as the rest of us.

As we motored through the inlet and out to the Gulf, a couple of dolphins splashed playfully nearby. I watched them with joy, treasuring these creatures of the sea.

We passed other boats and waited until we had plenty of room around us before Vaughn gave Robbie instructions to bring the boat head to wind and stand by for raising the mainsail and then the small genoa jib before falling off onto a port tack.

Vaughn helped trim the sheets as the wind filled the sails, and then he cut the engine and took the wheel. In the quiet that followed, we surged forward, making me feel as if we were flying in the wind.

I caught Vaughn's eye, and we smiled, content to be together sharing a love of sailing. Thank goodness, our children loved it too. Robbie stayed right at Vaughn's side, gazing at the sails with a serious expression, learning how best to keep the sails full. Liz had stretched out on the foredeck enjoying the downdraft from the jib. Chad sat nearby, holding her hand. Seeing this, my earlier worries about any tension between them evaporated.

Vaughn lowered himself onto a cushion next to me but stayed within safe distance should he need to take the wheel from Robbie.

He wrapped his arm around me and kissed me on the cheek. "Mmm ... glad I had these few days off," he murmured in my ear. "If we're lucky, all this fresh air will make Robbie sleepy after dinner."

"And?" I teased.

"And we can go to bed too," he replied, grinning.

The thought of it sounded wonderful. The coming days were going to be difficult at work, and he'd soon return to the City.

A gust of wind came up, making the boat heel and causing it to swing a bit off course. Vaughn got to his feet and stood behind Robbie, helping him guide the boat to a better setting, keeping the sails full, and making the wind work for us.

Observing the two of them, I thought how alike they were with their dark hair and brown eyes and wondered what it would've been like to have a child of Vaughn's. He was a great father to Nell and his son, Ty, who lived in San Francisco with June Chung, his new wife.

After we'd let the wind carry us back and forth, up and down the coast for an hour or so, Vaughn announced it was time to find a spot to picnic. He took the wheel from Robbie, and we drew close to a more protected area closer to shore. Vaughn brought the boat into the wind, and when it lost forward motion, he called to Chad, "Okay, drop the anchor!"

"Aye, aye, captain!" he answered, dropping the decorative anchor I'd bought for Vaughn when he'd purchased the boat. "So, you won't stray too far from home," I'd told him, loving his delight in it.

As if he'd read my thoughts, Vaughn caught my eye and grinned.

As we ate, Liz talked about the new display she'd put in their store window. Located among clothing stores and eating places along Fifth Avenue, their small storefront, Bits 'N' Bytes, attracted computer geeks, game players, and men whose wives were busy shopping. In addition to selling items, Chad ran his IT consulting business, overseeing computer and other technical programs for companies in the area.

I turned to him now. "I have a question for you. Bernie received an unusual phone call earlier today. It was someone claiming to be from the White House. He knew it was a crank call, but it showed up on his phone as coming from a number in Washington, D. C. That's an easy thing to do, isn't it? Set up a false Caller ID?"

Chad gave me a thoughtful look. "Yeah, it's not difficult. Why would the White House be calling The Beach House Hotel anyway?"

"The vice president," said Liz. "People in the store were talking about the vice president supposedly coming to stay at the hotel." She glanced at me and back to him. "But we're not to mention any possibility of it."

"It's important," I said. "Rhonda and I pride ourselves on offering our guests privacy. A good number of our bookings are due to this policy."

As soon as I got back home with some privacy, I would double-check with Tim to make sure the added security guards were patrolling the hotel property. The vice president's plan was already fraying.

###

Back at the house, after saying goodbye to Liz and Chad, I took a moment to slip into the library to call Tim, our assistant manager on call. He picked up right away. "Yes, Ann," he answered to my question, "we've taken care of it. I've also taken the liberty of speaking to the front desk people again to alert them that people who might appear to be dining guests might be snooping and to be careful what they say."

"Good idea. That's exactly right. I had no idea word would spread so quickly," I said, unable to hide the worry in my voice.

As I walked out of the library, Robbie came running toward me, his hair wet from his bath, his soccer pajamas from Christmas already looking small. He was going to be a large man. Even though they weren't biologically related, it was another way in which he resembled Vaughn.

I swept Robbie up in a hug. "Bed time! You have school tomorrow." He attended a private school and loved it. That attitude would undoubtedly change in the future, but I intended to encourage it, along with plenty of hugs for Mom. He was growing up too fast.

Vaughn and I both tucked him into bed and lifted Trudy up beside him, where she'd sleep until morning. It was sweet to see those two heads sharing a pillow.

"See you in the morning," I said softly, kissing his cheek. "Love you."

"Love you too," he said, smiling at me even as his eyelids began to droop.

Vaughn ruffled his hair. "Love you, buddy!"

"Yeah, me too, Dad," he replied, turning over on his side.

We left quietly, making sure to leave the door open a crack as he wanted. As we walked down the hallway, Vaughn put his arm around me and pulled me close. "I've been waiting for this all day."

He grinned at me, revealing white teeth in his tanned face, sending anticipation shooting through me. It sometimes took me a moment to distinguish between the way he looked on screen and the way he was with me. Either way, he was a sexy hunk of a man. And either way, he was mine.

CHAPTER FIVE

I lay in bed next to Vaughn, feeling very lucky to have a man like him. Robert hadn't been a generous lover. It was Vaughn who'd shown me what it was like truly to make love, giving and sharing the joy of it.

He turned to me and caressed my cheek. "As I said, it's good to be home. What did you want to talk about?"

I told him about the situation with Amelia Swanson and her sister, Lindsay.

He frowned. "That's a lot of responsibility for you and Rhonda."

"I'm worried about it, but after what that poor woman went through, we're both determined to keep her safe. It may be for only a week, possibly longer. Lindsay will decide once she's become acclimated to the hotel."

"I remember how awful the press was to Tina Marks when she stayed at the hotel. Can you help Lindsay in the same way by giving her privacy?"

"I think so. We're going to try." I cupped his cheek in my hand. "You said you had news too. You're not going to tell me Lily Dorio is back on the show with you, are you?"

"No, no. The producers have kept their promise to me to keep her off the show. However, they've hired another young actress to take her place, and they've told me right up front that if the public wants to assume that we're together outside the show, they, themselves, won't do anything to deny it. They loved all the publicity with Lily trying to make it appear as if she was my lover on the side."

I let out a sigh. "Who is the new actress? And what's she like?"

He trailed his hand down my back. "Her name is Darla Delaney. I swear she's not much older than our daughters. Though she's fairly unknown in the industry, she's very ambitious. I think the circumstances will mean a lot of the same bullshit as with Lily, but I'm in love with you. It's even difficult for me to play the role of the mayor in town having an affair with her, a school teacher. It doesn't work for me. I've mentioned it to the writers, but they don't care. They have this crazy idea I'll end up going for her." He let out a sigh. "I love my job. If I didn't, I wouldn't stay. I just don't want you to have to go through all the crap with her that you had to with Lily."

"Is Darla nice? Is she married? Lily wasn't a nice person, and no, I'd be unhappy if this Darla person wanted to pull the same stunts as Lily."

"Let's see. She's twenty-eight, attractive, and as self-centered as any other actress. But she has a stuffed dachshund puppy that goes everywhere with her, and that makes me think she's a whole lot better than Lily."

I sat up. "A dachshund? Really? I think I like her already."

He laughed and pulled me down on top of him. "I think I like you."

"Well, then, I'm not going to worry about Darla. Hopefully, she won't try to get publicity through you."

He nuzzled my neck, and all thoughts of Darla disappeared in a fresh surge of desire.

The next morning, while Vaughn was taking Robbie to school, I googled Darla Delaney. She was a stunning young woman with auburn hair, attractive facial features, green eyes, and a voluptuous figure. Darla was twenty-eight, from a small town in Iowa, and had won a scholarship to an acting school in New York. If she was half as good as her promotional materials claimed, she should be an easy person to work with unless her ego got in the way. Studying her photos, I was glad Vaughn wasn't attracted to her sexually. I wasn't willing to share one minute of our time together with any other woman.

I showered, got dressed, and prepared to leave for the day.

"What are you going to do today?" I asked Vaughn.

"I promised I'd stop by the high school and talk to a group of kids in their theater club."

"Nice. Since you're leaving for New York tomorrow, I'll try to come home early. We can have a quiet dinner ourselves. I've asked Cyndi if she'd have Robbie for dinner in exchange for having Brett here one day next week." Cyndi and Charlie Brigham lived next door and had a little boy, Brett, who was Robbie's age. The boys were best friends. It worked out well because Vaughn and I enjoyed Cyndi and Charlie, and the boys got along.

"Sounds good. I may have to stay over in New York next weekend. We'll see how it goes."

"Okay. Then I'll definitely be home early."

His eyes twinkled as he leaned over to kiss me.

When we pulled apart, I said, "While I'm gone, decide what you want for dinner. If you wish, I can get Jean-Luc to put something together for us. I don't know what's on the menu, but you like most anything he makes."

"And how! If I don't feel like grilling a steak, I'll let you know, and you can bring home something."

"Deal." I waved goodbye and left him to get in my car.

On the short drive to the hotel, I thought of Jean-Luc, a semi-retired chef originally from France who'd moved to

Florida thinking he might enjoy early retirement. Soon bored, he'd agreed to work for Rhonda and me on a part-time basis when we first decided to include an upscale restaurant at the hotel. He and Rhonda had butted heads a few times about his taking over *her* kitchen, but they'd ended up best of friends. Good thing because anyone who tasted his food wanted more.

Close to the hotel, I noticed news trucks parked on the street. Then as I drove through the gates of the hotel, a group of reporters swarmed my car, trying to stare inside intrusively. My lips thinned. Having to deal with the press was always an exercise in restraint. It was hard to tell someone off when you were trying to appear professional, and The Beach House Hotel was in the background.

I continued driving out back where I knew a security guard would be on duty during morning deliveries. Getting out of the car, I noticed Rhonda's Cadillac was already there.

After greeting the guard, I hurried inside the hotel. Before I could even get to the office, Rhonda met me in the hallway.

"Annie, we've got to get rid of these press bastards; they're making it difficult for our guests."

I let out a long sigh at the thought. There was only one thing we could do to make the press back off. "Guess we'll have to meet with them."

"Okay, but Annie, you're going to have to do the talking as usual because I'd like to wring their effin' necks, every one of them. One of the guests complained these jerks surrounded her as she was returning from her morning run downtown."

"We can't have that," I said, trying to form words in my mind that wouldn't offend the ghost of my grandmother, who'd raised me following my parents' deadly automobile accident. Growing up with a kind but distant woman who had very strict rules about etiquette, proper speech, and ladylike deportment, it had taken me a while to get used to Rhonda.

She was prone to say exactly what was on her mind with words that had never left my mouth. Even now, though she'd loosened me up a bit, I knew it was best if I did the talking.

As we had so many times for many different reasons, Rhonda and I descended the front steps of the hotel together. I stopped us midway and motioned the reporters toward us.

"We're here to answer any questions we can and ask you to go away then and leave the property to our guests. It's a fair proposition. We don't want your being here to escalate into asking the police for help."

"We heard the vice president is staying here. Is that true? And is she about to resign because of personal difficulties with the president?"

"All of you who've been to the hotel before know that we cannot confirm or deny anyone's presence, that we provide all of our guests, known or not, strict privacy. We've built our business on that promise. As to the other question, we would have no such information."

"If Amelia Swanson is here, do you have any news about her plans?"

"As I said, we wouldn't have any such information no matter where she might be staying."

"We have the right to know these things," protested a young woman, who clutched her microphone intently.

I stared right at her. "Unfortunately, you don't."

The woman started to protest.

"You heard her," said Rhonda, starting to move down the steps.

I grabbed hold of her arm. "Now, we're asking you all to leave. There's nothing we can tell you. If there comes a time when one of our guests would like to hold a news conference here at the hotel, we'd be glad to accommodate you."

Grumbling among themselves, the group of eight moved

toward the gates of the hotel.

Rhonda and I watched them go.

"Frickin' vultures," said Rhonda.

We stayed there watching as the last of the trucks pulled away from the curb outside the hotel.

A low-slung, bottle-green Jaguar came between the front gates and pulled up to the front circle at our feet.

I gripped Rhonda's arm as Brock Goodwin climbed out of the car and faced us with a look of triumph. "I'm hereby giving you notice that I'm filing a complaint against the hotel. Our peaceful neighborhood was disrupted by all the news trucks blocking our streets and making a nuisance that won't be tolerated."

"Brock, you bastard ..." began Rhonda, her hands fisted.

I elbowed her and quickly spoke. "Considering that your house is at the other end of the neighborhood and no one else seems to be bothered by it, we'll simply disregard your action. You continue to try to make our lives difficult, Brock, but your tactics won't work, as we've proved to you over and over."

"Disregard it? You can't do that. I will bring it up at the next Neighborhood Association meeting."

"I'm sure you will," I said, forcing a cheerfulness I didn't feel into my voice. I'd learned that you couldn't act defeated in front of him, or he'd pounce like a starving cat after a helpless mouse.

"C'mon, Annie, let's leave before I do something to that face of his," Rhonda said in a stage whisper that Brock heard.

He studied us and shook his head. "How the two of you can run an exclusive place like this is beyond me. But, believe me, the day will come when I'll shut you down once and for all. This estate was never meant to be a hotel."

Ignoring his words, Rhonda and I headed up the stairs and inside.

One of our guests was lingering at the door. "Who is that fellow, and why is he so angry?" he asked, indicating Brock's car roaring out of the property.

"A troublemaker," blurted Rhonda. "That's what he is."

"Sorry, I didn't mean to be nosy." He gave us a sheepish look. "I'm a writer, and we always like to know what's going on around us."

I laughed. I knew exactly who he was. "I loved your last thriller," I said to the famous author. "The ending really fooled me."

He grinned. "Me, too. Sometimes I'm as surprised as anyone when I'm writing it."

A pretty young woman joined him. "Ready to go in for breakfast?" she asked him. "I don't want to miss out on those cinnamon rolls."

As they walked away, I turned to Rhonda. "Who knew cinnamon rolls would be a part of our success?"

Rhonda beamed at me. "My recipe worked, didn't it? Consuela does a nice job with them."

"She's a blessing," I said, meaning it with my whole heart. While Jean-Luc reigned in the afternoons and evenings, Consuela was the early riser who ran the kitchen for breakfast. I was happy that Manny and Consuela had moved back into the apartment we'd built for them over the expanded garage, which now housed a commercial laundry and a wonderful small spa on the ground floor.

We returned to our office, and after spending time reviewing sales figures, I decided to talk to Debra about the problem with the news people.

"Want to come?" I said to Rhonda.

"I can't. I promised the kids' pre-school teacher I'd visit

today. It's a special day for mothers."

"Okay, see you later." With Bernie running the hotel, Rhonda and I had the freedom to come and go when we hadn't scheduled meetings and other events.

Instead of leaving through the front door, I went out back and took a secret path through the landscaping to the guesthouse. We'd purposely kept the path hidden as much as possible among the oleander bushes, hibiscus, and evergreens planted along this edge of the property. Lindsay Thaxton was just one of many people who'd sought refuge at the house.

Now, as I approached it, I thought back to when Rhonda first had the idea of turning a little caretaker's cottage into a small, luxurious home for me. I'd still been trying to figure out how I could start my life over again with no job, no money, no house of my own. The renovated cottage was where Vaughn and I first got together. That, alone, would make me love it better than any other home in which I'd lived.

I walked up to the front door and knocked.

After several seconds passed, the door was cracked open, and Debra peered out at me.

"Ah, it's you. Come on in. Lindsay and I have just finished our exercises."

"Thank you." I entered the house, and when I noticed Lindsay out on the patio, I took a moment to speak privately with Debra.

"I'm sure you may have noticed or heard people out in front of the hotel. Several reporters and their news vans were here asking questions about Amelia. As per our normal routine, we informed them we never discuss who's staying at the hotel. We have a policy of respecting our guests' privacy. All of our staff are trained as well."

"Good to have that in place," said Debra.

"Bernie told you about the phone call yesterday from the

so-called White House, didn't he?"

"Yes. It's a bit disconcerting, but nothing too outlandish. Lindsay has been instructed not to use the house phone here at any time. She can use my iPhone if she wishes."

I glanced at her lying down on a deck chair outside and asked, "How's she doing?"

Debra let out a long sigh. "Her physical injuries are healing. We're doing what we can to keep her body strong. The mental issues? That's another story. The woman was almost killed by a man she thought loved her and who became a monster."

"I have the name of a wonderful therapist if she wishes. One of our special guests used her and is still in touch with her."

Debra's eyes brightened. "I'll tell Lindsay."

"I'd like her to know we're doing our best to keep her safe. With you and the incognito security guards we've added, we don't foresee any problems."

"Yeah, I've noticed a landscaper hanging around who, I'm sure, is not a real gardener," said Debra. "His clothes are much too clean."

I grinned. "Hopefully, no one else will notice. May I speak to Lindsay?"

"She'd love to see you. I'm not the most exciting person around." Debra shot me a look full of humor.

"I'm sure she's very grateful to have you here with her. But I hope you have the opportunity to relax, go on the beach, and enjoy some of the delicious food from the hotel."

"Thanks. We both intend to do all that in good time," said Debra.

I liked Debra. She was pleasant and upbeat. And one good look at her well-muscled body told me she'd be a formidable match for most any adversary. The gun secured at her waist was another clue that this wasn't a game for either of them.

I walked out to the patio to say hello to Lindsay.

Seeing her in a bathing suit, I couldn't help but notice bruises yellowing on her thin torso as they healed. Her arm was in a removable cast and was resting on a table beside her chair.

"Good morning, Lindsay," I said quietly.

Startled, her eyes flew open, and she clasped a hand to her chest.

"Sorry, I didn't mean to scare you," I said. "May I sit down?"

"Certainly." She started to rise.

"No, no, please stay where you are. I just wanted a minute to see how you're doing and if there's anything else you need or want."

"Everything is very nice, thank you. I love being in a small house. It makes me feel safer to know that Debra is near if I need her." Her eyes filled. "I'm working on getting past the memories."

"I told Debra I know of a good therapist. Other special guests who've had traumas similar to yours have used her."

"Thank you. I'm still not sure what I'm going to do. Thomas's brother wants me to return to Washington, but I'm not about to do that. I've filed divorce papers, and after all I've been through, I want nothing to do with the president or his entire family." Her voice caught. "Some of them even thought it was my fault I made Thomas so mad."

"That's B.S. and you know it. That's the classic blame-the-victim scenario," I said, not caring if I was overstepping boundaries. The sight of this emaciated, wounded woman made me want to scream with frustration. It was never okay for a woman to be beaten up. Did they all live in a bubble? Or were they so concerned about their image they didn't want to face reality?

I reached over and took hold of her hand. "Whether you decide to stay after Amelia returns or not, I want you to know we're doing everything we can to keep you safe with us. We've had to send reporters away, but there's nothing for them here. We don't give out information on any of our guests. Aside from that, our security guards and Debra should help you feel comfortable."

Her eyes welled with tears. "It's something you don't get over. If Amelia hadn't forced me to sign those papers, I probably wouldn't have, thinking I was doing something wonderful for our country by keeping bad news about all of them private." She let out a sound of disgust. "Talk about bullshit."

I gave her hand an encouraging squeeze. "We're just glad you're here. By the way, I hope you're enjoying some good food."

Lindsay's face lit up. "It's delicious. Someday, I hope to meet the chef."

"Jean-Luc is a nice guy. He lost his wife two years ago in an automobile accident in Europe. I thought he might not be willing to stay on here at the hotel, but he's part of our hotel family. We're lucky to have him."

Lindsay smiled, and I could see what a beautiful woman she was beneath the bruises. "It's lucky for all of us he stayed."

I said goodbye to Lindsay and Debra and headed back to the hotel, my mind spinning.

Inside the kitchen, Jean-Luc was overseeing kitchen staff getting food prepped for dinner. He was in his late sixties, of average height, with brown hair graying at the temples and long enough to tie back behind his head. His clear blue eyes seemed to miss nothing as his staff, like soldier ants, did as he directed. Not a handsome man in the usual sense, his features were regular and pleasant. He carried an air of command about him that was intriguing rather than off-putting. Rhonda had once called him a French frog during their initial battles, but even though he had forced Rhonda to give up her kitchen, they were close friends.

"*Bonjour*, Ann! What brings you to my kitchen?" he said in his charming French accent.

"I have a favor to ask of you," I said, inhaling the aromas of a lovely meal being created.

"Ah, *oui*," he said. "For you ... yes."

"Thanks. A certain special guest has told me she'd love to meet you someday. As she's here recuperating, I thought it would be a nice gesture on both our parts if you were to take a treat over to her and her bodyguard."

He paused, looked around the kitchen, and turned back to me. "Okay. Later."

"I'll go ahead and send your photo to them, so they know who to expect. Is that agreeable to you?"

He bobbed his head. "Yes, I will do this for you."

"Good. Now tell me, what's for dinner?"

He grinned and rubbed his hands together with delight. "We have a variety today. A little beef, a little lamb, fresh snapper, a few other treats."

"It all sounds lovely. I told Vaughn I'd bring home dinner tonight if he didn't want to grill steak."

"Ah, he could grill the snapper. It's beautiful, and I'm putting together a special herbal blend to use in the oil to spread over the fish. *C'est magnifique!*"

"Wonderful! Please put some fish aside for me." I grinned. "And I'll take the herbal blend too."

"For you, always." He kissed me on one cheek, then the other in the French manner.

I beamed at him, grateful he was, as I'd described to Lindsay, part of our hotel family.

CHAPTER SIX

That afternoon when I arrived home, Vaughn and Trudy greeted me.

"Where's Robbie?"

Vaughn grinned. "He's already next door for the evening. He and Brett are playing a special game, something about space cowboys, and he didn't want to miss out."

"I'm so glad he has a friend like Brett. Growing up, I was pretty lonely living in a neighborhood of large homes separated by a lot of land and with a grandmother who didn't think sleepovers and such were a good idea."

Vaughn wrapped an arm around me. "Poor little girl. Tell you what, I'll happily be your playmate."

A thrill of anticipation wove through me. "You're such a tease."

"How about joining me in the pool, and I'll show you how serious I am?" Vaughn wiggled his eyebrows playfully.

Chuckling happily, I turned to go to our bedroom.

"Where are you going?" he asked.

"To get my bathing suit on," I replied, liking his idea of a swim. "By the way, I left the snapper packed in ice and the herb mixture I told you about on the kitchen counter. Will you put it in the refrigerator?"

"Yes. Hold on." He slid the fish inside the refrigerator, hurried over to me, and swept me up in his arms. "How can I think of dinner when I know you're going to take your clothes off?"

He carried me into the bedroom, nuzzling my neck all the

way. I loved that we were always willing to play these games. It was something new and wonderful for me. Looking back at my relationship with Robert, I realized it had always been about his wanting my business and my money to pay for it. The thought hurt.

I nestled closer to Vaughn. As he placed me atop the bed, I looked up at him and saw the love that I'd always wished for there in his eyes.

Later, wishing Vaughn didn't have to leave for New York the next day, I strolled into the kitchen in my bathing suit. While Robbie was next door, I intended to have a glass of wine or two in the pool with Vaughn before worrying about dinner. When Robbie first came to live with us, it was an adjustment to having him around, forcing us to delay times like this.

Vaughn joined me from outdoors. I took a moment to study him. For a man in his fifties, he was in excellent shape. He had to watch his weight for the show, but he enjoyed being outdoors and ran almost every morning, giving him a healthy physique.

"Would you like some wine?" he asked. "I picked up a nice pinot noir from the Willamette Valley at the store. A Chandler Hill wine from the Lettie's Creek Vineyard."

"Mmm, sounds delightful. I'll get things ready for you to grill, and then I'll join you."

While Vaughn and I lived in my house on the hotel property, we delighted in being close to the beach. But gazing out the kitchen window at the pool and beyond it to the water, I was pleased we'd been able to find this quiet spot. And even though it was just Robbie living with us, we had plenty of room for guests with enough privacy for everyone.

I set the table, got out the salad bowl and dressing, and

headed out to the pool.

Vaughn was in the heated water lounging on a step in the shallow end. I joined him there.

He handed me my wine in a plastic glass and raised his. "Here's to us! May we always be this happy!"

"Hear! Hear!" I said, clinking my glass against his.

We watched the sun gradually lower toward the horizon.

I turned to him with a smile. "Maybe we'll see the green flash tonight. The sky is clear enough."

He drew me closer. "Whether we do see it or not, I don't need it to tell me that with you by my side, I have all the luck I need."

But he, too, studied the sky as the sun began to slip below the horizon. If the sky was clear and conditions just right, one could see a green flash at the exact moment the sun dropped from view. I had yet to see it, but I never tired of looking for it. And I wasn't the only one. Sunsets on the Gulf Coast were highlights for visitors and residents alike.

In the dark that followed, the pool lights lit the water in a blue shimmer, and I decided to swim a few laps before going inside. The moment I pushed off, Vaughn followed, and we swam side by side.

A chill entered the air as we got out. He wrapped a towel around me and hugged me to him. "I'm going to miss this in New York. But I'm hoping you'll come to visit me. That would be a great way to meet Darla."

I thought about it. "That might work. Angela is due to have her baby soon, which means I'll have to cover for Rhonda at the hotel, but, perhaps, after that, it will be a good time to come to see you. Hopefully, before Nell, Clint, and the baby come here for a visit."

"Sounds good," said Vaughn. "I'm getting hungry. How about you?"

"Yes. I'll get dressed and then get dinner started."

We hurried to the bedroom together.

After getting dressed, I went into the kitchen to fix the salad while Vaughn grilled the fish that he'd rubbed with the herbal spices as Jean-Luc had instructed.

These quiet evenings, with a comfortable sense of peace between us, were what I'd wished to find with Robert. I'd given up hope of ever having them until I met Vaughn. He was, deep down, a man with simple tastes for someone comfortable in the trappings of fame. I loved that about him.

We'd just finished our meal when Robbie burst into the kitchen. "Guess what? Brett and I had dinner at the Burger Palace! And we played Space Cowboys! See!" He held out his arm where he'd drawn an X on his arm. "X stands for the secret code."

I hugged Robbie. "Sounds like you had a perfect evening. I hope you thanked Brett's Mom and Dad."

Robbie glanced at me with a proud look. "Yep. Just like you said."

"Good. That makes me happy." I glanced at Vaughn. "I'll have to thank them myself."

Vaughn winked at me, and I returned his smile.

Dropping Vaughn off at the airport was always a sad time for me, but I understood how much he enjoyed his job and was grateful for all it provided us. And knowing I might be traveling to New York to see him made the departure easier.

I pulled up to the curb and waited for him to retrieve his luggage. Then with a kiss and a last wave goodbye, he entered the terminal, and I pulled away before the policeman could reach my car to tell me to move on.

As I made my way back to the hotel, I thought of the days ahead. Amelia Swanson had said she'd be gone a week. I hoped the remaining days of Lindsay's stay would encourage her to find a refuge somewhere where she could heal and rethink her life and what she needed to do to recover from her trauma. I knew what it was like to suddenly lose your identity as someone's spouse and be forced to forge a new life.

The hotel gates were crowded with reporters once more as I drove into the property. As before, I continued past the front entrance out to the back, where I'd be assured of privacy.

Wondering what had happened to cause new interest, I parked the car and hurried inside.

On my way to my office through the kitchen, I snatched a warm cinnamon roll, thanked Consuela, and kept going.

Rhonda was in the office when I got there.

"What's going on?" I asked her.

"Amelia's back. She's going to hide out here for a couple of days while she and the president work out the final details of the announcement about the female news reporter who was taken captive in Guatemala has now been freed."

"What does this mean for the hotel?" I asked. "Will they have all the equipment they need?"

"She told me not to worry about it. Her press secretary is working things out with one of the local television stations." Rhonda grinned. "She said it should be good publicity for the hotel."

The thought warmed me. The hotel business could be spotty, depending on weather and other factors we couldn't control. Heads in beds for every day of the year was a goal we always strived to meet.

"Vaughn has gone back?" Rhonda asked.

"Yes." I took a seat at my desk and began nibbling on the

sweet roll that had helped introduce The Beach House Hotel to the public when the recipe and article about the hotel were featured in a New York magazine.

Rhonda rose. "How about a cup of coffee? I'll bring it to you."

I gave her a thumbs up.

After she left, my thoughts flew back to Wilkins Jones, a free-lance writer who'd died at the hotel while doing the article for a New York magazine on the sweet rolls at the hotel. His death while in bed with a woman who wasn't his wife was my introduction to the need for Rhonda and me to be discreet when it came to our hotel guests.

Rhonda returned with the coffee, handed me a cup, and sat in her desk chair facing me. "I talked to Angela this morning. She asked me to meet Katherine at the airport." Rhonda gave me a worried look and let out a sigh. "I know she wants us to be friends, but as much as I love my daughter, I will never be friends with her mother-in-law. Especially after Angela told me she's planning to have Katherine be with her at the hospital while the baby is born."

"Oh," I said, doing my best to hide my surprise. I knew how upset Rhonda was. It took me a moment to come up with something to say. "But you'll be there too."

"Yes, but Angela is *my* daughter, not hers."

"But you're both grandmothers to this baby," I said.

"I know. Will says that too. But, knowing Katherine, she'll take over. Angela says she's asking her to come here to help Reggie repair his relationship with his parents. But the reason his parents are upset is because of me and Will. They don't think we're good enough." Rhonda's chest heaved with the release of another sigh. "That, and the fact Reggie chose to work with Will."

I leaned forward. "Listen, Rhonda; you have nothing to be

worried about. I'm guessing Katherine will be on her best behavior. After Reggie overrode their wishes for him to marry someone else and stay in New York, his relationship with them changed. While that can't be denied, no mother wants to lose contact with her child."

"I'm going to do my best to be pleasant to her, Annie, but if she gives me a whole lot of trouble, I'm not holdin' back."

"One day, one step at a time, remember?" If Rhonda vowed not to hold back, I could only imagine what might come out of her mouth. "When is Katherine due here?"

"That's another thing. She's coming tomorrow, a whole week before the baby is due. She says she's going to take care of Evan, but I bet it's to try to get Reggie to change his mind about New York. And then what would I do? I love having Angela and Reggie and the baby here. And if this new baby is a girl like I think, I'd be devastated to have her live close to Reggie's parents. She'd become as pretentious as Katherine."

"Mmm. Like I said, one day at a time. Better not project too much. Give Katherine a chance to make up to you for the horrible way she acted toward you before and after the wedding."

"I'll try," grumped Rhonda. "Now, let's talk about Amelia. She called, but I think you and I better go see what's happening."

"Good idea. I want to know where all the extra security people are going to stay. I don't think we have any rooms for them here unless Amelia made those arrangements directly with Bernie."

As we walked over to the guesthouse through the back path, I thought of all the changes we had made to the property since Rhonda and I worked to turn it into a hotel. On my first visit, I was awed by the beauty of the seaside estate, the number of rooms, the fact that it sat right on the beach. It had at one time been a small hotel. It seemed natural to see it that way again. The path ended at the guesthouse driveway where a compact mobile home now sat, complete with what looked like satellite gear atop it.

"Guess we have our answer," said Rhonda. "Looks like security has already set up there."

We walked up to the door and knocked.

After several seconds, the door cracked open, and Debra waved us inside.

A man sat at the kitchen counter, sipping a cup of something that smelled like coffee. Though he did nothing more than look at us, I'm sure he noted many details about us, what we were wearing, and if there was any reason for him to be alarmed. I gazed out the sliding glass door in the living room and saw that Lindsay and Amelia were sitting at the outside table talking.

"Is it okay if we speak to Amelia?" I asked Debra.

She glanced at the man in the kitchen and then nodded. "Come this way."

It wasn't until I stepped onto the patio that I saw a man in the far corner lounging in a chair under an umbrella. His shoulder holster distracted from the short-sleeved, Hawaiian-print shirt he wore.

Amelia looked at us and smiled. "How are you both?"

"Good, thank you. We thought we ought to see what you might need from the hotel and how we could help in any way," I said.

Amelia waved us over. "Come sit. I was just talking to Lindsay about what she wanted to do in the future. With your approval, she'd like to stay here in the house for the next several weeks. Debra would stay with her, of course."

Rhonda and I exchanged glances. *Did they realize how difficult it might become if word got out Lindsay was here?* I looked at Lindsay. There was no way we could say no. She looked much better, but I suspected she would still need more time to recover.

"We'll work it out as best we can. If needed, Lindsay is welcome to stay at my house. It worked well for Tina. I'm in a small, gated community where people pretty much mind their own business."

"Unlike some guy named Brock," said Debra, standing by. "I met him on the beach this morning."

"Brock Goodwin is an asshole," said Rhonda. "Don't worry about him. Someday I'm gonna take care of him permanently." She gaped at the man with the gun sitting in the corner and clapped a hand to her mouth. "Hold on! I didn't mean that the way it sounded."

We all laughed.

"He's been a constant pain, trying to interfere with any plans we make," I said. "He was dying to get me to tell him if you were at the hotel, Amelia. I explained that we never give information about our guests to anyone."

"That's why we're here," said Amelia smiling. "But I'll do you a favor. With your permission, I'll make an announcement from the front steps of the hotel about the recent release of one of our news reporters. It will appear as if all transactions took place at the hotel, not during a secret trip to Guatemala."

"That would be nice," I said. "Perhaps we could invite a few of the city officials to the announcement."

Amelia thought about it and nodded. "We could work that out. Perhaps it would be better if the announcement came from the library and not the front of the hotel. If I remember correctly, there's a small stage and room for a few reporters there."

"Yes," said Rhonda. "It's a versatile room. My daughter was

married there."

"How nice. Okay, then, let's go with that plan."

"Are you going to be comfortable here at the house?" I asked.

"Oh, yes. Lindsay and I have a couple of slumber parties planned. Don't we, hon?" Amelia's features softened with affection.

Lindsay's lips curved into a smile I liked seeing. "It'll be fun. Jean-Luc has promised us a couple of nice meals."

I observed how the mention of his name had sent a flush to her cheeks. I hadn't paid much attention to his comings and goings, but he must have come here more often than I'd thought.

"He and I have been talking about France," Lindsay continued. "I was once a foreign exchange student there, and I loved it."

"Hey! Maybe you and he ..." Rhonda started to say, ending abruptly when my foot stepped on her toe.

"Sorry," I said, catching myself, not meaning it at all. Rhonda thought she was a terrific matchmaker. To this day, she still thought she was the reason Bernie had married Annette. But it was not an appropriate time to introduce the idea of Jean-Luc becoming more than a friend to Lindsay.

"I've yet to meet Jean-Luc, but I can't wait to have him join us for lunch. The dinner he prepared for us last night was scrumptious," said Amelia.

"Yeah, he's a great chef and a good man. He's been lonely since his wife died," said Rhonda, moving away from me. She knew I was about to pinch her.

"I'll send a list of things we would like the hotel to do before my announcement, which I will make tomorrow afternoon," said Amelia. She turned to Lindsay. "Anything you want to add?"

"I just want to thank you both for your hospitality. I don't know if you've heard, but I'm meeting with Barbara Holmes as Ann suggested, and I like her a lot. That's one reason I want to stay here. Even though I've filed for divorce and soon will be free from the past horrors, I want to work on me before I move ahead."

"Oh, right," said Rhonda. "That makes sense."

"As I said, no matter what, we'll have room for you here in town," I said.

Amelia stood, and I knew the time for talking was over.

Rhonda and I said our goodbyes and left.

Outside, Rhonda rubbed her hands together. "I see another love match coming up."

"Patience. It's not even close to the time to think of it."

"Aw, Annie, for once, just let go."

I turned to her. "I didn't say I don't like the idea. I just said it was too early."

"That's better." Rhonda threw an arm around my shoulder, and we walked back to the hotel. Rhonda was as good for me as I was for her.

That afternoon as I was thinking of leaving, Rhonda popped into the office. "Time for girl talk and a margarita."

"Sounds wonderful," I said. "Meet you in the hotel bar in fifteen minutes. We can pretend we're guests and do some undercover spying on the staff."

Rhonda grinned. "I'll wear my sunglasses, so nobody recognizes me."

I laughed. If she wrapped herself in paper and tied a bow around herself, Rhonda would still be recognized by her boisterous voice and the colorful caftans that were the signature pieces of her wardrobe.

After making sure Elena would pick up Robbie from school, I entered the lobby, walked into the bar, and headed to the far end. The bar offered comfortable seating arranged for private conversations and was a welcome opportunity for me to see the hotel as others did. Working behind the scenes, I sometimes forgot what a stunning property it was.

Rhonda sat in a corner chair and waved me over. "I've already ordered. Margaritas at The Beach House Hotel. What could be better?"

"At this moment? Nothing," I said, happily sitting beside my best friend.

CHAPTER SEVEN

The next morning, I'd just dropped off Robbie at school when my cell rang. *Rhonda.*

"What's up?" I asked.

"Annie, I know we talked about it, but I just can't do it. That woman is such a bitch. You know what Katherine told Angela? She said she'd rather have a cab meet her at the airport than me."

I could hear the hurt in Rhonda's voice, and if I didn't know Katherine Smythe, I might think Rhonda was overreacting. But Katherine wasn't a pleasant person. It was a miracle her son was. But he'd spurned a lot of his mother's ideas about being superior to anyone else and had mellowed nicely here in Florida.

"How did you leave it with Angela?" I ventured.

"I told Angela that if she asked me to pick up that woman, then I was going to do it whether Katherine liked it or not." She paused. "But, Annie, promise you'll go with me. Please?"

The thought of Rhonda facing Katherine alone was frightening for so many reasons. "Sure, I'll go with you."

"Bless you!" said Rhonda. "I owe you big time for this."

"No worries. I'm happy to help you out. You've done so much for me."

"Okay. Come to my house. We can have coffee and try to relax for a while. I have to pick her up in an hour and a half."

"I'll call Bernie and let him know we'll be late. There's nothing on my schedule until this afternoon when I meet with Lorraine Grace about upcoming weddings."

"Right. I'm meeting with Dorothy to talk about the next Neighborhood Association meeting. Brock is still against our putting up a gate on our back property."

"See you soon."

A few minutes later, I pulled into the circular driveway of Rhonda's enormous, two-story house. I parked, grabbed my purse and phone, and headed inside, hoping Willow and Drew hadn't left yet for their pre-school. I loved her children. At just four, Willow looked more like her dad with light-brown hair and hazel eyes. But she had an attitude just like Rhonda. Drew, thirteen months younger, was a combination of Rhonda and Will in appearance and was both easy-going and then stubborn under Willow's constant supervision. Luckily, he adored her.

I rang the doorbell expecting Rita Ramos, their housekeeper, to answer the door. Instead, Willow beamed at me. "Hi, Auntie Ann!"

As she threw her arms around me, I hugged her close. "How's my special girl today?"

"I'm going on a field trip," she said, grinning.

"Nice. Where are you going?" I asked, gazing into her sparkling eyes so full of excitement.

"To the Naples Zoo. And Drew isn't coming." She folded her arms in front of her and looked at Drew, who'd approached us.

"No fair," said Drew.

"Babies can't come on the trip," Willow said. Seeing Drew's face begin to crumple, she put an arm around him. "But I'll tell you all about it."

Mollified, Drew let me pick him up. He was a cuddler, so I held him as often as he'd let me.

Rita joined us. "Hi, Ann! Rhonda said to come on up to her room. I just delivered coffee for you there."

"Thanks, Rita. What would we do without you?"

"More like what would I do without my Graysons?" she replied smiling.

Rita was the sister of Elena Ramos, who worked part-time for me. Both were attractive, ambitious women who attended courses at the local community college. Neither Rhonda nor I could imagine our lives without them. As soon as Rhonda unexpectedly became pregnant after Willow, she immediately gave Rita a huge raise that ensured Rita's decision to stay.

Upstairs, Rhonda was in the sitting room off the master bedroom, a favorite spot of hers. It was a cozy space that overlooked a back garden and pool area. We'd shared many secrets, worries, and decisions here.

Rhonda was sitting in a comfortable, upholstered chair in front of the French doors leading to an outside balcony and waved me to the chair opposite hers. "Thanks for coming Annie. I need to build up my confidence so I can pull off this meeting with Katherine."

"She isn't easy for anyone, Rhonda. But there's no reason for you to feel less about yourself when you're around her. You're a good person, beloved by all. She, on the other hand, may have her summer cottage in Newport and penthouse in New York, but she doesn't have the circle of friends and supporters that you have. That's priceless."

"I keep telling myself that, but she's never going to 'get' me. Ya know?" said Rhonda.

"Probably so," I said, being honest. "In-laws can be either wonderful or not so great. I like Chad's mother, but we have such different lives it's hard to keep close."

"But she and Vaughn have worked together in Community Theater projects. So that helps."

"Yes, it does," I admitted. "The kids want us all to get along. And that's what Angela wants. Especially with this second baby coming."

"That's why I'm going to try my best."

"By the way," I said. "I'm glad we have this time to talk about Lindsay staying at the hotel. I've offered to have her at my house, and I will gladly follow through. But I think she's probably safest at the hotel. Don't you agree?"

"Yes. As long as we have those extra security guards on duty, she should be fine. That's something we have to discuss with Amelia. Will told me we shouldn't have any problem being reimbursed under these special circumstances."

"I wondered about that. It seems only fair. But thank Will for that piece of advice." Rhonda's husband was a successful financial consultant who had extensive experience dealing with government contracts and reimbursement procedures.

"How's Reggie doing?" I asked Rhonda. Reggie had joined Will's company and was learning a lot even though he'd at one time pooh-poohed the idea of working in a company that wasn't his father's international firm.

"Will says Reggie is bright, courteous, and creative. No wonder his parents are angry he decided to stay in Florida and work with Will."

"It was a blow to them. That's another reason to be kind to Katherine."

Rhonda shrugged. "I guess. Finish your coffee, and we can take off. I'd rather be early than late."

We traveled up I-75 to Ft. Myers to the Southwest Florida International Airport. We'd meet Katherine there in the baggage claim area.

As we parked the car and climbed out, I observed the

tension in Rhonda's body. Beneath her caftan, her body was stiff with worry. I noted the diamonds sparkling on her ears, fingers, and wrists and knew she'd put them on like a coat of armor. In truth, as Rhonda had mentioned earlier, she was wealthier than Reggie's parents; she just didn't have their connections and pedigree. Having come from a somewhat rough background in New Jersey, she couldn't compete in that arena. But while Katherine claimed to know a lot of people, I thought it was more like a name-dropping game than real.

I stayed right at Rhonda's side as we entered the baggage claim area. We checked incoming flights and saw that Katherine's plane had already arrived. In the stream of passengers entering the area, I saw Katherine striding toward us with purpose.

When I'd first met her, I'd thought that with her long legs, sharp nose, and narrow neck, Katherine resembled a blue heron on the hunt. She still had that intimidating air about her.

Rhonda waved at her and stepped forward.

Katherine frowned and stopped.

As we approached, Rhonda said, "Welcome, Katherine. We're here to take you to Angela's."

Katherine drew her lips together. "I expressly told Angela that I'd take a cab to their house."

"I know," said Rhonda cheerfully. "But my daughter asked me to pick you up. So here we are. Nice to see you again."

"Okay, thanks. I guess I'm stuck." Katherine retorted and then turned to me with a sly smile. "How are you, Ann? And that handsome husband of yours? I've told everyone whom I know that Vaughn and I are friends. They all envy me." Her voice held a note of triumph, and I realized all over again why I'd never liked her.

Still, I tried to be pleasant. "We're all fine, thank you."

"Did you have a nice trip?" Rhonda asked, smiling. I knew her well enough to understand what effort she was making to be pleasant.

"Not really." Katherine shook her head. "Travel isn't what it used to be. Now, anyone and everyone are aboard the plane with all their backpacks and pillows and things of that kind."

"But surely you traveled first class," said Rhonda innocently.

"Of course," Katherine said. "I'd never travel any other way."

"In that case, it couldn't have been too awful," Rhonda said.

Noticing Rhonda's flared nostrils, I quickly added, "And for such a wonderful purpose."

Katherine looked directly at Rhonda. "Angela asked me to come help with Evan and then told me she wanted *me* with her at the hospital when the new baby comes."

Rhonda's eyes widened. Her cheeks flushed. "It was very nice of her to extend that invitation to you. As her mother, I'll, of course, be there too."

"Well," I said, trying to ease the tension between them, "let's get your luggage, Katherine, and then we can be on our way. I'm sure you're anxious to see your grandson."

"All right. It's two Louis Vuitton suitcases. I doubt we'll see any others."

Rhonda rolled her eyes and followed us to the conveyor belt.

After we retrieved her luggage, we headed to Rhonda's Mercedes station wagon, where we quickly loaded up. She usually drove a Cadillac convertible, but for this occasion, she'd chosen something more practical.

"Where's Manny? I thought he was your driver," said Katherine.

"I'm perfectly capable of driving," said Rhonda. "He's busy

with something at the hotel. We're very busy with some special guests."

I glared at her.

Smiling, I turned to Katherine. "But then, if you remember, all of our guests are special. Your friends, the Larkins from Palm Beach, have been back to visit a couple of times."

"Yes, Bettina has mentioned it," Katherine said quietly.

Rhonda held open the door to the back seat. "I think you'll find it roomy and comfortable back here. There's a bottle of cold water there waiting for you."

"Thank you," said Katherine. "But it's such a waste to have plastic water bottles."

Rhonda's lips thinned.

I sent her a warning look. "That's why we try not to abuse the use of them. But it's good to be sanitary. And we do recycle them."

"Oh, yes, Ann. I agree with you."

After Katherine had settled in her seat, Rhonda walked around the back of the car to get into the driver's seat, and I climbed in front beside her.

Trying to keep things smooth, I asked Katherine about her weather and what was happening in the City.

Katherine, pleased to be the center of attention, spoke of the weather both at her home in Newport and in the City. Making sure, I suppose, that we realized once more her social status.

I noticed Rhonda's grip on the steering wheel tighten and asked Katherine if she'd seen any interesting plays recently. Broadway plays were something I loved to see whenever I got to New York.

She chatted about the latest one she'd seen and then asked nicely, "And how is Robbie, that adorable boy of yours? He looks so much like Vaughn."

"He's doing very well in school and has become quite a sailor, thank you." I glanced at Rhonda. "He loves getting together with Willow and Drew. Rhonda and Will have created a beautiful outdoor playground behind their home for the kids."

"Oh, nice," said Katherine. "With the weather in Florida enjoyable much of the year, children can be outside a lot. You'll have to bring Robbie to Newport one day, Ann. Sailing is the big sport there. He'd love it. And then I could introduce my friends to Vaughn."

"We'll have to see. Vaughn's schedule can be erratic."

"I understand he has a new love interest in the show. She's beautiful but so young."

"So, I've heard. I haven't seen her on screen yet. But Rhonda and I try to see the show as much as possible." I knew I was impolite, but I couldn't help myself. "Vaughn adores Rhonda and always asks for her opinion on the show."

"Really?" said Katherine. "I'm surprised."

"Yeah," said Rhonda. "Vaughn and I are close."

"Looks like we're here," I said as Rhonda pulled into a cute neighborhood.

Katherine sighed loudly. "I don't understand why Reggie would buy anything here when he could have a much bigger, nicer home elsewhere."

"It's all about Evan and the baby. This is a neighborhood where Evan already has playgroups. And Angela and Reggie have made a lot of friends here," said Rhonda. "It's why I helped him pick out the house."

Katherine let out another noisy sigh. "Things could be so different."

Rhonda pulled up in front of a white, one-story stucco house. From the curb, it was impossible to see how large it was because it extended into the oversized, fenced-in back yard where a screened-in lanai and pool still left room for a swing set and other toys for a toddler.

As we climbed out of the car, Angela emerged from the house, looking every bit like a woman about to deliver a baby. Holding onto Evan's hand, she called out, "Hello!" and released him.

He immediately raced to Rhonda. "Hi, Gammy! Up! Up!"

Rhonda swung him up in her arms and hugged him tightly.

Katherine approached. "Hi, Evan. I'm Grandmother. I'm here to see you."

Evan hid his face in Rhonda's caftan.

"Here, I'll take him," said Angela. She held Evan for a moment and then placed him into Katherine's arms.

A smile crossed Katherine's face, and I realized that she was quite attractive without the constant pinched look she wore.

"My! He's grown so much! He's heavy," she declared.

"He's going to keep you busy, Katherine." Angela glanced at her mother.

"Yes, he's a busy boy," Rhonda said crisply.

I gave Angela a hug. "How are you feeling?"

"Like I'm ready to pop," she said, laughing. "They say the jump from one child to two is a big one."

"You've got that right," said Rhonda. "But, if you're lucky, the baby and Evan will be friends like my two."

"Depends on whether the baby is a boy or a girl. We don't want Evan playing girl games," said Katherine.

Too astonished to speak for a moment, I glanced at Angela, who was frowning.

"My two do very well together," said Rhonda. "As you might not remember, Katherine, I have both a boy and a girl. Willow and Drew."

I exchanged worried looks with Angela.

Angela, bless her heart, caught on. "My half-sister and half-brother are adorable. Willow and Evan play together all the time."

"Oh, well," sniffed Katherine. "I didn't mean to upset everyone. It's just that I always wanted Reggie to have friends who had similar, appropriate interests."

"Reggie's learned to be a big help around the house vacuuming, cleaning, taking care of Evan. Isn't that right, Angela?" said Rhonda.

Aware of the game being played, Angela hesitated, then nodded. "He's a good father and husband. You'll see for yourself, Katherine." She faced Rhonda. "Thank you for picking up Katherine, as I asked. I appreciate it."

"I'll help with the luggage," I offered. "Then, Rhonda and I need to get back to the hotel."

"You can't stay for coffee or something?" Angela asked, looking as if she desperately wanted us to agree.

"Sorry," said Rhonda, not acting sorry at all. "We have some important things to take care of." She kissed her and headed to the car, waving her ringing phone in the air. "I have to take this call."

I helped Katherine inside with her luggage and wheeled a suitcase into the guest room. Angela had placed a vase of fresh flowers in the room. A nice touch. I glanced at the plastic bottle of water sitting on the bedside table and wondered whether Katherine would comment on it negatively as she'd done with Rhonda. No doubt about it, Katherine was a difficult person.

I gave Angela a hug and left. As soon as I settled in the car, Rhonda sputtered. "That woman is impossible!"

"Yes, she is. But you're stuck with her. Good luck!"

Rhonda frowned. "That's it? That's all you're going to say?"

"Yes."

"But, Annie, I need you to say more," said Rhonda.

"Alright, she's a frickin' bitch," I said.

Rhonda grinned at me. "Ah, that's better. Now I don't feel so bad."

We laughed together.

CHAPTER EIGHT

I followed Rhonda into our office and took a seat at my desk. During the night, something had niggled at my brain. I checked the reservations, and, sure enough, we'd promised Tina Marks the use of the guesthouse for an extended stay after her and Nicholas Swain's baby was born sometime in May, just a few weeks away. I made a note to myself to mark that time on the calendar for Lindsay to come and stay with me. As much as I loved Tina, I thought the guesthouse would be a better place for her to stay.

I made a few phone calls regarding our upcoming annual spring event. Each year, after most of the snowbirds had left and we'd reclaimed our town, Rhonda and I hosted a Sunday brunch for the locals. This year, we'd hoped to take the time to thank everyone for their approval of the gate to the property. But because Brock Goodwin was gathering support against it, that wasn't going to happen. Instead, we'd thank them for their understanding of any inconvenience when we had someone famous in the hotel.

Rhonda handed me a note. "The Neighborhood Association is meeting tonight. Will and I will attend with you, but you'll have to speak, as usual."

I hated confrontation. No matter how polite and willing to compromise we were, Brock would keep any disagreement nasty. I always found these meetings difficult. But as we both agreed, it was best if I represented the hotel. Rhonda would not be able to hold back when Brock played his nasty word games.

I called Elena to make sure she could pick up Robbie and stay through the evening with him. She'd married Troy Taylor, the head of the spa at the hotel, and lived nearby, making it convenient for both of us. Though she was no longer working as a full-time nanny, Elena was more than happy to continue part-time. When the time came that she could no longer do it, a younger sister was ready to take her place.

With plans laid for the rest of the day, I went into the kitchen to check on Jean-Luc. He was in his small office off the kitchen doing paperwork.

"Good morning," I said, waiting for him to respond.

He looked up at me. "*Bonjour*, Ann. How are you?"

"I'm fine, but I'm curious. I understand you've been spending some time at the guesthouse. You've seen Lindsay, and Amelia mentioned dinner together last night. How do you think things are going? Lindsay looked a little better to me. And now she's decided to extend her stay."

The features of his face softened, and a smile played at his lips, chasing away his typical stoic look. "On my time off, Lindsay and I have done a lot of talking. We talk of France. It's been beneficial for us both, I think. I remember good times with Sabine, and it helps to speak about her. Lindsay understands how much I miss her, how guilty I feel about that automobile accident that took her away."

"It's wonderful you can open up to one another."

"I know," he said. "It makes me furious to see Lindsay so wounded in spirit and body."

"It's very upsetting."

"She's a lovely woman," said Jean-Luc. "So genuine. I'd heard of this terrible husband of hers, but until I saw what he did to her, I didn't understand."

"It's shocking," I agreed. "The fact that his family was willing to sweep his behavior away as if it was nothing is frightening. It was only after the judge forced him to go into rehab that the news finally got out. By then, she'd filed for divorce."

Jean-Luc gave her a worried look. "He still doesn't want to give her up."

"Too late, I'd say."

"Well, I've agreed to continue to see her as a friend. For some reason, she can talk to me. Her therapist told her it was a good thing."

My lips curved as I studied him. He was a proud man, comfortable with authority, but I saw through what others said was a crusty presence to the man beneath. I leaned over and kissed his cheek. "Have I told you how much I admire you, Jean-Luc? You're a sweet man."

"Bah!" he said, waving away any sentimentality.

But I saw how pleased he was.

Late that afternoon, as soon as I could get away, I left the hotel to see Robbie and change my clothes for the upcoming neighborhood meeting.

When I arrived home, Trudy greeted me at the door with barks and wiggles and then raced out back to where Robbie was swimming in the pool with Elena. One of the conditions we made with Robbie when Vaughn bought his sailboat was he had to continue with his swimming lessons. Not only for safety reasons but because he needed a healthy physical activity. Liz had been a good swimmer growing up, and Robbie had the same effortless grace in the water as she.

"Hi, Mom!" Robbie waved at me and then did a handstand in the shallow end of the pool.

I laughed, loving the way he showed off to please me.

"How are things going, Elena? Schoolwork going well?"

She let out a sigh. "I'll have two more courses completed at the end of this semester. I'll take courses through the summer too."

"Great. At this rate, you'll get your Master's degree in Psychology before you know it."

"From my position, it isn't as easy as that. But yes, I'm hoping to move forward as quickly as possible between work and helping Troy. How are you, Ann? You said you have another Neighborhood Association meeting to attend. That's never easy."

"Don't I know it." I sat in a chair by the pool and gazed up at the sunny sky, watching puffs of clouds drift by like dollops of marshmallow. Neighborhood meetings under the presidency of Brock Goodwin were always annoying because he repeatedly forced us to defend ourselves, our actions, and our hotel.

"Troy and I think we've found a house to buy. It's not in the best of condition, but we're willing to work to renovate it. The neighborhood is going through a revitalization, so it makes sense to get in before the improvements drive the house values way up."

I turned to her. "That makes me so happy. You two are such a wonderful pair." At one time, everyone at the hotel had been a little in love with hunky Troy, who was as nice as he was handsome.

Just then, Rhonda showed up. "Figured it was margarita time. I brought a pitcher of them we all can share. I don't know about you, but with everything that's going on, I need a little girl-time break."

"Sounds wonderful. Elena, join us when you can. I'll set things up on the lanai."

Sitting with my best friend, sipping a tasty cocktail, I felt my body begin to relax. I treasured these moments away from the hotel and work, a time to share other things going on in our lives. And I knew after the morning with Katherine, Rhonda needed a lot of soothing.

After Robbie got out of the pool and changed his clothes, Elena joined us. She eagerly showed us photos of the house she and Troy were considering.

"Better grab it quick," said Rhonda.

"We had first right of refusal, but Troy just called to tell me he made an official offer."

"Sounds good. Rhonda is right. When something like that comes along, it's a good idea to move quickly. It's an attractive house that hasn't received much love lately. But I can tell the bones of it are good."

Later, I told Rhonda I'd see her at the meeting, went into my bedroom, and changed clothes. Dorothy was on the board and had promised me we'd get lots of support.

When I walked into the meeting room, I was relieved to see Will and Rhonda had saved me a seat next to them. After going through so many of these gatherings, I told myself there was no need to be worried, but upon seeing Brock and his cronies at the front of the room, my pulse quickened.

Dorothy hurried over to me as I sat down. "Hi, Ann. Glad you're here. I've requested your topic be brought up right away, so you don't have to spend the whole evening here. Hopefully, Brock will follow through."

"Thanks, Dorothy. I appreciate it," I said, skeptical that it would happen.

"Don't get your hopes up, Dorothy," grumbled Rhonda.

"Guess we'd better get ready for a long night," I said.

"I'll stay as long as I can," said Will. "We promised Rita we wouldn't be too late. She's had a tough day."

"What's going on?" I asked.

"Drew has decided to become a painter, using peanut butter instead of watercolors."

"He painted an entire wall of the playroom with it before Rita caught him," said Rhonda. "He used it like fingerpaints. Actually, he's pretty artistic."

I laughed. Rhonda adored her son.

"The meeting of the Neighborhood Association will now come to order," Brock announced, pounding a small wooden gavel on the table.

As we listened to various reports, I grew nervous. The gate we wanted would keep people on the beach from traipsing through our hotel, disturbing our guests. It was a very reasonable request, especially considering it would be on our own property. I couldn't imagine why others in the neighborhood would object to it. But, with Brock, there was always a twist.

Tonight was no exception. By the time the board got to our request, some of the people in the audience were getting ready to leave.

Dorothy, sitting at the head of the room with other board members, stood. "Please don't leave, people. This will be a quick, easy decision." She turned to Brock. "It should never have come to this. Ann and Rhonda informed the board what they were doing out of courtesy. You've made it into something that it shouldn't be."

Brock's blue eyes blazed with fury. "As president of the board, I must protect my neighbors' interests. It's well and good they so-called informed us, but it's up to me to see that things are done in such a way that it doesn't damage our neighborhood. Trying to deal with Rhonda and Ann hasn't been easy."

"Read your statement, Brock, so it can be discussed quickly

and voted on," said Dorothy, her eyes sparking with anger behind her thick glasses.

Brock stood. "The owners of The Beach House Hotel have requested the board's approval of their putting in a gate leading from the beach onto their property. Some members of the board feel that a gate will change the way our section of the beach is perceived and may lead to others doing the same, discouraging people from using the beach."

I stood. "As one of the owners of the hotel, may I speak?"

Brock pounded his gavel. "You have just a minute to make your case."

I ignored his attempt at riling my temper, while Rhonda fidgeted in her seat beside me, unable to hold back.

"This issue should never have become a problem for the board. I want to assure all our neighbors here tonight that the gate is being erected on our property, not on the public beach, and is designed to be unobtrusive to those walking by. It is, however, necessary to protect our guests from intruders joining them by the pool, as one person recently did."

"I say we bring this to a quick vote," said Dorothy. "All in favor, raise your hands."

Several hands were raised.

"Anyone object?"

Brock responded, clearly irritated, "Dorothy, I, not you, have the right to ask those questions. Now let's start again. Any discussion?"

The room was quiet.

"All right. For the time being, we won't object to the request by The Beach House Hotel to go ahead and install a gate. However, have it noted that a group of us will take a look at it after it's in place."

"Bullshit!" Rhonda said in a stage whisper everyone around them heard.

"You're out of order, Rhonda," yelled Brock, pounding his gavel on the table.

I turned and faced the crowd still on my feet. "You know us well enough to be assured it will be done nicely."

"That's right," said an older man who'd supported us in the past. "Before Rhonda bought the property, it was in need of many maintenance issues that the former owners couldn't afford. It's been a blessing to all of us that Ann and Rhonda have turned the estate into such a beautiful property."

"It adds to the values of our homes," another man said.

"I see no reason for our board to keep making a problem over every request you make," added a woman in the audience.

"Remember that the next time the election of officers takes place," said Dorothy.

Brock pounded his gavel. "Without further ado, this meeting has ended."

He stood and walked over to me. "I hope you're satisfied that you've turned this into a vendetta against me."

I smiled sweetly while I just wanted to slap his face. "I haven't said a word about that. Other people in the neighborhood have spoken about it. Not me."

Will and Rhonda drew close.

" 'Evening, Brock," said Will. "I hope you're not threatening Ann. I'd hate to have to bring it to someone else's attention."

"I haven't threatened her at all, but I am disappointed that Ann and Rhonda don't respect the others in the neighborhood."

"You mean they don't respect you," Will said, nodding. "I'd agree with that. Me too. Good night."

"That bastard," mumbled Rhonda as we headed out the door.

We'd won this battle, but I knew there would be more.

CHAPTER NINE

When I arrived home, I was bone-tired. Brock Goodwin always made me feel as if I'd been dealing with a serpent.

I bid Elena goodnight and crept down the hallway to check on Robbie. I quietly opened the door. Trudy's eyes studied me as I walked over to the bed.

Stretched out atop the blanket, Robbie seemed as if he'd grown inches overnight. My heart filled with love. Who knew my ex-husband, who'd treated me so cruelly, would end up giving me such a gift? When I looked at this sweet boy, I tried to remember the good times I'd shared with Robert. After all, he'd also given me my precious daughter.

I bent over and kissed Robbie's cheek. Trudy's tail thumped against the blanket, and I patted her, then left the room. The best way I knew of to move past a meeting with Brock was to talk to Vaughn.

I locked up the house and went into my bedroom. After taking care of my nightly ritual, I slid into bed and lifted my phone to make the call.

He answered right away. "Hey, hon! I was just about to phone you. I called earlier, and Elena told me you were at a Neighborhood Association meeting. How did that go?"

"As well as could be expected. It was a non-issue that Brock placed at the bottom of the list of things to be discussed. Typical behavior for him."

"The guy is a total ass. I get it. So, no problem with the gate?"

"He's now saying it will be inspected after it's installed. Honestly, the man is impossible. But no matter how hard he tries, we'll fight him on this issue and the next and the next."

"Some people get a thrill out of being in a position like his. Why doesn't someone run against him?" asked Vaughn.

"He has a small cadre of people who like what he's doing. Besides, no one else wants the job."

Vaughn lowered his voice. "Enough of him. I'm missing you. What are you wearing, Mrs. Sanders?"

Even though he couldn't see me, I felt my cheeks heat. We loved playing this game, wishing we were together. "Well, if you were here, you would see that I'm wearing my PJs, not the usual filmy stuff I wear when you're here."

"It doesn't matter. Whether I'm there or here, I imagine you with nothing on."

"When do you think you'll be home again?" I asked, playing my own imagination game.

"Not soon enough," he growled. "The producers have us on a tight schedule because of Darla's introduction to the show. Rumors are already spinning, but I had a talk with Darla, and she's agreed there will be no romance between us."

"That sounds like a big improvement over Lily. I'm glad," I said. "With Angela's baby due in a week, my visit to New York won't be anytime soon."

"How's that going? Wasn't Angela's mother-in-law due to arrive soon?"

"Katherine arrived this morning. Rhonda made me go with her to the airport to pick her up, and I have to say, Katherine Smythe is a difficult woman. You'll be pleased to know she's told all of her friends that you and she are pretty close."

Vaughn surprised me by laughing. "So, I've heard. She's requested eight seats in the audience for our annual open rehearsal, telling the producers that we're good friends."

"Well, it's going to be a long two weeks with her here with Angela."

"How are things going with Lindsay and the vice president?"

"Amelia is going to hold a press conference in the library at the hotel. I haven't heard anything else about it."

"I'm proud of the way you and Rhonda handle prominent people at the hotel. A class act."

"Thank you, Vaughn. We try our best, even when guests don't make it easy."

"I spoke to Robbie earlier. How do you think he's doing? He still seems excited about school."

"He's a bright boy who likes learning. I'm hoping to keep that enthusiasm going. He had another swim lesson today with Elena. We'll get him signed up for sailing at the Yacht Club as soon as the program opens for the summer."

"Sounds good. I'd better go. I have to get up early."

"Good night, sweetheart. I love you," I said, wondering if he realized how important he was to me. He'd shown me in so many ways that I was loveable, and I could trust him.

"Love you too," he said and clicked off the call.

I lay back against the pillow. I'd learned making small talk discussing the day's activities was as important as the physical aspects in building a friendship within a marriage.

The next day, when I was sitting in my office going over the invitation list for our spring brunch, I was surprised to see Amelia and her Secret Service agent at the door.

"Hi! C'mon in. Rhonda and I are just working on plans for our annual spring brunch."

"You're not hiding out anymore?" Rhonda said.

Amelia shook her head. "No, I want people to know I'm

here so Lindsay can have a little break. Jean-Luc has asked her to his house for dinner and a walk on the beach away from here."

"Sounds like a good idea," I said. "We don't want her to feel like a prisoner at the hotel, and his house is in a quiet spot."

"Well, like it or not, it's important to lay low. Thomas Thaxton is used to getting his way, and he's upset about divorce papers being served to him." Her lips thinned. "Some jerks don't get it. I'm sorry I ever introduced them. Edward Thaxton isn't like his brother, but he should've warned me that Thomas was a troubled man."

"Isn't he in a rehabilitation program?" I asked as a shiver traveled across my shoulders. I'd read enough stories in the news about women being stalked after spurning a man. And divorce was a huge, final break in a relationship.

"For the time being, he is," said Amelia. "But Debra will stay with Lindsay until I feel it's safe for her to be alone. The president and I have discussed the situation, and though he won't tell his brother where she is, he'll try to reason with him about the circumstances."

"When is the news conference?" I asked.

"That's what I want to talk to you about. I'd like to hold it here at noon tomorrow if that's all right with you. Bernie has cleared the room for me but said I should discuss it with you."

Rhonda and I exchanged satisfied glances. We liked that Bernie included us with the running of the hotel though he'd made it plain he was in charge, as we'd hired him to be.

"That's great," said Rhonda. "We thought we'd invite a few of the city council members. Does that sound okay to you?"

"We like to keep close ties with them because the president of our Neighborhood Association can make things difficult," I explained.

Amelia laughed. "I get it. Politics are the same everywhere.

No problem with inviting them to come. We've invited Governor Horne to attend. We'll finalize plans with the local networks to provide coverage for the major ones. And Terri Thomas from the Sabal *Daily News* has requested an interview following the announcement."

"That should take care of everyone, I imagine," I said.

"There's plenty of room in the library for all of them," Rhonda added. "But not much more with all the equipment."

Amelia's lips curved. "I'm delighted I thought to come here. It's been perfect so far."

"I'm pleased to hear it," I said. "If it's at all possible, I'd love for you to join Rhonda and me for margaritas later this afternoon. It's become a ritual every so often, whenever we can squeeze it into our schedules, to take a moment to relax in our hotel and remind ourselves of what's important in running the place. It's easy to get caught up in stuff that doesn't matter."

"Oh, I know what you mean. I'd love to join you. Sounds like fun. You're so lucky to be friends as well as business partners."

"I wasn't always sure it would happen," said Rhonda, grinning at me. "We're quite different."

"Oh, really?" said Amelia, grinning at us. "You two are a great team. Anyone who's met you says it."

I glanced at Rhonda. We were as different as could be. In looks as well. While she was tall, blonde, and well-padded, I was short and thin, had blue eyes, and had dark hair worn straight to my shoulders. When we'd first met, she'd told me not to be so beige. This coming from a woman who dyed her hair, wore colorful caftans, used too much makeup, had huge diamonds sparkling on fingers, ears, and toes, and had a loud, raucous laugh.

"Rhonda's the best," I said, meaning it.

"Annie's come a long way," said Rhonda, bursting into loud laughter.

Amelia and I looked at one another and joined in.

On a whim, I decided instead of going home for lunch, I'd take a selection of tea sandwiches and little pastries to Angela as a surprise. Angela was like my own daughter, and I wanted to see for myself how she was doing with her mother-in-law.

I drove up to the house, surprised to see Angela's van in the driveway with a couple of doors open and nobody in sight.

Curious, I pulled up behind the vehicle and got out. Carrying the food I had carefully boxed up, I went to the front door. From inside, I could hear a child crying and voices raised in argument. I rang the bell and waited.

The voices quieted, and Angela opened the door. Her eyes were red-rimmed, but her lips curved when she saw me.

"Surprise! I brought some treats for you for lunch. A gift from the hotel."

"Oh, Ann, that's very nice." Her voice shook. "I'm sure Katherine will love it as much as I will. Come on in."

Katherine was standing in the living room holding onto Evan's arm. He was crying and reaching out for his mother.

"We're having a tough morning," said Angela with a brightness I knew to be fake. "Katherine went to pick up Evan from pre-school, and he didn't want to ride with her in the van. I think he's getting temperamental because he knows the baby is coming soon, and he wants me, not anyone else, to take care of him."

"I can understand that," I said.

"He's a willful child," Katherine said, disapproval dripping from her voice.

"It might be confusing to have new people in the house," I

offered. "But after he has some quality time with you, I'm sure things will be easier."

"Ann brought us some treats for lunch," Angela said. "Evan, come into the kitchen with me. You can sit with us."

Evan pouted. "I want a picnic outside. You said I could."

"Evan, you heard your mother. Do as she says," Katherine said sharply.

Angela gave me a helpless look.

"If he eats lunch outside, it'll give us a chance to relax and talk," I said.

"Right," said Angela. "Katherine, do you want to fix him a peanut butter sandwich on white bread with the crusts cut off? I'll set the table and get the food set out for us." Angela turned to Evan. "You may eat your lunch in the play yard, but no fussing, and you have to eat everything, including the fruit cup Grandmother made for you. Understand?"

Evan, too, must have heard the desperation in Angela's words. He gazed wide-eyed at his mother and slowly nodded.

"Well, then," I stated brightly. "That's settled. Let me help you, Angela. You should be resting."

Angela rolled her eyes at me, took Evan's hand, and walked outside with him.

I went into the kitchen to talk to Katherine.

"That child is so spoiled," Katherine hissed at me. "And look at this! Crusts have to be cut off the bread?"

"It's not that unusual. And Evan is usually a sweet little boy. Super active, but nice. I think Angela is right. He's aware of what's happening and is fighting for attention."

"Angela is too easy on him. Lord knows, he won't listen to me," Katherine huffed.

"Have you played with him on his level?" I asked, doubting she had.

"I'm trying to teach him checkers, but he doesn't want to

play," Katherine said. "It's been years since Reggie was his age, but he played that game with me back then."

"At age four?"

"He was a bright child," Katherine declared.

"How about playing Legos with him? Something to help with his eye-hand coordination?"

"When I tried to show him how to build a house like the picture on the box, he got mad." Katherine's eyes filled. "I'm not used to children his age."

"Let him guide you as to what he wants to do, not what you're telling him to do. See the difference? Evan's a bright boy too, but nobody likes to be ordered around."

Katherine gave me a woeful look and sighed. "Here comes Angela now. Let me get this sandwich made. I'm sure I won't make it right."

I patted her arm. "A peanut butter sandwich is pretty easy. Relax."

She gave me a grateful smile.

"Let's see what you brought, Ann! You know I'll love anything from the hotel." Angela stood at the counter and clutched her back. "If this baby doesn't come soon, I don't know what I'll do. I'm more than ready."

"I told Angela it's going to be a couple more days," said Katherine. "The baby hasn't dropped yet."

"But it has," Angela protested. "At any rate, when the time is right, the baby will come."

"Still don't know the sex yet?" I asked.

"No," said Angela. "We wanted to wait and be surprised."

"I told Angela it would be so much easier for everyone if they knew, but she and Reggie insisted on waiting." She glanced at Angela. "But it'll be fun to be surprised. Won't it, dear?"

"I think so. Ann, will you pour us drinks? I've made some

iced tea the way Katherine likes it."

"Sure." I went to the refrigerator and opened it. Inside were several boxes from various restaurants. "Wow! You guys have had lots of different foods."

"Katherine doesn't like to cook," said Angela.

"I've never had to, you see, and I thought it would be a treat for them if I bought take-out food from some of their favorite places." Katherine turned to Angela. "It's worked out well, don't you think?"

"It's been nice that I haven't had to fix meals," said Angela politely.

I knew her well enough to understand the effort she was making to be friendly and loved her for it. She and Reggie had a healthy relationship, and I knew from earlier conversations that it was important for him to have his mother present during this time. A coming together of the families.

As we sat and ate, I worked to keep the conversation light.

"Is Vaughn in town?" Katherine asked me.

"No, he's not. But I'll be sure to tell him you asked about him. How's Arthur?"

I'd liked Reggie's dad the few times I'd met him.

"He's busy as always and waiting to get the word the baby has arrived so he can fly down here himself. He's anxious to talk to Reggie about some of the international deals he's working on."

I swallowed my bite of sandwich and reached for my glass of iced tea. This was precisely what Rhonda had been worried about.

"Reggie's doing very well with Will," said Angela. "But it's always nice for the guys to talk business. Especially as one business owner to another."

Katherine shot Angela a look of surprise.

"It's official, Reggie and Will are now equal partners," said

Angela, her eyes shining with pride.

"I didn't know ..." Katherine patted her face with her napkin with a look of distress.

"Reggie's planning to tell Arthur when he's here. I hope I didn't ruin it for him," said Angela. "I'm so proud of him."

Katherine sniffed. "You were fortunate to have found him."

"And he's lucky to have discovered Angela," I said, speaking for Rhonda.

Katherine and I studied each other.

Evan came inside the kitchen holding his empty plastic plate. "See? I was a good boy."

"You're a good boy, all right," said Angela taking the plate from him and wrapping an arm around him. "Now it's your quiet time. Katherine, will you please help Evan choose a book to listen to on his electronic player so he can rest in his room?"

Katherine rose. "Of course. Come along, Evan. You can show me which book you want and how to set it up for you. Okay?"

Evan stared at her for a moment and then headed for the door.

I watched them leave and turned to Angela. "How are you holding up?"

She emitted a long sigh. "If I didn't love Reggie so much, I swear I'd ask Katherine to pack her bags. It's been tough. You can't be a dictator. It works better if you're able to make children want to do things. You must have talked to her. That's the nicest she's been with Evan."

"She's got a lot to learn. She really does."

"Mom is in a dither because I've asked Katherine to be with me in the hospital. But Katherine needs to be a grandmother to both of the children."

"I agree, even if Katherine doesn't make it easy. I'm here to help any way I can." I rose. "I'd better get back to the hotel.

We have some big things coming up. Vice President Swanson is going to hold a news conference at the hotel tomorrow. And later today, your mother and I are going to treat her to margaritas at the hotel."

"Sounds like another fun event at The Beach House Hotel," said Angela in a wistful voice.

I hugged her. "Don't get overtired."

As I walked to my car, I stopped and closed the doors of the van, guessing an argument had taken place. After talking to Katherine, I thought she truly cared about Angela and Evan. It just wasn't within her to show it easily. Poor Angela!

CHAPTER TEN

Rhonda and I walked together into the small, intimate bar of the hotel to meet Amelia. I noticed a young man I remembered as one of Amelia's security guards seated on a love seat next to a blonde wearing dark glasses, a sun hat, and a brightly-colored, floral-print sundress.

"Hello!" I said, approaching them.

The man rose. "Hello." He wore tan slacks and a bright-blue shirt that did nothing to hide the strength in his muscled body. His eyes surveyed the room before he sat.

Rhonda and I pulled our chairs up to the coffee table in front of the love seat.

"You look great," Rhonda said to Amelia. "If I didn't know we'd arranged to meet, I might not have guessed it was you."

"I thought I'd try blonde for a while. A little less obvious in these surroundings," Amelia said quietly. "Clyde and I arrived early so we could take a tour of the hotel."

"Oh, yes, for security," I said. "Have you ordered?"

"No, we were waiting for you," said Amelia.

I turned and signaled the bartender for service. Immediately, a pleasant young man appeared at my side. "Yes, Mrs. Sanders."

"I've raved about the margaritas here." I turned to Amelia. "You'll try one?" At her nod, Clyde spoke up. "And I'll have a club soda with lime, please."

"Okay, three margaritas and the club soda. And please put this on my tab."

He gave a little bow and left us.

"You've trained your staff so well," said Amelia.

"Bernie is a big part of that, but that's always been our philosophy," said Rhonda.

"We may not be a big operation, but we're rated at the top in the industry for service and attention to detail," I said proudly. It had been a struggle at first to make staff understand we operated at a much different level from some other hotels. Pleasant, excellent service and discretion were absolute necessities.

"I'm pleased I've had the opportunity to see for myself how lovely The Beach House Hotel is," said Amelia, giving us both a big smile. "Several people in Washington, D. C. had told me about it, but it's not the same as experiencing it."

The bartender arrived with our drinks. After he had served them, Rhonda raised her glass. "Here's to a successful visit by all."

We clicked glasses, even Clyde. Though he wore no shoulder holster, I'd noticed a shape of something in his lower pant leg and figured he had a weapon there. Usually, firearms weren't allowed in the hotel, but under these circumstances, we accepted it.

We were exchanging pleasantries when I felt rather than saw someone approach. Clyde's attention focused on someone behind me.

I whipped around. "Brock! What are you doing here at this time of day? Don't you usually appear later, just before sunset?"

Brock glanced at Amelia and said, "A friend of mine, a councilman, said Amelia Swanson is giving a news conference here tomorrow. I'm hoping to see if she's around so I can get an invite for myself."

"Brock, you're not invited," said Rhonda firmly.

He glared at her. "As president of the Neighborhood

Association, I should be included in any major event in the area."

"Sorry, but you're not on the list," I added, praying Brock would leave.

"Well, guess I'll have a look around. I don't need the two of you to permit me to speak to her. I want to discuss ways I can perhaps help her in the future with all my business connections overseas."

As he left, I turned to Amelia. "Sorry about that. He's a constant pain ..."

"... in the ass," Rhonda finished for me.

"He reminded me of several people back in D. C. Right, Clyde?" said Amelia.

Always professional, Clyde merely nodded.

"How is it having someone guarding you constantly?" Rhonda asked.

Amelia shrugged. "Not always comfortable, but you get used to it. Especially if you have a good guy like Clyde around. If your friend had made any move toward me, he'd be flat on his back on the floor wondering what had happened to him."

Clyde chuckled. "Got that right."

"Lindsay left to meet Jean-Luc?" I asked Amelia.

"Yes. I see a real friendship forming there. Neither one is interested in anything more, which is a good thing. It's going to be a while before Lindsay is able to heal from a relationship gone so bad."

"Jean-Luc is a very nice man," said Rhonda. "And lonely too."

"Oh, yes, and talented too," Amelia said, patting her stomach. "He prepared a simple meal for us last night. It was out of this world. I'm grateful he's getting Lindsay interested in eating again. I was afraid she was heading into anorexia." She glanced at Clyde.

He stood. "Why don't I give you some privacy? I'll sit at the bar and keep an eye on things from there."

"Thank you," said Amelia. She turned to Ann and Rhonda. "Now, tell me more about yourselves. The fact that you two put this operation together is a fascinating story I want to tell to others. As you know, I continue to do a lot of work on women's rights in the home, the workplace, the nation."

At a signal, the bartender brought another round of margaritas along with three glasses of water, a bowl of assorted nuts and crackers, and a variety of olives on a glass dish.

As we talked, I discovered Amelia was an interesting person. She spoke very frankly about being raised in a household by her abusive father and the political maneuvering it had taken to get noticed in what was still very much a male-dominated arena.

"Your work is so important," I said.

"Bullying needs to be addressed, too," Rhonda told her. "Believe me; I know all about it. I didn't fit in with the other girls in school, and they made sure I did not attempt to do so. My brother helped some, but he couldn't control the million mean things they did and said."

I patted Rhonda's hand. "And look how you turned out! Everyone here loves you."

"Some just for my money," Rhonda said. "But I've got their number." She glanced at me and grinned. "Annie, here, didn't want any help from me. But we got that worked out. I'm one of those rags to riches stories. Several years ago, I won the Florida Jackpot for one hundred eighty-seven million dollars, so I had a little to spare."

"Rhonda's a very generous person," I said, remembering how, when I had no job and no house, she had come to my rescue. She'd convinced me to live with her and use my business expertise to help her convert her mansion into a hotel.

I looked up as Brock came hurrying through the bar from the outside.

"What's going on?" I asked.

"Yeah, why are you in such a rush?" Rhonda asked him suspiciously.

"Someone told me the vice president is just leaving the hotel. I want to try and catch her before she goes," he said, moving away.

"Good for you, Brock." Holding in my laughter, I glanced at Amelia. She was laughing too.

Not long afterward, Amelia got to her feet. "I have to leave as I'm meeting someone for dinner. Thank you for the opportunity to get to know the two of you better. I'm very excited to share your story with my women's group and hope you'll agree to come to speak in Washington."

Rhonda and I glanced at one another and smiled. We were accustomed to having VIPs at the hotel, but this seemed different. More like friends helping friends.

That night, lying in bed talking to Vaughn, I shared a good laugh with him over Brock's self-importance preventing him from noticing the vice president in disguise. But then his focus tended to be on young, voluptuous women, not someone older like Amelia.

The next morning Rhonda and I stood by as cameras were set up in the library for the news conference. A few years ago, we'd transformed the library into a special room where private, secure meetings could be held. Later, we added a few features like a raised dais where people could speak and small musical groups could perform. Today, the vice president would make a significant announcement there. Bernie made sure the American flag was on one side of the platform, and a special flag with the hotel's name and logo stood on the other side.

After most of the camera crew had set up their equipment, they and we waited for Bernie to escort our guests into the room. A few minutes later, we all applauded as Vice President Amelia Swanson entered the room with Clyde and a thin, young woman. The governor had sent a message he'd be unable to attend.

Shivers traveled down my spine as I observed Amelia in her role, one of the most prestigious in the world. And then tears of gratitude stung my eyes. Of all the places she could've chosen to hold the news conference and, more importantly, to keep her sister safe, she'd chosen the hotel Rhonda and I had worked so hard to create.

I glanced at Rhonda and, from her expression, knew she too was awed by this moment.

Amelia spoke about the courage of the young newswoman seeking information about life in Guatemala and Central America and the need to know the truth behind the headlines. "We need and want to support these truth finders. It is with extreme gratitude for the cooperation of the government of Guatemala that I'm now able to present to you, Carlotta Morales."

Applause erupted as a young, dark-haired woman walked toward the microphone. Thin to the point of being emaciated, she moved slowly. I realized then that what the papers had reported was true—she'd suffered in captivity.

Amelia met her at the steps of the dais and helped Carlotta onto it. "Now, ladies and gentlemen, I'm sure you all have a lot of questions."

A reporter waved a hand. "Before we get started, where is your sister, Lindsay Thaxton? You must know where she is. She hasn't been seen in Vermont."

A pained expression crossed Amelia's face. "You know I won't discuss my sister's personal business."

"Is she safe?" The persistent reporter asked.

"If you're asking if she's still with Thomas Thaxton, the answer is no. And that's all I'm going to say on the subject." She turned to Carlotta. "We welcome you home, Ms. Morales. These journalists would be interested in your statement about your time in captivity."

"There's not much I'm able to share, but I do want to publicly thank Vice President Swanson for her dogged persistence in managing an exchange so I could return to the country I love. To those who may have forgotten, I suggest you remember and cherish the freedoms we in the United States take for granted and others don't have."

As the room became full of questions shouted at Carlotta and the vice president, causing a din of confusion, Bernie appeared at the door and signaled me to join him.

"What's up?" she asked him.

He waved me outside.

As I stepped into the hall, I faced Brock Goodwin. "Hello, Brock," I said coolly. "What are you doing here?"

"I'm here to speak to the vice president." He glared at Bernie. "I haven't been allowed inside the room, but I'm a citizen and have the right to speak to her."

"Then I suggest you wait in the lobby. She'll be coming through there. After she finishes her talk, she's heading for the airport with Carlotta Morales for a flight back to Washington to meet with the president."

"Okay. I'll wait there."

"Just so you know, I'm not promising any of the guests will be able to spend any time with her."

"A crowd of people is waiting outside," Bernie said. "Her Secret Service contingent is keeping an eye on the limousine waiting to drive them away."

"Maybe we'd better use our security staff to help."

Bernie shot me a satisfied grin. "Already on it. They've kept everything under control elsewhere."

"Good." I knew he was thinking of Lindsay staying in the house.

When I entered the library, the news conference was ending.

"Thank you, everyone," said the vice president. "We'll release a statement after Carlotta Morales and I return to Washington. With her staying in the area for a couple of days recovering, we wanted to give you local news people the opportunity to share our good news. Now, we leave to visit the president."

Another member of the security team joined Clyde as Amelia made her way past the news people and out the door, stopping briefly to greet the dignitaries invited to the press release.

"There's a crowd outside," I overheard one of the guards say to Amelia. "No stopping for anyone."

Amelia took Carlotta's elbow and followed the guard, moving quickly.

Outside, Rhonda and I stood on the front steps and watched as Amelia and Carlotta disappeared into the limo. It took me a minute to register that not everyone in the crowd was friendly. Some were holding signs saying: *"U.S. Stop interfering in Central America!"*

The Secret Service contingent stepped into their black SUV, and both the SUV and the limo made their way out through the hotel's gate.

Brock came up to us. "Is she coming back? Those guards of hers kept me away from her."

"Not anytime soon."

"You lose," said Rhonda. Her smile was almost cheerful.

Brock's gaze settled on Rhonda. "Someday, you're going to be sorry for the way you treat me."

"Be careful what you say, Brock. It isn't right for you to threaten us or others in the neighborhood." Though I spoke softly, nobody could mistake the warning in my voice.

He waved away my words. "Everyone knows you don't show me the respect I deserve."

"Respect is earned, not dictated," I said, watching a security guard head our way.

"Everything all right here?" he asked, studying Brock and turning to us.

"He was just leaving," Rhonda said.

Brock let out a noisy sigh and headed down the stairs.

I turned to Rhonda. "I don't like how Brock threatens us. I'm going to speak to Bernie about alerting the guards to keep an eye on him whenever he shows up at the hotel. Especially now, with Lindsay."

"Good idea. We never seem to get past our troubles with him. He's more of a pest than a frickin' mosquito."

"Or the alligator they found on the golf course nearby," I said, commiserating with her.

Bernie approached. "Glad there were no disruptions here. When the sign bearers arrived, there was a small skirmish."

"How did you think it went overall?" I asked.

"Good publicity for the hotel. We'll see how that translates into heads in beds," Bernie said.

"We need some cold spring weather up north," said Rhonda.

"That, too," Bernie agreed. "I'd better leave you. We have a big wedding party coming in soon."

"Good luck with it," I said. "Rhonda and I will come to say hello at the reception for them."

Bernie acknowledged my words and walked away.

Rhonda turned to me. "You know, Annie, I didn't like having those protesters here. They looked like a rough bunch. I'd feel better if we checked on Lindsay and made sure she was all right."

"Probably a good idea. There was enough of a crowd that someone could easily slip by and walk into the non-public areas."

We took the back path toward the house. It was a hidden way to go from the hotel because it was tucked into the trees and landscaping that we had added around the house. So as not to disturb anything, we walked quietly.

We'd gone halfway when I pulled Rhonda to a stop.

Ahead of us, a man wearing a baseball cap and sunglasses had a camera with a telephoto lens around his neck, and he was talking into his cell phone. "No signs of her here."

I pressed the number for hotel security on my cell phone and then approached him.

"You!" I shouted. "What are you doing here?"

The man whipped around, saw us, and took off running.

I ran after him, but he came to an abrupt stop when a security guard stepped in front of him.

I hurried to catch up to them. "Who are you? And what are you doing here?"

"None of your business," he protested, giving me a defiant look.

"Officer, call the police. I want him arrested for

trespassing." His earlier words made me believe it wasn't just a matter of trespassing. He'd been spying.

At that, the man, dressed in jeans and a golf shirt, laughed. "Trespassing? I am just a potential guest looking over the property and got lost. That's all. You can't prove it was anything more than that."

I faced the guard. "I want you to get all the information you can from him and mark it on our records that we found him in an area marked private, and he was obviously trespassing."

"Again, you have no proof of it," the man asserted with a sneer.

Another security guard showed up. "What's going on?"

I gave him the details.

"We'll take care of it," the security guard said. "Feel free to go about your business. He's not going anywhere but off the property."

"Make sure of it," said Rhonda. She took my arm and led me into the hotel.

"What's going on?" I said, turning to her inside the lobby.

"I'm sure I saw that man last night, poking around the lobby when we were having margaritas with Amelia. I don't like it. He's after something."

"Do you think he's suspicious about Lindsay, or was it simply an interest in Amelia?"

"That's something we'll have to wait to find out," said Rhonda. "We need to get information on him. Let's get Bernie to join the security people, so the guy will think it's just hotel routine and not that we have something or someone to protect."

Bernie was in his office when we approached.

We quickly told him what happened and asked him to join the security people out front.

He returned shortly. "We couldn't get much information.

Security did get him to show them his license. His name is John Denver, from Maryland."

"John Denver? Sounds like a name someone would make up," I said.

"You don't remember 'Rocky Mountain High?'" said Rhonda. "My mother used to listen to that all the time."

"My grandmother listened to only classical music," I said with a note of sadness. "That, and opera."

"Anyway," said Bernie. "We've got that much information on him. The guards have taken his photo on their phones and will post them in their office so we can watch for him should he try to return. They'll also run a background check on him."

"Thanks, Bernie," I said, feeling more urgency to go to the guesthouse to check on Lindsay. There was no way John Denver or whoever he was, was a tourist lost on the property.

CHAPTER ELEVEN

Rhonda and I headed back to the house to check on Lindsay.

"I don't want this to become a battleground for the Thaxtons," said Rhonda. "We have the reputation of our hotel to protect."

"I agree. And I don't like the idea of spying going on here. I wonder when Thomas Thaxton is due to get out of rehab. From the way Lindsay has to hide, it's not likely to be a happy scene."

"He's never going to get his hands on her as long as I'm around," growled Rhonda. "That man is dangerous whether he's sober or not."

"That's what frightens me. But even though I'm worried, I'm not sorry we're helping her out."

As soon as we knocked on the door, Debra cracked it open. "You alone?"

Rhonda and I glanced at each other and nodded to her.

"Why?" I asked.

"We had a visitor a short while ago." Debra opened the door, swept a good look all around, and motioned us inside.

"Let me guess. The visitor was a guy wearing a baseball cap, jeans, and a golf shirt, and with a camera. Is that right?"

Debra grimaced and bobbed her head. "Yep. I don't know him, but I'm pretty sure I know where he came from."

"Thomas Thaxton?" Rhonda asked.

"No. His brother," said Debra, looking grim.

"The president?" My heart rate leaped. "Why would he

send someone here?"

Debra let out a little laugh that wasn't humorous at all. "*He* wouldn't do it. He'd have someone ask someone to do it, if you get my drift. He is a man who must be in control at all times. The word I get from some of my friends in D. C. is that he's totally pissed that the vice president won't reveal where Lindsay is."

"Oh, boy! This isn't good," said Rhonda, giving me a worried look.

My stomach churned. I didn't want to get caught in a game of cat and mouse with the president of the United States.

"I've already put in a call to Bernie," said Debra. "Whenever there's a major event at the hotel like the news conference, he needs to alert us. Luckily, Lindsay wasn't here."

"Not here? We should know if and when she's off property," I said. "If we don't, how can we help protect her?"

"That's my concern. The fewer people who know her whereabouts, the better," Debra said with a firmness I suddenly understood.

"All right. But if she's with Jean-Luc, he needs to be warned about the situation. We don't want anything to happen to him."

"Yeah. He's one of the good guys," Rhonda said.

"Understood on both counts," said Debra. "I've already called in someone else to help me." A pretty blush colored her cheeks. "My old boyfriend, Whit Evans, is ex-CIA. I trust him to help keep Lindsay safe."

"So, he'll stay here with you?"

"Unless Lindsay is staying elsewhere. She's very comfortable with Jean-Luc. I've checked out his house, and with a little rearrangement of things, I'm satisfied it's safe for short visits as both she and Amelia Swanson want. She's begun to feel like a prisoner. But I told them I'm not comfortable with that. From now on, when Lindsay goes to Jean-Luc's house, Whit or I will accompany her while the other stays here at the house, so no one else is aware when she leaves the premises."

"I get it," said Rhonda, turning to me. "Wow! This is like a television show. Or one of Vaughn's soap operas."

I grinned. We'd both been fascinated a few years earlier when *The Sins of the Children* came to The Beach House Hotel to film a large segment of the show. Even now, we continued to watch it together whenever we could squeeze it into our schedules.

"Seriously, I don't want you to worry," said Debra. "Both Whit and I are good at our jobs."

"I feel better knowing there will be two of you. When we agreed to help Lindsay, we didn't realize there might be this kind of search to find her."

"Not with the president getting involved," said Rhonda. "I didn't vote for him, and now I'm glad I didn't. Seems to me he's hiding a whole lot of issues."

"All right," said Debra. "Whit is arriving this afternoon." She held out her cell phone to them. "Here's what he looks like."

Rhonda and I studied the picture of a large man with light-brown hair, dark eyes, ruggedly handsome features, and what looked like a scar above his right eyebrow.

"Don't worry, he'll fit in with your typical guest," said Debra. "And for his own knowledge, he'll make sure he knows this place inside and out. So, you might see him wandering around a bit."

"Be sure Bernie and the head of security see his picture and know what his job is here," I said. "The last thing we want is for staff to create a scene while confronting him."

"Or to make our guests uncomfortable," Rhonda added.

"This is a lovely hotel. I'd hate to see it caught up in this and getting bad publicity because of your kindness." Debra held out her hand, and we both shook it.

As we were walking back to the hotel, Rhonda elbowed me. "Did you get a load of that hunk Debra says is her ex-boyfriend? Just looking at that picture made me feel hot. Or maybe it was another hot flash coming on."

I laughed. "Probably both. Whit Evans would make any woman under eighty want to call for his help."

Rhonda flung her arm around my shoulder. "Too bad I'm so out of practice. With the kids running us ragged in the evenings, Will and I are too pooped to do much in bed except to roll over and go to sleep." She let out a dreamy sigh. "He was such a good lover when we first met. We were more like ..."

"Ach! TMI... Too much information! You guys need a vacation. That's all."

"Maybe after Angela has had her baby, Will and I can go away for a while."

"Let's hope the issue with Lindsay is resolved by then," I said, more worried about it than I'd let on.

That afternoon, I pulled into the driveway of my house, grateful for the home I loved. Here, peace and quiet were welcome gifts.

I got out of the car and waited for Trudy to bound through the doggy door to greet me.

Not seeing her, I went inside to the kitchen and gazed out at the pool and backyard.

Neither Robbie nor Elena were there. But I noticed

movement on the sailboat tied at the dock, and my heart beat with joy. *Vaughn?*

I ran outside and headed down the hill, smiling and laughing. It was always such a wonderful surprise when he came home unexpectedly.

Robbie appeared topside on the boat and shouted, "Hi, Mom! Dad's home!"

Vaughn joined him, grinning at me. He stepped off the boat and came to greet me, easily sweeping me up in his arms and twirling me around.

"I'm so happy to see you!" I cried. He was my rock who could steady me on my feet when I felt overwhelmed.

His lips met mine, and I melted against him.

"That kissing stuff is gross," said Robbie, making a face.

Laughing, Vaughn and I pulled apart.

"Someday, you're going to like it," said Vaughn. "Trust me." He winked at me. "More later."

"Yes," I said happily. With him working in New York and gone so much of the time, each reunion was sweet. "What brings you here?"

He frowned. "Darla was having some trouble with one of the producers and called in sick. I'm not sure what's going on, but she's asked for some time off. And, Ann, she wants to come and take a break here at the hotel. Is that possible?"

"I'll have to check. If we're booked, the Presidential Suite might be available. Would she be willing to pay for that? I could maybe give her a special room rate, but it would still be expensive."

"Either way, I'm sure she'd be willing to pay. She was quite agitated," said Vaughn.

"When I go back inside, I'll call reservations. Are you boys going sailing?"

"Not tonight," Vaughn said. "But tomorrow."

"Oh, well, then, when you're ready, come up to the house. We can have wine before dinner."

"I bought some chicken and am marinating it to get ready to grill," said Vaughn.

I beamed at him. "How did I get so lucky to find a man who loves to cook?"

He cocked an eyebrow. "That's not all I'm good at."

Still smiling, I walked up to the house to change my clothes and check on reservations for Darla.

After discussing it with Bernie, we agreed to give Darla the Presidential Suite for a discounted price. As I hung up the phone, I drew a deep breath, wondering how I'd gotten caught unaware in all things presidential.

That night though, as I enjoyed my time with Vaughn and Robbie, all thoughts of the president and his family disappeared.

It wasn't until I was lying in bed with him after a thorough, satisfying welcome home that my worries reappeared. I discussed them with Vaughn, and he, too, became concerned.

"Are you sure you have enough security coverage?" he asked. "I don't like the idea of people possibly nosing around the hotel."

"We've added security staff to our hotel team, and Debra has solicited additional help. Her old boyfriend is ex-CIA, and by the looks of his photograph, he'd have no trouble taking down anybody."

"Who's paying for all this?"

"Amelia Swanson. She's paying for extra help on the hotel staff, too."

Vaughn drew me to him and kissed me. "Let's not worry about this now. I want to enjoy being here with you. I'm hoping we can do some sailing tomorrow, and in the meantime ..."

The sound of my cell cut off his words. I knew from the ring it was Rhonda and picked it up. "Hello?"

"Annie, sorry for the late call, but I need your help. What are you doing right now?"

"Mmm, actually, I'm with Vaughn. He came home to surprise me."

"Oh, well, uh ... If I know the two of you, it's horizontal mambo time."

I laughed. "Rhonda!"

"What? It's true, isn't it?"

Ignoring her question, I said, "What's going on with you?"

"Katherine called. She's heading for the hospital with Angela and Reggie. Angela wants me to meet them there. I thought maybe you'd go with me. For moral support."

"You mean to keep you from saying something awful to Katherine," I said, understanding.

"Yeah, that too," Rhonda admitted. "But it's more important for you to stay with Vaughn. Tell him I said hi. I'll talk to you later."

I clicked off the call. "Angela's about to deliver her baby. Rhonda wants me to go to the hospital and be with her while she waits with Katherine Smythe for the baby to arrive. They just can't seem to get along. Rhonda's already an emotional wreck."

Vaughn cupped my face in his broad hands. "If you want to go, go. I'll be right here when you come home."

I let out a long sigh. "Would you mind?"

"No. Rhonda, wouldn't ask if she didn't really need you. The two of you are each other's bestie. Go, help her."

I gave him a lingering kiss, and satisfied that he wasn't unhappy about it, got out of bed and went into the bathroom to get ready to leave.

CHAPTER TWELVE

At the hospital, I found Rhonda, Katherine, and Reggie in Angela's room on either side of her bed.

"How're you doing?" I asked Reggie, who was looking a little concerned.

"Okay, I guess. But I could never do this."

"The pains are two to three minutes apart," said Katherine, checking her watch.

"Sounds like it's getting pretty close," I said to Rhonda. "At least she won't be delivering her baby on my kitchen floor."

Katherine glanced at me with a look of horror. "Surely, you jest."

"No, it really happened." Rhonda had delivered Willow in my kitchen when we realized it was too late to even try to get her to the hospital. "Let's hope this little one decides to come in a hurry. How long have the pains been going on, sweetie?"

"Since eight o'clock this morning," interjected Katherine with a smugness I knew irritated Rhonda.

"And you didn't call me?" Rhonda said, facing Katherine with a frown.

"Angela and I decided it could wait until we were more certain the baby was on its way. Wasn't that the plan, Angela?"

"I guess," she answered, grimacing as another pain rolled through her.

When Angela stilled, I walked to her side and kissed her on the forehead. "You're doing a great job. It seems like it won't be too long. When's the last time a nurse checked in with you?"

"A nurse was here four minutes ago," said Katherine. "She should be here again soon."

Just as the words left Katherine's mouth, a nurse appeared with a gray-haired female doctor I recognized. "I think it might be time to clear the room except for Mom and Dad," the nurse said. "Dr. Benson will take it from here."

Rhonda and Dr. Benson exchanged warm smiles. "Looks like another little one for you to love, Rhonda. Congratulations."

"Make this one a girl," said Rhonda.

"But I want another boy," Katherine said.

Dr. Benson glanced at them with amusement. "Well, ladies, we don't get to choose. That's already been done for us. Now, please excuse us, as Angela, Reggie, and I are about to deliver a baby."

I saw the way Reggie gripped Angela's hand and wondered if he still felt the same about wanting to cut the baby's umbilical cord as he'd once announced.

"Come along," said Katherine, motioning for Rhonda and me to follow her. "By my estimations, we'll be back here before we know it."

"In the meantime, can I get coffee or water for anyone?" I asked, needing a moment away from the tension.

Neither Katherine nor Rhonda answered as they marched from the room.

I wondered if it was a good idea to leave those two alone for a few minutes. Right now, they looked as if they were backing into corners of a boxing ring. Sooner or later, they'd have to work things out between them.

Regardless, I went to the coffee and drinks station on the floor and poured myself a cup of water.

When I returned to the waiting room, Rhonda was staring out the window, and Katherine was sitting on the couch checking her watch.

"It might be some time before we can go back to the room," I said gently.

Katherine's shoulders slumped. "I suppose. It's been a long day of timing pains with Angela, keeping Evan busy."

Rhonda turned around. "If you'd called, I would've come to help."

"You know perfectly well, I'm capable of handling the situation alone," said Katherine.

"No worries," I said. "It's a good thing you did. But we all need help from time to time dealing with young children. Let's face it. It's exhausting." I gave her an encouraging smile. "And if you're busy now, think what it'll be like when the baby comes home."

"That's why I'm trying to convince Angela to recover at home with me in New York," said Katherine. "I've hired the best nurses to come in and help. There, she can just relax."

Rhonda's dark eyes flashed her annoyance. "She doesn't need to go away to get that kind of help. I can hire good staff too. Besides, Evan is used to me. That's important. I know from experience. Willow would've freaked out to be in a new place with a new baby."

"I'm Evan's grandmother too," snapped Katherine. "Don't forget it."

"How could I forget it? You're constantly trying to take him away from me," Rhonda said.

Reggie appeared in the doorway, a big grin on his face. "It's a girl!"

"Wonderful!" cried Rhonda, clasping her hands together as if her prayers had been answered.

"Can we see her?" said Katherine.

"Yes, but Angela is asking for Ann first," said Reggie, winking at me.

"Ann? But ... but ..." sputtered Katherine. She turned to me. "You're not the baby's grandmother!"

"No, but she's as close to one as anyone could be," said Rhonda, coming to my defense. "I'll go with you."

Reggie shook his head firmly. "No, just Ann for now."

Letting out a puff of surprise, I waved to the other two and followed Reggie into Angela's room.

She was sitting in bed, holding the baby to her breast.

I hurried over to her. "How are you, sweetie? Let me see." We'd always been close.

"Take a look. She's so sweet." Angela held the baby, so I could see every perfect little finger and toe. "And see, she looks like Reggie." Angela gave her husband an adoring smile that made me unexpectedly tear up.

"Your mom and Katherine are waiting to see her," I gently reminded Angela.

"I just wanted a quiet moment with you. I know you've been waiting to hear news of Liz being pregnant, and I thought ... well, I thought you'd enjoy seeing my baby first before all the fighting begins." She gave me a long look. "It's been awful."

"I'll leave so you can talk to them," I said.

"No, Ann! I want you to stay while we tell them her name," said Angela. "Don't you agree, Reggie?"

"Yeah, you're a calming influence. I'll get them. You stay here."

After Reggie left, I leaned over and kissed Angela's cheek. "I love you as if you were my daughter, you know."

She took hold of my hand. "I love you too."

I looked up as Rhonda and Katherine rushed over to Angela's bed.

I deftly moved aside and watched. Babies were such a miracle. I hoped this adorable little girl would help draw her grandmothers together. I glanced at Angela and Reggie and saw worried expressions.

"What are we calling this sweet little girl?" Katherine said.

"It should be after someone from my family," Rhonda said, looking at Angela for confirmation.

Angela smiled sweetly at both of them. "A name from each one."

"Her name is Sally Kate," Reggie announced proudly.

"Do you mean Sarah?" asked Katherine.

"Do you need the Kate?" Rhonda asked, shooting a glance at Katherine.

"No, it's not Sarah," said Angela. "She's named Sally after my father, Sal."

"And she's named Kate after my mother," said Reggie.

Rhonda and Katherine looked at one another with tears in their eyes.

"Perfect," said Rhonda.

"Oh, yes," Katherine said. "I'm so proud."

"Sally Kate is a wonderful name for such a beautiful little girl," I said. "Congratulations to all of you."

I eased out of the room, pleased I'd come to help Rhonda and had, instead, shared a special moment with Angela—one I'd never forget.

When I got home, I eased into the house quietly, not wanting to disturb anyone, most especially Trudy, whose bark could wake the whole neighborhood.

I tiptoed down the hall to the master bedroom expecting Vaughn to be asleep. But the moment I walked into the room, he stirred and murmured. "Hi. How'd it go?"

"Great. The baby's beautiful, and Angela's doing fine. I'll tell you all about it in the morning." I quickly undressed and slid into bed beside him. "I thought you'd be sleeping."

He rolled over and smiled sleepily at me. "Was waiting for you. Didn't want to miss out on another cuddle."

I snuggled up against him and closed my eyes.

CHAPTER THIRTEEN

The next morning after Robbie was off to school, Vaughn and I sat on the lanai with mugs of coffee while I shared last night's events.

"Poor Angela has had to work hard trying to keep Katherine and Rhonda on friendly terms. And when she wanted me to see the baby alone, I was very touched. She knows I worry about Liz not being able to get pregnant."

"They haven't been married that long," said Vaughn.

"I know, but I would've had many more children if I could. I don't want it to be the same disappointment for Liz. That's what concerns me."

He took hold of my hand and squeezed it. "Liz, the child you made, is a marvelous young woman. Someone who should make you very proud. I'm honored to be her stepfather."

"You always say the sweetest things," I said, realizing how much his words meant to me.

"I meant to ask, did you and Bernie work out an arrangement for Darla?" Vaughn said. "She'd like to come next week. She and a friend."

"Yes, they can have the Presidential Suite. No one has booked it for the next two weeks, so we're putting her there with a special discounted price. She needs to call reservations to confirm it."

"Thanks. She seems like a nice young woman. Not at all like Lily. But there's tension on the set, and I don't know why. One of the producers hasn't liked her performance. It's made it hard on all of us."

"Maybe she'll be able to figure things out after a rest here," I said. "You say she's young. Perhaps she's just sensitive."

Vaughn rubbed a hand through his dark curls. "I've tried talking to her, but she won't discuss it."

"The producer you're talking about isn't Roger Sloan, is it?" His name sent a shudder through me. He and others had conducted a smear campaign against Vaughn.

"No, oddly enough, Roger isn't part of what's going on. This is someone I don't know very well. A man named Simon Merrill." He got up and took my empty mug from me. "I'll call her now and ask her to speak to the reservations office at the hotel."

"I'm afraid I won't be able to spend much time with her because of our annual spring brunch. Rhonda and I will be busy putting together last-minute arrangements, along with doing all our other PR work."

"I'm sure she'll understand. Besides, she's coming here for a rest."

After he walked away, I thought about all the years Vaughn had been working on this show. He'd seen actors come and go, but his character remained the center around which other stories were told. I supposed working together for so long forced members of a large, extended family to get along. Thinking of Darla, I decided no matter how busy we were, I'd make time to get to know her.

Lifting my phone, I called Rhonda to see how things were.

She answered with an out-of-breath, "Hello?"

"What are you doing?" I asked.

"Riding my exercise bike," she puffed out.

"Wow! You haven't done that in ages," I said.

"Yeah, well, with Katherine around, I thought I should start doing it again."

"You aren't trying to compare yourself to her, are you? You

know you're perfectly fine as you are."

"Yeah? I'm still carrying the extra weight from Drew's birth. And before that, I was carrying extra pounds from Willow, and before that, well, I'm Italian, and I cook a lot," said Rhonda, breathing hard.

I thought for a moment. Rhonda wasn't thin, and she wasn't obese either. But I knew how much Katherine intimidated her. "Exercise is great, Rhonda, but if you think by losing weight you'll be more acceptable to Katherine, please stop right now. Katherine is almost bony in appearance. You don't want that, and neither does Will. Angela and I and everyone else like you exactly as you are—healthy and loveable."

"Oh, good," said Rhonda, "because I don't think I could do this every day for very long. I work with my trainer a couple mornings a week, and that should be enough." She hesitated. "Do you think I should change up my wardrobe? You know, wear all that linen stuff Katherine does?"

"Why? We need to be comfortable working both at the hotel and at home. You always look nice. Why are you so charged up about this?"

"Angela let it slip that Katherine thinks I look like a tropical bird in my caftans. All I could think of was me as a big, fat parrot."

I held in a laugh. "And what should we call her? A skinny, slithering snake?"

Rhonda let out a roar of laughter. "That's perfect! Oh, Annie, what's wrong with me that she makes me so crazy?"

"Honestly?" I hesitated. "I think you're afraid of losing Angela, Reggie, and the babies to Katherine and her big ideas for them up north. But they're happy here in Sabal. They're not going to change their minds."

"I guess you're right," said Rhonda, sighing loudly. "I

shouldn't worry about it. It's good for Angela and Katherine to get along."

"Angela is committed to being nice to Katherine, but she told me it's been a struggle. If the two of you were nice to one another, that would help."

"I'll try. But she makes it so hard. She's trying to get the kids to call the baby Sarah Katherine."

"I don't think it'll work. Both Reggie and Angela seemed pretty firm about the baby being named Sally. I think it's a wonderful tribute to Sal."

"Yes, it is," Rhonda agreed. "Frankly, I was surprised. But just before he died, Angela found a way to forgive him for leaving us. He was a good father and husband until we had all that money."

"I liked him," I said. During his waning days of fighting cancer, he and I had become good friends.

"Are we meeting at the hotel to go over the guestlist for the spring brunch?" Rhonda said.

"Yes. I'm going to head there soon. The young actress working with Vaughn is coming to The Beach House Hotel for a rest, and I want to make certain reservations for her are set."

"Can't wait to meet her! See you later. I'm dying to get out of these workout clothes."

Rhonda clicked off the call.

No one would believe beneath that loud, self-confident manner of hers, Rhonda was still the young girl who'd been picked on for her size.

When I got to the hotel, I went directly to Bernie's office. There was a time when the man had appeared forbidding, but now, after being part of the hotel staff and married to Annette, there was a new softness about him. We were fortunate to get him back after he'd been forced to leave by the hotel company that had briefly taken over The Beach House Hotel.

"Good morning, Ann," he said cheerfully after I'd knocked and entered his office. "What can I do for you?"

"Hi, Bernie. I wanted to check to make sure everything will be ready for Darla Delaney and her friend's visit. She's to call you today to confirm the days she wants to book for the Presidential Suite. If she is to stay through next Sunday, we need to explain about our spring brunch." We had told all guests wanting to stay on that Sunday that the hotel would not run normally that day, that the hotel would be taken over by us entertaining townspeople, and dinner would not be served.

"No problem. I'll wait for her call and explain our routine for the spring brunch. The staff is already excited about it."

"Great." After serving guests and scrambling to see that everything went smoothly, the staff was allowed to have their own post-party. It had become something they all looked forward to celebrating.

Bernie frowned. "Ann? I've wanted to talk to you about Lindsay and her security. I understand they've been taking her over to Jean-Luc's house for early-morning walks on the beach. Do you think that jeopardizes our protection of her?"

I hesitated. "I don't think so. She can't be made a prisoner here. As long as she has her security team with her, I think she'd be safe. And once they're off property, it relieves us of that responsibility."

"All right, but I'd hate for anyone in his neighborhood to catch sight of their comings and goings," he said.

My stomach churned. "You mean someone like Brock Goodwin?"

He grimaced and nodded. "He's often an early-morning walker on the beach. Who's to say he wouldn't see anything going on here at the hotel?"

"I see your point. How's the progress on installing the gate between the beach and us?"

"Because it's a special size, there's been a bit of a delay," Bernie said. "But I'll call them this morning and make sure things are moving along."

"Good, because the last thing we need is for Brock or anyone else to poke around." The thought sent a shiver through me. "After I look at the Presidential Suite, I'm going to walk over to the guesthouse and tell them our thoughts."

I left his office and climbed the stairs to the second floor. We'd converted Rhonda's original master suite into the Presidential Suite after she moved out following her marriage to Will.

I unlocked the massive door and walked through the foyer into the main living room. As I stood there, my vision took in the pale blue walls, whose color was repeated in the overstuffed chairs and couches. The plush, cream Oriental rug with accents of blue and red echoed the blue in the sky and the magenta of the bougainvillea viewed through the windows. It was a comfortable, sunny area.

Nearby, a dining room held a large mahogany table and eight chairs above which a crystal chandelier glittered in the sunlight. An efficient kitchen with top appliances added to the space beside it. The bedroom with its massive bed and private balcony overlooking the beach was another luxurious feature. It could be connected to a standard guest room, providing two bedrooms to those who needed it. The bathroom off the master bedroom was lined with marble on the floor, the walls, and inside the massive shower that could easily handle two.

Of it all, my favorite spot was the large balcony off the living room that faced the private garden sometimes used by brides for their ceremony. There, the whisper of the wind was a nice relief on a summer day, bringing the tang of salty air with it.

Giving a last look around, I filled with pride. Darla and her friend should be happy here.

Satisfied, I left the hotel to head to the guesthouse. My mind spinning, I made my way across the front lawn of the hotel and over to the drive leading to the house. As I walked, a pink hibiscus flower bobbed its head at me, making my lips curve. Manny and his nephew, Paul, waved to me, and I waved back. They did an excellent job of keeping the plants nicely trimmed and weeded.

Thinking of Manny, I wondered how he and Consuela had enjoyed a few days off. They'd gone to Miami for a wedding and had asked to stay a couple of extra days. Of course, we said yes. Consuela and Manny were the very heart of our original team, more like family than staff. They now enjoyed living on the property, no doubt remembering when the hotel had simply been Rhonda's sprawling estate.

I continued my walk up the drive to the home I'd so proudly owned after being left without one by my sly ex-husband. Though the house was now part of the hotel, it still gave me a thrill to see it.

The moment I arrived at the front door, it was opened, and I faced a large man who studied me intently.

Debra appeared from behind him. "Don't mind Whit. He's just doing his job. How are you, Ann?"

"A bit worried," I said honestly. "Can we talk?"

"Sure, come on in. First, let me introduce you to Whit Evans. Whit, this is Ann Sanders, one of the owners of the hotel."

"How do you do?" he responded, giving my offered hand a firm squeeze and looking directly into my eyes.

"I'm delighted you're here," I said, feeling as if I'd been examined and placed onto a list of suspects he'd store in his mind.

He moved back and waved me inside. "Welcome."

I stepped inside, saw Lindsay out by the pool, and gave her a wave. Even from a distance, she looked better, healthier.

"How's it going?" I asked Debra.

She glanced at Whit. "Much better, don't you think?"

He nodded. "My guess is she's feeling more secure. The two of us together do a good job of protecting her."

"That's what I wanted to talk to you about. Bernie is concerned about your taking Lindsay in and out of the property so often. He knows you're going to Jean-Luc's house to walk on the beach there, but he's worried there's a possibility you'll be seen leaving and returning."

Debra gave me a thoughtful look. "I understand. But there's something very beneficial going on between Lindsay and Jean-Luc. She's been able to unload a lot of her trauma talking with him. My thought is that it's worth the risk. Why would a hotel guest bother with us?"

"That's just it. It's those in the neighborhood who might be most curious. One man, in particular. Brock Goodwin."

Debra made a note on a piece of paper. "We'll look into him."

"Also, I wanted to tell you that next Sunday, Rhonda and I will be holding our annual spring brunch. The hotel will be overrun by local people. Our staff will be on site after the close of the party, holding their own celebration. You're invited, of course, but I'm not sure how that would work. We'd be glad to send over a couple of plates of food."

Debra glanced at Whit and turned back to me. "We'll think about it. Thank you."

"May I speak to Lindsay?" I asked, curious about the changes in her.

"Sure," said Debra. "We're right here."

"Actually, I'm going to take a look around the property,

make sure all is in order," said Whit. "Nice to meet you, Ann."

"Yes, nice to meet you too. As I said, we're glad you're here. We feel a great responsibility to keep Lindsay safe."

"And so do we," he said, studying me.

I left them and walked out to the pool.

"Mind if I sit beside you?" I asked Lindsay.

She smiled and patted the chair next to her. "It's all yours. How are you? I haven't seen you for a while."

"You look great. We've been busy, and so have you, I hear."

"Yes. I've been doing calls with Barbara Holmes, seeing Jean-Luc, and walking on the beach at his house. It's all been helpful. For a while I was so scared that Thomas would turn up and I'd be left to fight him on my own that I didn't dare move. I don't mean fight him physically, but mentally. It's amazing how one person can take control and steal someone's self-confidence, break their spirit, and leave nothing but pieces."

"I understand completely. Thinking back, I realized how easily I had allowed my ex-husband to take over the business I'd created and financed. He'd even made everyone believe most of the ideas were his."

"You? Caught like that? I'm surprised. You seem so self-assured," said Lindsay.

"It's taken some time to change my thinking, but abuse can happen so effortlessly, it's frightening."

Lindsay gave me a steady look. "Jean-Luc says everyone admires what you and Rhonda have done at the hotel."

"Thanks. It hasn't been easy, but we keep on trying."

"I'd like to stay here for as long as I can. Is that possible?"

"This house is booked for a couple of weeks from now, but if we can't make other arrangements, I'll be pleased to offer you a private guest wing at my house."

"Oh, thank you. That's so sweet." Lindsay's eyes filled.

"Jean-Luc would let me stay with him, I'm sure, but I'm not ready for anything like that. Though I have to admit he's becoming a dear friend."

"That's good. He's a wonderful man, and I know he's been lonely. No word from your ex?" I asked, hoping I wasn't prying.

"No, and that worries me a bit. No matter what he says about being sober and a better person, I'll never trust him again. Especially after he made me think I was at fault."

"How's your sister doing with all this?" I asked.

"She's happy I've found a safe place to stay for the moment and gain my strength. She, too, doesn't trust Thomas or his family."

"Doesn't that make it difficult for her to do her job?"

Lindsay's lips curled. "In Washington, no one trusts anyone else, so it's nothing new. Just adding a few people to the list. That's all."

"That's awful," I said, knowing what she said was the truth.

"I know," she said softly.

CHAPTER FOURTEEN

Before we met with Dorothy to go over the guestlist for the spring brunch, I told Rhonda about my conversations with Bernie, Debra, and Lindsay.

"We've got to get that gate up right away," said Rhonda. "In the meantime, why don't we put a security guard there right next to the beach?"

"Good idea. The thought of Brock Goodwin or any other neighbor or some random person strolling on the beach snooping on private hotel property sends shivers down my spine."

"Yeah, we've fought enough bad stuff to do everything we can to make this hotel succeed," said Rhonda. "Most of the trouble came from Brock Goodwin, but still, we don't want anything to stop us now."

"You're right," I said, firming my resolve. "Now, let's build up some good public relations and plan that party. Dorothy should be here any minute."

As if by magically hearing her name, Dorothy Stern knocked at the door.

I opened it and smiled at the short woman who carried an air of authority like a fur stole around her shoulders. Barely five-two, the elderly, gray-haired woman peered at me through thick glasses that added to the suspicion she missed nothing going on around her.

"Hello, Dorothy, good to see you. Are you ready to oversee the invitations to the party as you normally do?"

"You bet," she answered, stepping inside the office. "I want to make sure certain people are coming. It's important for the cooperation you gals need from the city." She grimaced as she continued, "Of course, Brock Goodwin is coming. Says he wouldn't miss it for the world, that if he hadn't given his permission, you two would never have been able to open the hotel."

"What an ass," said Rhonda.

"Truly," I said, thinking of my grandmother and stopping myself from saying more.

"Well, only the new people in the neighborhood would believe such a thing. They and the one or two friends who've stayed close to him," said Dorothy, shaking her head. "I did hear from Father Donnelly. He's coming. He wants to thank you two for all your donations to his secret charity."

Rhonda and I gave each other high fives. We'd decided his charity was one way to give money for a good cause without making a fuss about it.

We left Dorothy and went into the kitchen to speak to Consuela.

The short, round, gray-haired woman who smiled at us filled my heart with affection. Consuela was like the mother I never had the privilege of knowing. Warm, kind, hard-working, encouraging, she'd been with us from the beginning when she was a housekeeper for Rhonda.

"Hope we're not catching you at a bad time," I said, hugging her. "We just wanted to make sure we've ordered all the food for the brunch."

"And a lot of it made and frozen." Rhonda beamed. "Even after all these years, our sweet rolls are still a favorite."

"*Si, si*, they're made," said Consuela, waving away our concern. "What we can't freeze ahead of time will be made on Saturday and Sunday mornings. Are you prepared to help the staff and me?"

"Oh, yes. That's what makes our brunch so special. All original recipes with the best ingredients," I said.

"Some of my mother's favorite recipes and mine," said Rhonda proudly. She was an excellent cook. She and Jean-Luc loved to tease one another as to who had better family recipes.

We left Consuela to take care of the lunch menu and decided to walk down to the beach to check on the gate area. To one side of where we wanted to place the gate sat a large, bohio-style, open-sided hut where guests could enjoy cocktails and nibbles while watching the sunset. It had been reconstructed after a suspicious fire had burned the original to the ground.

I stood and faced the water. Waves rolled in and moved away in a pattern I'd never tire of watching. Some people strolled the beach, their faces to the ground, looking for shells. Others trotted or jogged by intent on clocking steps. But others like me seemed content to lose themselves in the rhythm of the waves or delight in the shorebirds that scurried along the packed sand at the water's edge, looking for food.

Rhonda turned to me. "This makes me think of many times in the early days when we'd both come to this spot as a way to escape our worries." She smiled at the memory. "Sometimes, it's hard to believe all that's happened. Right, Annie?"

"I wasn't at all sure we'd make it. But we've had each other to help us through tough times. That and hard work have made our success." I turned and faced the hotel. The pink, two-story building, which stretched like a sleeping flamingo across the span of land we owned, was stunning. Balconies and patios of the thirty-six rooms offered views of the Gulf or private gardens. The pool and patio areas were multi-functional and enhanced the accessibility of the outdoors. On rainy, windy, or cold days, the lobby and dining areas were happily used by those who chose not to stay in their comfortable rooms.

"Sure is pretty. Don'tcha think?"

"Gorgeous. We have to get that gate up so our guests are protected."

"Until we can provide a little more security, I'm going to be worried about Lindsay. Any idea when her ex is getting out of rehab?" said Rhonda.

"No. Nothing's been mentioned."

"Let's hope it's not soon," said Rhonda. "I have a feeling he's not the kind of guy who's going to let her walk away."

"I wish I didn't agree with you," I said, checking my watch. "I think I'll head home. Vaughn is cooking dinner."

"I'm going over to Angela's to check on her. 'Sure you don't want to come with me? Arthur is here."

I glanced at Rhonda. At the way she was shuffling her sandal in the sand I knew how much she wanted me to say yes.

"I'll stop by with you for just a minute on my way home," I said.

"Aw, thanks, Annie. Reggie's father makes me almost as uneasy as Katherine."

"Arthur? On his own, he's a pussy cat. He just doesn't dare to defy his wife."

"Katherine's still fussing over the baby's name."

"Okay, let's go. Poor Angela needs some support."

A few minutes later, I was in my car headed to Angela's house. When my cell phone rang, I eagerly picked up a call from Liz on my car's blue tooth system.

"Hey, darling! How are you?"

"Not so good," said Liz. "I'm feeling a little down about things." She sniffled, and I drew in a shaky breath.

"I'm sorry, Liz. I really am." I knew what was bothering her.

"Listen, I'll be home in a little while. Do you and Chad want to come for dinner? Vaughn's home, and he's cooking."

"Thanks, I'll ask him," said Liz, sounding like a young girl instead of her usual competent self. "It might do us both good to do something different. After we close the store, we'll come over unless I call you."

"Okay, my darling. I hope to see you soon."

We clicked off the call, and my eyes teared up. I was disappointed too that Liz wasn't pregnant. After seeing Angela with her new baby, I wanted the same for Liz. A few years ago, they'd talked about having children at the same time so their children could become best friends. Now, Angela was way ahead.

I parked in front of Angela's house so there wouldn't be any problem with cars when I was ready to leave.

Rhonda pulled her Cadillac behind my SUV and got out. "Thanks for coming Annie." She stopped and stared at me. "What's wrong?"

"It's Liz," I couldn't hold back a sigh. "She's feeling down about not having any baby news."

"Oh, Annie, I'm so sorry. I know how much you worry about her." She swept me in a big hug that smelled of her favorite perfume, Poison.

I leaned against her for a moment and pulled myself together. I wouldn't let Liz's disappointment mar my joy for Angela.

Katherine met us at the door. "Sh-h-h! The baby is sleeping."

"Is Angela awake?" I asked.

"Yes, she's spending time with Evan." Her lips thinned. "He doesn't want to leave her side no matter how hard I try."

"I'll talk to him," said Rhonda, brushing by Katherine.

"And I wanted to stop by to say hello to Arthur. How's

grandpa doing?" I asked, smiling at her.

"He's doing better with Evan than I am," said Katherine, sniffing and looking annoyed.

"How ... nice!" I said in what I hoped was an upbeat tone. A four-year-old was as perceptive as an adult when it came to personality.

When I entered the living room, Angela was sitting on the couch with Rhonda, who was holding Evan in her lap.

"Hi, Ange! How's it going?" I asked softly, kneeling at her feet and taking her hand.

Angela's lips trembled. "I'm trying very hard to be with Evan and the baby and ..." she paused "... and everything."

"It's overwhelming when that second baby comes," said Rhonda. "Believe me, I know. Why don't I take Evan to my house overnight and give everyone a break here?"

I heard a gasp from Katherine and turned to see the outrage on her face. "You can't take Evan away from us! We're here to help him."

To Rhonda's credit, she clamped her mouth shut, but the look on her face told a story of its own.

Angela looked from one to the other. "Thanks, anyway, Mom, but we're fine here. It's just going to take some teamwork."

Arthur walked into the room.

I stood. "Hello, Arthur. Do you remember me? Ann Sanders?"

He smiled politely. "Of course. It's good to see you. I'm sorry I didn't hear you arrive. I was taking a nap."

He walked over to Rhonda and lifted Evan from her lap. "Hey, Buddy. You and I were to take a nap together. What happened?"

"No nap!" screamed Evan. He wiggled to get down and then ran toward the kitchen.

"Come here, young man!" said Katherine striding quickly after Evan.

Arthur hurried after the two of them.

Rhonda and I gave one another helpless looks.

"If there's anything I can do for you, Angela, please tell me," I said softly.

She whispered. "Take Katherine out for coffee or lunch."

I leaned over and gave her a kiss. "I'll call tomorrow morning. I promise. Try to relax."

"Okay, I'll try. Reggie has promised me your new-mother spa package at the hotel as soon as they leave."

"I'd better go, too," said Rhonda. "I love you, honey, but I don't want to make matters worse. And if I stay much longer, I will."

Angela laughed. "I'll call you when I can. Thanks for stopping by."

Rhonda and I said our goodbyes and made our way back to our cars. Halfway there, Rhonda stopped, stared at the house, and said, "I'm going to do it. Tell them to go the fuck home."

"No," I said calmly, "we're going to our cars, and then *we're* going home."

Rhonda held up her hand, her forefinger close to her thumb. "C'mon! I'm this close to telling them to fuck off and leave my daughter alone."

"Stop and think about it, Rhonda," I warned.

Rhonda heaved a sigh. "You're right. Reggie and Will have to work together, and I don't want to screw that up. I'm going to call Reggie on my way home and tell him he'd better step in to help Angela. Arthur shouldn't be napping on the job, and Katherine doesn't know the first thing about taking care of a toddler who's just been 'dethroned' from being prince of the castle. Evan is nothing compared to how Willow was when we brought Drew home, but still ..."

"Yeah, I remember what that was like. Willow went from being enthralled with Drew to being furious with you for bringing him home." Like her mother, Willow wasn't one to hold back her feelings.

"I'll tell Will he has to make sure Reggie takes some time off. Will's offered, but Reggie said he didn't want to disappoint and irritate his mother by taking over." Rhonda placed her hands on her hips. "I'm tellin' ya, Annie, if things don't change for Angela, I'm going to let them all have a piece of my mind. And I won't hold back from saying all the frickin' things I've wanted to say for days. It's been killin' me to keep quiet."

"Okay, draw a deep breath," I said, placing a calming hand on her arm. "Are you going to make it home safely?"

"Yes. Ya know, Annie, I'm tryin' hard not to interfere."

"I know you are. Keep up the good work. Wish we could do our margarita time, but I have to get home." I gave her a hug and climbed into my car. Chad's mother and I weren't close friends, but when the time came for Liz and Chad to have children, I hoped it would be easier than this.

When I arrived home, Liz's car was in the driveway, and all was quiet. Curious, I went into the kitchen to see where everyone was. I looked through the window and could see Liz and Robbie down by the water, sitting on the dock together, Trudy between them.

Vaughn walked into the room. "Hi, glad to see you!" He swept me into his arms and kissed me. "I'm not sure what's going on, but Liz arrived and said she wanted to spend some time with her brother."

"She's feeling a little down. I'm sure it'll pass, but in the meantime, I think it's a good idea for her to spend some time here."

"Ah, that's it. She looked as if she'd been crying." He stared out the window. "I'm sorry. I hate to see her this way."

"I think some of her desire to have children is because of her guilt for not being able to take care of Robbie after her Dad died. She understands logically why we were a better choice, but she's always been a responsible person, and I think it bothers her."

"She couldn't be a better sister to Robbie," said Vaughn. "Seeing them together like this isn't unusual."

My eyes filled. "She's always wanted a lot of children."

Vaughn hugged me tighter. "It hurts to see our kids unhappy."

"It's only been a short while, but her hopes were so high that she'd get pregnant right away," I said, swiping at my eyes.

"Chin up! Here they come," Vaughn said.

Robbie burst into the room at a run, his dark eyes shining. "Lizzie and I are going to build something with my Legos."

"Nice," I said, opening my arms to Liz.

She came into them and nestled for just a moment before she pulled away. "At the rate I'm going, I'll be an expert," she said, attempting humor.

"You're very sweet to play with him. When you're ready, come sit with me before dinner. Vaughn's cooking, so I'll be relaxing by the pool."

Liz nodded, and, taking hold of her brother's hand, they left the room.

Vaughn put his arm around me. "C'mon, Mom, let's relax together. How are things at Angela's?"

I made a face. "Let's pour some wine, and I'll tell you all about it."

After Chad arrived, Liz joined us by the pool. "Robbie is

still working on a spaceship that looks more like a whale."

Chad stood, drew her into his arms, and kissed her.

Her eyes filled, and she looked out at the inlet. When she turned back, her smile was wobbly. "I stopped at Angela's on my way over here. The baby is adorable."

"How were things there?" I asked. "Rhonda and I stopped by earlier, and it was a chaotic scene."

"Evan wanted to go home with me. That should tell you a lot," Liz said. "I didn't stay long because Katherine informed me Angela was receiving too much company."

"Oh, for heaven's sake," I grumbled. "Better not tell that to Rhonda. She's ready to unleash a whole bunch of anger on Reggie's parents. Thank goodness, I managed to drag her away."

"How are things going at the store?" Vaughn asked Chad. While they talked, Liz signaled for me to follow her down to the dock.

Silent, we walked together and took a seat on the bench at the end of the dock.

"You okay?" I asked quietly.

"I guess," Liz said. "I know it hasn't been long, but I worry I'm going to be someone who's never going to have a baby of her own."

"It's too early to talk of such things," I said, reaching for her hand and squeezing it.

"I know you're right, but it's hard when I see Angela with two kids, and Nell has her little girl."

"When your time comes, it'll all work out. You'll see. Now, how are things going at the store? You said you wanted to put in a new inventory system. Is that helping to keep track of all the bits and pieces your store carries?"

Liz's face brightened. "Yes, it's much better. I thought you might want to take a look at the program for the hotel. I can do a demonstration for you, Rhonda, and Bernie anytime you want."

"Great! After our annual brunch, we should have some time. I'm glad you're thinking of the hotel. Rhonda and I eventually want you and Angela to run it for us."

"After seeing what Angela is going through, it won't be anytime soon," Liz said. She grew serious. "I love you, Mom. Thanks for not freaking out over my not being pregnant. It's hard enough for me to handle as it is."

"I love you. Things will work out." I hugged her, grateful I'd been able to hold back my tears. As Vaughn said, it was hard to see your child so unhappy.

The next morning when I called Katherine to see if she wanted to meet for coffee, she said, "Thank you, but no thanks. I'm needed here at Angela's."

"I just thought you might need a break, too," I said, remembering my promise to Angela.

"That's not necessary. I know you and Rhonda think I'm not capable, but I assure you that I am. Things are calmer now with Arthur here. We both want to enjoy our grandchildren while we can. Reggie has informed us that they'll try to visit us this summer, but that's all it'll be—a visit. You can imagine my disappointment at his turning down an offer most young men would dream of having. And, with us, Angela could have a cultured life."

"I'm sorry for your disappointment," I said, warning myself to end the conversation before it became a battle. Angela certainly had a "cultured life" here in Florida.

I clicked off the call, wondering if the time would ever come when Katherine could let herself go and simply be nice.

CHAPTER FIFTEEN

Two days later, I left a message at the front desk to alert me when Darla arrived. I was working in the office with Rhonda, going over expenses for the upcoming brunch, when I received a call that she was checking in.

"I'm going to meet Darla. C'mon, let's greet her together," I said to Rhonda. "She's bringing a friend."

"A boyfriend?" Rhonda said as we left the office.

"I guess so," I answered.

When we walked into the lobby, I studied the young woman at the reception desk. Even wearing a baseball hat, her auburn hair was a giveaway. That, and her voluptuous figure in cut-off jeans and a tank top. Beside her stood a tall, thin, striking blonde in a short skirt and knit golf shirt.

I hurried over to them. "Darla?"

She turned and faced me. "Oh! You're Ann, Vaughn's wife. I recognize you from the pictures he has of you."

"Welcome to The Beach House Hotel." I urged Rhonda forward. "And this is my partner, Rhonda Grayson."

"Welcome," said Rhonda. "And who are you?" she asked, facing the blonde.

"Hello. I'm Meredith Wilkinson, a friend of Darla's."

Darla and Meredith smiled at one another, and I understood she was more than a friend.

"Vaughn told me you're here for a rest. We've put you in the Presidential Suite, which should give you some privacy."

"Thank you," Darla said. "We appreciate it. I'm hoping I have a chance to speak to you alone during our stay."

"Of course," I said.

"And you're both invited to our spring brunch," said Rhonda. "You'll find information about it in your room."

"How nice," said Darla.

Another couple approached, and I said, "We won't keep you. Enjoy your stay, and we'll talk later."

My mind was filled with ideas as I left with Rhonda to return to our office.

"I didn't know Darla was gay," said Rhonda.

"I had no idea," I said. "Vaughn's never mentioned it. I wonder if that's the problem she's having on the set."

"Both Darla and Meredith are beautiful women. I'm surprised the gossipy talk shows haven't made a big deal of it."

"I'm sure the producers of *The Sins of the Children* wouldn't like it. Not when they're trying to promote Darla as the one Vaughn is interested in both on the show and maybe, just maybe, on a personal level. A promo trick I despise them for."

"I can imagine. But anyone who knows Vaughn well would know he'd never wander."

"It doesn't make it easier," I said, feeling vulnerable.

We went back to our budgeting, and then it was time to leave to pick up Robbie from school. I treasured the moments when he emerged, saw me standing there, and came running to me smiling.

At the school, I stood with Cyndi Brigham catching up on neighborhood news. I was grateful for her friendship. As busy as I was with the hotel, I had little time to socialize with others, so it was always special to be with her. The fact that Brett and Robbie were best buddies made it even better.

"I ran into Rhonda yesterday," said Cyndi. "She told me she's a grandmother again. How nice. And so sweet the little one is named after her deceased first husband. Sally is an old-fashioned name, but I like it."

"She's a darling baby. Very calm, unlike her big brother," I said, unable to hold back a smile. "Evan's having a hard time with the new baby."

"I remember those toddler years so well," said Cyndi. "How about you? Are Liz and Chad thinking of children, making you a grandmother?"

"Thinking of it," I said, careful not to give anything away. No wonder Liz was feeling pressure.

"Mom! Mom! Look!" cried Robbie running toward me. He held up a piece of paper.

I took it from him and admired the two gold stars at the top of a sheet of practice writing. "Excellent! Let's go home and show Dad."

I turned to Cyndi, who was talking to Brett. "See you later!"

She gave me a friendly wave, and Robbie and I headed toward my car.

"Are we going sailing?" Robbie asked.

"We'll have to ask Dad," I said, realizing I hadn't checked my messages recently.

As I settled behind the wheel of the car, I looked at my cell, saw a message from Vaughn, and listened to it.

"Guess we're going sailing," I said to Robbie. "With some new friends." Vaughn had invited Darla and her friend to come on an evening sail with us, telling me not to worry, he'd take care of everything.

Surprised by this, I called him back. "Hi. I understand we're having guests this evening. Need me to pick up anything?"

"No. I have it under control. Hope you don't mind, but Darla sounded anxious to get together."

"It's fine. I said hello to her and Meredith this morning."

"Meredith?"

"Yes, her special ... friend."

"Ah, that's it," said Vaughn. "Okay, good thing we're meeting right away. I think I can help her. See you soon. They're just pulling up now."

When I got home, I saw a yellow jeep sitting in the driveway. I pulled into the garage and got out, curious to see why Darla had been in such a hurry to make contact with Vaughn.

Robbie ran into the kitchen ahead of me and out to the lanai, waving his starred paper in his hand. "Look, Dad!"

Vaughn stood and took a moment to look at it. "Good job, Robbie! Hi, Ann!" He ruffled Robbie's hair and kissed me on the lips before saying, "You met Darla and Meredith this morning?"

"Yes. Good to see you again," I said, smiling at Darla and Meredith, who were sitting on one of the couches and wearing what looked like colorful bikini tops and white shorts. They were already showing a bit of color. Trudy, the traitor, was sitting between them, enjoying their attention.

"I told them it's a perfect evening for a short sail on *Zephyr*," said Vaughn with a note of pride. He loved any excuse for a sail.

"We hope we're not intruding, but I thought it was important for me to speak to you both," said Darla with a look of concern.

"Let me get Robbie settled, and then we'll relax here for a moment before we get ready to sail. Is that okay with you?"

Darla nodded agreeably. "Sure. Take your time."

While Vaughn took orders for drinks, I got a glass of juice for Robbie and suggested that he play in his room until we were ready to go.

When Vaughn and I returned to the lanai, Darla and Meredith were quietly talking, holding hands.

Vaughn handed out glasses of pinot noir, and we sat down in chairs on either side of the couch.

"As I'm sure is evident, Meredith and I are more than friends," said Darla. "While we're happy together, I've been careful not to make this known around the others on the show." She faced me. "Especially with their idea of trying to promote something romantic between Vaughn and me. It's a foolish idea, but I don't want to lose my place on the show, and I've played along."

Meredith glanced at Darla. "We're both unhappy with it."

"What I haven't told anyone else is that one of the producers is sexually harassing me," said Darla.

"Is that why Simon Merrill has been so hard on you on the set?" Vaughn asked, his face an angry mask.

"I think so. I've refused to be alone in his office with him." Tears filled her eyes. "You can understand how awful it's been on so many levels. The way he touches me, the things he whispers."

My lips thinned. "Abuse of women at work has gone on for years. It's time to put a stop to it. For every woman out there."

"I agree. But to keep my job, I have to figure out a subtle way to take care of it. That's why I wanted to talk to both of you. First, Ann, I have no romantic interest in Vaughn, and, Vaughn, I'm asking for your help."

Vaughn and I exchanged grim looks.

"Of course, we'll both help," I said.

"What do you want us to do?" asked Vaughn.

"If you would approach Simon and tell him you are aware he's been harassing me, it would be huge. It would put him on notice that someone else knows what's happening on set. And it would hopefully put a stop to Simon's actions," Darla said.

"It's all about ratings and audience and money," said Vaughn. "I've never liked it and hate having you and others hurt by untruths being spread. Until the group finally gets rid of Roger Sloan, the nonsense won't stop."

"He's another slimeball," said Darla.

"I had no idea that all this shit was going on behind the scenes," said Meredith.

"It wasn't always that way," said Vaughn. "And there's no reason it should continue. We'll put an end to it once and for all by not playing any games."

"How?" asked Meredith.

"That I don't know," Vaughn said. "But we'll figure it out."

"Thank you so much," gushed Darla. "Getting this role means so much to me. My agent is trying to build interest in my playing bigger roles in movies."

"Good for you. When the time comes, let me know. My agent was able to make a deal with the producers to allow me time off to make films. Lately, I haven't found anything I'm interested in doing."

"Now, let's relax and enjoy that sail we've talked about," I said, knowing it was one way to erase the angst on Vaughn's face.

Vaughn got to his feet. "Let me get my young skipper, and we'll be off."

After everyone was handed a life jacket and Trudy was bundled into one, we all climbed aboard and sat while Vaughn and Robbie motored us out onto the open water where we could set sail.

True to his word, Vaughn had provisioned the boat with heavy hors d'oeuvres of every kind, it seemed, and plenty to drink, including margaritas made with the hotel recipe that had become a favorite of Rhonda's and mine.

As the breeze filled the sails and we glided smoothly across the bay, we faced one another in the cockpit. The hissing sound of the bow cutting through the waves and the cries of seagulls circling above us soon put us in good spirits.

"Ah, this is so nice," said Meredith. "I grew up on a lake in Michigan and did some sailing when I was younger."

"I've never done anything like this," Darla said shyly. "After growing up on a farm in Iowa, I've learned and done so many new things." She turned to Meredith. "I have Mere to thank for a lot of it."

"You two seem very happy together," I said. "It's nice to see."

"My parents don't think so," said Darla, her mouth down-turned. "They've disowned me."

"Oh? I'm sorry to hear that," I said, meaning it. I thought every parent wanted to see their children loved and happy.

"I'm glad we came here," said Darla to me. "It's making me feel a lot better about things."

"That's important. As you go forward, the two of you are going to have to rely on one another for support," I said. "I have an idea that may be helpful in the long run."

"Okay, spill," she said eagerly.

I thought of the words I wanted to say without sounding too preachy. "I've always found it's best to be honest. I see the way you and Meredith are together. Why hide that from your fans? You have a loving relationship and are kind and supportive of one another. It's your life to live, and it's not up to the producers to create one that's not real. Tell them about the harassment from Simon and, in return, find a way for you to be true to yourself."

Darla's eyes widened, and then a broad smile crossed her pretty face. "Okay. Good. I can do that."

She seemed so young, so innocent. No wonder Simon wanted to play his dirty little games with her.

###

Later, lying in bed with Vaughn, I told him my thoughts.

"I'll start by telling Simon to keep his hands and words to himself," said Vaughn. "If it doesn't stop, I'll go to the top and let them know the liability and bad press they'll face if this is made public."

"That might help," I said. "After dealing with Lindsay and now Darla, I'm determined to support women's groups fighting to bring an end to this kind of harassment."

"It's well past time," said Vaughn grimly. He nestled me closer. "I'll always protect you and the kids."

"I know," I said, remembering how he'd fought against Roger Sloan in the past.

CHAPTER SIXTEEN

On this early May morning of the Spring Brunch, blue skies shimmered above us like a blessing. To prevent the Neighborhood Association from grumbling about too many cars parked alongside the road, vans we'd hired were delivering guests from the nearest grocery store parking lot to the hotel. Manny and Paul directed traffic for those who'd chosen not to take a van or who'd walked.

Rhonda and I stood together on the front steps of the hotel, welcoming the locals who'd been forced to share their town and beach with snowbirds for several months. Now that things were quiet again, they were ready to settle down before some of them traveled north to mountains and lakes for a respite from the summer heat.

It was a quieter time at the hotel. During this "shoulder season" between winter and summer, we were still busy, but not at the usual hectic pace of the high season. It was a time of year I liked.

"Another brunch," said Rhonda. "Remember our first one?"

"I was a nervous wreck, hoping people would love what we'd done, hoping I hadn't made the biggest mistake of my life."

"Second biggest mistake after marrying that A-hole of a husband of yours," said Rhonda.

I laughed. Rhonda had an unmistakable way with words. As a group of people headed our way, I gave her hand a squeeze of encouragement. "Let's hope this party is as successful as the others."

"Uh, oh. Brock is headed this way."

"We can't let him ruin this," I said, pasting a pleasant smile on my face for the people in the neighborhood who deserved my best attention.

As I spoke to each new arrival, I marveled at how many friends I'd made in the last six years. I'd come to Florida without knowing anyone in the area.

After most of the guests had arrived, I went inside to check on things. The buzz of pleasant conversation filled the air. Staff members circulated among the guests with trays of food or drinks, and the delicious aromas caused me to fill with pride. Those guests with bigger appetites headed into the dining room, where a buffet table displayed a wide selection of appetizers, salads, and entrees.

I noticed Brock in a corner of the living room talking to a gentleman whose back was turned to me. The eager expression on Brock's face was unsettling. *What is he up to now?* I glanced at Rhonda in conversation with Father Donnelly and Dorothy and decided to let it go.

In the kitchen, Consuela was in charge, working with others to keep the food coming. One of the big reasons why our brunch was so successful was the delicious food everyone loved.

I went into the office I shared with Rhonda to check on the latest reservations. Bernie had told me about a last-minute one that had come in last night. Every "head in a bed" reaped rewards for us.

I checked the reservation. T. Hyde from Virginia, not a regular.

A tap sounded at the door, and a middle-aged gentleman entered the room. His craggy features seemed almost haggard.

He seemed familiar to me, and then I recognized the sport coat he wore and realized I'd seen him talking to Brock.

"Hello. You're Ann Sanders, one of the owners," he said. "Am I right?"

"Yes. And who are you?"

"We've never met. But my sister-in-law was here recently ..." he began.

I studied him closer and froze, certain now I knew who was speaking. Thomas Thaxton was thinner and grayer than his pictures, but there was no mistaking his face—the same face that continued to haunt Lindsay. Fighting the urge to flee, I gripped onto the edge of my desk and told myself to remain calm.

"You may know her as Vice President Swanson," he continued smoothly.

"I'm sorry, but we don't discuss our guests," I said primly, my heart pounding inside me. "Their privacy is of utmost importance to us."

His lips curved into a smile that didn't begin to warm the cold frown he gave me. "I'm sure by now from the look on your face that you've figured out who I am and why I might be here. For a vacation, yes, but to see what you can tell me about my ex-wife." His gaze drilled into me. "She and I have some unfinished business."

Though he was of average height and build, he sent shivers of fear through me. My God! No wonder Lindsay had been intimidated by him. I felt as if I were a little mouse about to be pounced on by a large, feral cat. This was a man used to having his way in all matters.

Swallowing hard, I pulled myself together. "I haven't any idea why you'd think I'd know anything about your ex-wife. That's your business. Not mine."

"We'll see. In the meantime, I intend to enjoy the hotel. It's as lovely as Amelia told my brother it was."

Pulling out all the self-confidence I could, I said, "I hope you find your stay as relaxing as you want. In the meantime, feel free to enjoy the annual spring brunch we put on for the locals."

"I've already talked to some of the people here," he said. "Your neighbor, Brock Goodwin, and I have an arrangement of sorts. He's promised to keep an eye on things here for me in exchange for a business opportunity for him." Again, his smile wasn't friendly. "He seemed pretty excited about it."

"Oh," I said, forcing myself to act nonchalant while my stomach was filling with acid.

I stood, walked to the door, and held it open. "If you'll excuse me, I have to get back to business. I hope you have a pleasant stay."

"I intend to," he said, and then, having no choice, he left.

I closed the door behind him and leaned heavily against it, too weak to stand on my own. I had to get word to Debra, but I had the sense I shouldn't go there myself. Any chance of being overheard or seen was too dangerous.

I typed up a text on my cell, telling Debra what had happened and warning her that both Thomas and Brock Goodwin would be snooping around the hotel for any information that might help Thomas find Lindsay. I gave her the pseudonym he'd used for the reservation and told her I thought Thomas might have left the rehab center on his own because he'd used a fake name. I suggested moving Lindsay to my house for a while, certain Vaughn wouldn't mind.

My hands trembled as I hurried into the kitchen and approached Consuela. Pulling her aside, I asked her to walk over to the guesthouse with a tray full of food to deliver to Debra. I slipped her a note I'd hastily written with Thomas' additional information on it and gave her as much information as I could. "This is an emergency, but I need you to act as if this is a normal duty. And if anyone sees you or asks about the people staying there, say nothing according to our usual policy. For anyone's information, the couple staying there is on their honeymoon and doesn't want to be disturbed. Come back with any message for us. Got it?"

Consuela gave me a look of concern. "Don't worry, Annie. You can trust me."

I hugged her. "I know. That's why I need you to do this."

I walked her to the back entrance and watched as she headed down the path to the guesthouse with a tray of food. The thought of Thomas Thaxton blindsiding Lindsay sickened me all over again.

After seeing her off safely, I hurried back to the office and locked the door. Pulling out the card with Amelia's private number, I called it.

An unfamiliar voice answered. "The Swanson residence."

"Is the vice president there? It's Ann Sanders calling from The Beach House Hotel."

"Hold on. I'll see."

A few minutes later, Amelia said, "Hello? Ann?"

"Yes, it's me. Bad news. Thomas Thaxton is here at the hotel, asking about Lindsay."

"Oh my God! I thought he was still in the rehab center," said Amelia. "Does Lindsay know?"

"I sent a text to Debra, and one of my staff is making sure they know what's going on," I said. "I've suggested moving Lindsay to my house until he leaves. He's registered for only two days."

"I agree she'll be safer there. But I'm sick with worry. Thomas has threatened to kill Lindsay in the past. I doubt being sober will change his mind. He was furious to be served divorce papers." Amelia's voice wobbled. "Thank you so much for handling this. I'll speak with Debra and discuss how best to handle things. We don't want to do anything to make him suspect we're hiding Lindsay there. Did he seem sober?"

"Yes, but he's a terrifying person," I said, remembering the way he'd looked at me and smirked when he talked about the deal with Brock. "I understand why Lindsay wants to stay hidden until she feels stronger."

"Once the mask came down, the bastard became pretty scary and for good reason. When his bad side came out, we all realized how easily he had fooled us. He can be as smooth as his brother," said Amelia. "Go ahead with your normal activities, so he doesn't suspect a thing."

"Understood," I said. "We're having our spring brunch today. I'd better get back to that."

"Thank you, Ann, for all you're doing. My appreciation can never be enough."

I clicked off the call and told myself to calm down.

When I walked back into the party, Rhonda gave me a questioning look. I ignored it and checked on Brock. He was talking to Meredith, who, when she saw me, gave me a look of desperation. I kept on walking. Thomas was talking to Darla, who looked as unhappy as Meredith. Ordinarily, I'd help the women out by stepping into their conversation, giving them a reason to leave. But I couldn't do that now. I needed them to keep both Brock and Thomas occupied while I sought Vaughn.

He was talking to an older woman who was all but fluttering her eyelashes at him.

"Mind if I have a word with my husband?" I asked pleasantly and led him away from the crowd and over by the front door.

As we were standing there, I noticed Debra's SUV leave the

property and guessed they were taking Lindsay away. Relieved, I told Vaughn what had happened.

"I'll go check on them," Vaughn offered. "I don't like the idea of having the creep around. Here or there."

"I'm so scared," I whispered, clutching my hands together.

"I'll come right back. Be careful and stay by Bernie." He kissed me. "Everything's going to be okay. You did the right thing by contacting Debra and getting Lindsay away from here. I don't trust either man—Brock or Thomas."

"Me either. Love you."

Bernie and Annette walked over to me.

"Everything all right?" Bernie asked, giving me a look of concern.

"Vaughn just needs to check on things at home. Something with the babysitter," I said, finding it easier than I thought to lie about this. The secret to having Lindsay remain safe was keeping as much information to myself as possible.

"It's such a lovely party," Annette said. "Everyone seems to be having a good time."

Pleased, I gave her a warm smile. "This and our Christmas party are two of my favorite events."

Annette leaned closer and spoke softly. "I'm not sure, but isn't that Thomas Thaxton talking to the tall blonde over there?"

I exchanged glances with Bernie. "I'm afraid so. But I'm trying not to draw attention to him."

"I assume the real matter has been taken care of," said Bernie.

I nodded, grateful he understood the situation. "For the time being. I want to keep it quiet until all the guests have left."

"Okay," Bernie said. "Then we'll talk and come up with a plan."

Beneath the calm I projected, my heart pumped with anxiety. I watched with dismay from a distance as Thomas took one drink after another, openly at first, then surreptitiously. He became louder and drunker. After he made a scene with another guest, shouting and pushing him, I asked security to remove him from the party and hold him at their office.

After the crowd around him broke up, Rhonda followed me into our office and faced me. "What the fuck is going on? We've never had to escort a guest out of a party."

"Sit down. We need to talk. But first, I have a call to make."

Her eyes widened when she heard me ask for Amelia Swanson. "Oh my God! Was that drunk guy who I think it was?"

I gave her a grim nod and then spoke to Amelia, giving her the latest news.

When I was through talking, Amelia said, "I'm informing the president. We'll have someone escort Thomas off the property and accompany him here to Washington, where his relatives can step in to help him." Her voice grew wobbly. "How can I ever thank you enough for keeping your cool and protecting Lindsay?"

"Rhonda and I said we'd do our best to protect her," I said simply. But I wondered, as I often had, if we'd been foolish to take on such a responsibility. Then I thought of all Lindsay had been through and knew we were right to step in and help. Especially after meeting her tormenter myself.

After I hung up, I faced Rhonda. "I'll fill you in on everything."

"Why didn't you tell me before? I would've bruised that guy's balls so badly he wouldn't be able to speak in anything but a squeak for the rest of his life."

"See why?" I said. "I knew you'd be upset and didn't want

to take the chance on giving away anything."

A sheepish grin crossed her face. "I'm not too good at hiding my feelings, huh?"

"You think? But as long as Brock believes he's got a deal with Thomas, we'll have to be careful about his roaming the property."

"After the party and after Thomas is gone, we'll set up a meeting with security," said Rhonda. "They can make up a story about this guest and send around his picture to warn all the staff that he's not supposed to be anywhere on the property."

"That's a good idea," I said.

"I also like the idea of telling everyone a honeymoon couple is staying there." She grinned. "Debra and Whit? Maybe something good will come of it. I'm pretty talented at predicting these things."

I was unable to stop a laugh from rolling out. "Don't try to play matchmaker, Rhonda. We've got enough on our hands."

"Wha-a-a-t? You don't think a little nudge in that direction might change things a bit? What does 'old boyfriend' mean, anyway? I'll bet you ten bucks I'm right."

I placed a hand on her arm. "Okay, ten bucks says you're not. For now, let's just get through the party and get Brock Goodwin away from here."

"I wish there was some way to bar him from the property."

"So, do I, but that's not going to happen."

"Okay, then, we'll play detective and make sure either we or one of the staff follows his every move."

"Sounds about right," I said, sighing.

As soon as everyone left the party and the staff was holding their own party in the dining room, Rhonda, Bernie, and I, along with our spouses, met in Bernie's office to discuss what was going on with Thomas and Brock.

"For now, Lindsay and Whit are staying at our house," Vaughn said to the group. "The guest wing will give each of them privacy."

"Do you think you need to ask her to stay inside?" Bernie said.

Vaughn shook his head. "Remember, we live in a gated community in an area where access is limited to the few houses in our cul de sac."

"Did you ask Whit how long he wants Lindsay to stay with us?" I asked him.

"It didn't come up. Though, it can't be too long because Nell and the baby are arriving in three days."

"Maybe she can move to Jean-Luc's place temporarily," I said.

Bernie gave me a quizzical look.

"She and Jean-Luc have become friends," I explained.

"Oh, I didn't realize ... I've been to his house. It's set back from the beach and is pretty private," he said.

"Why don't I talk to Debra and see what she and Whit have in mind for protecting Lindsay going forward?"

"Lindsay was pretty upset by the news of Thomas being around," said Vaughn.

"If she needs to, she can always stay with me," said Rhonda. "It's a bit hectic, though."

"I'll say," said Will. "But no one would think to look for her there."

I got to my feet. "Rhonda, let's go speak to Debra now while everybody here is busy with the clean-up and staff party."

Loosening his tie, Bernie turned to Vaughn and Will, "I know where some cold beer is."

"Sounds good," Vaughn said, taking off his sport coat.

"Peace and quiet? I'll take it," said Will.

Rhonda and I left them and Annette and took the hidden path to the guesthouse, being careful no one was around to see us. It bothered me that Thomas had spoken to others. Had he also asked them to keep an eye on our property? If so, it was going to be a tough battle to keep Lindsay safe.

Debra met us at the door.

"Ah, the honeymooner," Rhonda said with a gleam of mischief in her eyes.

Debra gave her a puzzled look, but the flush on her cheeks gave away her interest.

I shot a glance at Rhonda. She was beaming at Debra.

"Come on in," said Debra. "We need to talk. I got a call from Amelia, and she's very concerned."

"So are we," I said, stepping inside the entry hall.

Debra waved us into the living room. We sat in a group—Rhonda and me on the couch, Debra in a chair beside it.

"When we got the news that Thomas was around, Lindsay became hysterical. She's doing well on her recovery and dealing with the therapist, but she's not ready to face him." Debra gave me a worried look. "I've seen other people afraid, but this was terrible. I'm not sure what he did to her, but it was more than physical."

"I admit he scared me to death, and I talked with him for only a few minutes," I said. "There's something so predatory about him, it's frightening."

"Lindsay didn't want to leave, but I convinced her it was best," said Debra. "I explained we thought it wise for me to stay here in case Brock or Thomas came here."

"Do you think she'll want to move away from Florida?" asked Rhonda.

Debra shook her head firmly. "No. She loves her therapist, and frankly, she loves her time with Jean-Luc."

"Would she ever consider moving in with him until we all feel she's safe here?" I asked.

"As much as she likes Jean-Luc and considers him a friend, she wouldn't entertain the idea of moving there alone," said Debra. "Not for some time. Amelia has spoken with her and promised her that Whit and I would stay here with her."

Rhonda and I exchanged glances. Somehow, we'd make everything work. But at the moment, I was afraid something awful was about to happen. There were too many loose ends to make me feel comfortable.

CHAPTER SEVENTEEN

L ater, after sharing information with Bernie about hotel protocol, I headed home with Vaughn, anxious to see what awaited us there.

Before Vaughn pulled into the garage, he let me out by the back door, and I hurried inside. It was quiet. I walked out to the lanai and found Lindsay, Whit, and Elena talking softly while sitting in the pool with Robbie.

"Hi, Mom!" cried Robbie upon seeing me. "We have secret company."

"Yes, I know." I walked over to the edge of the pool and gazed down at Lindsay. "How's it going?"

She glanced at Robbie and back to me. "Can we talk privately?"

"Of course." I faced the others. "How are you?"

Whit smiled pleasantly and nodded.

"Good, thanks," said Elena. "Just keeping things quiet here."

Lindsay climbed out of the pool, wrapped a towel around herself, and followed me inside. "Thanks for taking us in," she said as we headed into the guest wing.

"We couldn't let you continue to stay at the guesthouse while Thomas was around," I said. "He's now in custody for creating a disturbance at the party. Someone will fly up to Washington with him tomorrow. I'm sorry to say he got totally wasted."

"It only makes things worse," Lindsay said. "When he's like that, he doesn't remember the things he says or does." A shudder crossed her shoulders as she took a seat on the private patio off the guest room. "At least that's what he says."

I sat opposite Lindsay and studied her. Her brown hair was streaked blond in places from the sun. Her blue eyes, almost opaque when we first met, were alive now with interest. A thinner version of her sister, her features were more delicate than Amelia's. Her hunched shoulders had straightened a bit, and I realized with a pang of sorrow how much someone could hurt another and how a sense of safety could help.

"I'm sorry you've had to go through this scare," I said, taking her hand in mine.

"Me, too. I wonder if it'll ever end." She looked out at the water.

"As long as you're here or at the hotel, we'll keep you as safe as we can. Debra and Whit seem very good at their jobs."

A smile crossed Lindsay's face, softening the lines of it. "I think they're falling in love all over again."

"Really? That would make Rhonda very happy. She claims she's an excellent matchmaker. Believe me, if it does happen, she'll come up with some reason she helped them along."

"They're so sweet together," said Lindsay. "I didn't realize you were married to *the* Vaughn Sanders. How do *you* handle his being in the spotlight?"

I took my time to answer, thinking of all the embarrassment I'd had to endure because of the lies Roger Sloan had spread about Vaughn and Lily being together. "It can be difficult," I said. "But Vaughn is a good man, and we live a pretty quiet life."

"I envy you that. Especially now with all the furor over my divorcing Thomas while his brother, a Roman Catholic, is president." A long sigh escaped her. "Thomas never could get beyond envying his brother. He always felt cheated out of a life he wanted for himself."

"Maybe that's part of why he is the way he is," I said.

"Definitely," said Lindsay. "When we first met, he was charming. And loving. I was the one person he said he'd ever truly loved."

"What changed?"

"The election," Lindsay said. "The attention Edward was getting and the way people disregarded Thomas broke him in some way. He became someone I didn't know, and as he sank into addiction, tearing our life apart, I grew to hate him."

"I've met him now, and he scared me," I admitted to her. "I don't know how you managed to stay alive. He looked as if he were capable of murder even when he gave me a disingenuous smile."

"Almost like dual personalities," Lindsay said. "It was bizarre. Totally scary."

"What can we do for you here?" I asked, squeezing her hand.

"Just be yourselves. Debra said she'd come to spend the night with me if I needed her to. But with Thomas in custody, I'd like to allow Debra and Whit to have the house to themselves."

"Sounds like a plan. Does Jean-Luc know you're here?"

"Yes. I called him."

"Would you like to have him join us for dinner? The hotel restaurants are closed today because of the brunch."

Lindsay's face lit up. "That would be great. He's become such a dear friend."

"I'll call him and ask him to join us. Dinner will be something simple. Hamburgers or chicken on the grill."

"Sounds delicious," Lindsay said. "Guess I'll change my clothes."

Jean-Luc was pleased with the invitation when I phoned him, even after I warned him about the food. And Whit, reluctant at first, agreed that Lindsay would be safe with us with Thomas out of the picture. He'd seen how secure the neighborhood was.

It was interesting to see Jean-Luc in a different setting. At the hotel, he was a man on a mission, definitely in charge. With us and beside Lindsay, he was a comparatively gentle soul, quite willing to listen to others before adding to the conversation. From the way he gazed at Lindsay, he was obviously falling for her. Hopefully, he realized it was much too soon for her to consider him more than a friend.

Later, after a simple meal of grilled chicken, tossed green salad, and garlic bread, I rose. "Time to tuck Robbie in for the night."

"May I join you?" Lindsay asked.

"Sure. He'd love it. Robbie has school tomorrow, so we keep to a schedule."

While Robbie brushed his teeth and got ready for bed, Lindsay spoke softly. "One of the reasons I was attracted to Thomas was that he wanted children. How quickly all that changed. But I love kids and hope to have a family of my own someday."

"Robbie has been a blessing to Vaughn and me," I said. "Liz, my daughter, is trying to have a child. I'm hoping it happens soon."

After Robbie was settled beneath the covers, I said, "Tonight, Ms. Lindsay and I will share reading a book. Just one story, though, because we have special guests."

"Okay," said Robbie, smiling shyly at Lindsay.

It was touching to hear Lindsay's lilting voice as she finished reading aloud a picture book about sailing.

After Robbie's eyelids closed, I stood and stared down at

the little boy with such a complicated past. He'd found his way into my heart.

"So sweet," Lindsay murmured before tiptoeing out of the room with me and joining Jean-Luc and Vaughn out on the lanai.

A short time later, Jean-Luc rose. "I'd better go. Thank you for a delightful evening."

Vaughn stood and shook his hand. "I'm pleased that you could come."

"Yes. I'm glad you were able to join us," said Lindsay, smiling at him from her seat on the couch.

"I'll walk you out," I said, wanting to make sure he was okay. He'd been upset to learn why Lindsay was staying with us.

Outside, he turned to me. "Thank you, again, for a pleasant evening. It's always good to see you and Vaughn away from the hotel." His brow furrowed. "Is Lindsay going to be all right? It's frightening that her ex-husband was actually at the hotel. How did that happen?"

"He used a pseudonym to get a reservation. But don't worry, he's in custody and will be on a plane out of here tomorrow. A security guard is accompanying him back to D. C."

"Let's hope he stays there," said Jean-Luc.

We stood a moment, each having something to say but keeping quiet, letting our affection for one another speak for us.

The next morning when I parked behind the hotel, I noticed Darla and Meredith on the beach and decided to say hello. I slipped off my sandals and walked out onto the sand, loving the feel of the warm, soft mixture between my toes.

When I'd lived on the hotel property, I'd spent a lot of time on the beach and still loved the liberating feeling it gave me.

They saw me coming and strolled toward me, happiness lighting their faces.

"Good morning, you two! How are you?"

"Good. I'm getting some rest and thinking things through," said Darla. She looked up at Meredith and turned to me. "As much as Mere and I love one another, we've decided to keep it quiet for now. Not out of shame, but out of the necessity for me to keep my job."

"We're not hiding anything," said Meredith. "We're just discreet."

"Allowing me to nail Simon for his harassment," said Darla. "I've had my agent draw up a complaint, and she'll present it to them next week. Is it possible for us to stay here for a few extra days in the suite? I don't want to be in the City when she tackles the situation at work. I will, of course, testify if needed."

"Sure, we'd love to have you. I'm glad you've taken steps to put an end to your harassment, Darla. It's important not only for you but for women and men everywhere."

"He's a creep," said Meredith. "Speaking of which, who were the two creeps at your party yesterday?"

"The one looked an awful lot like Thomas Thaxton," said Darla.

"Yes. And the other one I saw talking to Meredith at one point is Brock Goodwin, a neighbor of ours."

"He told me he was the president of the Neighborhood Association," said Meredith. "He made it sound like a big deal."

"Oh, it is. To him, but nobody else. I'm sorry I couldn't bail you out," I said.

Meredith grinned. "No problem. I shook him off as fast as

I could. He was still talking as I left."

I grinned at the thought. Brock was such a bore.

"See you later!" said Darla. "Thanks for your help. I'll speak to the office to have them change our reservations."

"Sounds good. If there's any trouble, let me know."

Instead of following them back to the hotel, I walked down to the water's edge. A salty breeze played with my hair, and I breathed in the scent of it. I closed my eyes and stood facing the water, letting my thoughts unravel. Things would settle down soon, I told myself. Lindsay would be safe, Darla would get her work issues straightened out, and Liz would become pregnant as she wanted. Lately, Rhonda and I had missed our margaritas at the hotel, but I decided as soon as Vaughn went back to work, I'd initiate those times together. One drink in the late afternoon, lots of conversation, and much laughter kept us moving forward, leaving the stress of overseeing the hotel manageable. Thank God we had Bernie.

I sensed someone approaching me and whipped around to face Brock.

"Ah, just the person I was hoping to see," he said smoothly. "I had an interesting conversation with one of your guests yesterday."

"Oh?" I said, playing dumb.

"Yes, Thomas Thaxton and I now have a partnership of sorts. I'll be doing investigating for him in return for a favor to me."

"I can't imagine what you're investigating," I said. "Besides, he left for D. C. this morning."

The look of surprise on Brock's face was telling.

"I guess you didn't know that," I said.

"Well, I'm sure he'll call me when he's back and settled," said Brock.

"You left before he was escorted from the party," I said.

"He's a troubled man. I'd stay away from him if I were you."

Brock glared at me. "Are you threatening me?"

"What? No! Absolutely not. I just believe he's a problem to everyone with whom he comes in contact."

Brock jabbed at his chest with his thumb. "I'll be the one to decide that. Having contacts in D.C. could prove very beneficial to me and my business."

"Good luck with that," I said, trying to sound sincere. As I moved away from the water and headed back to the hotel, he followed me.

"I see the gate is going up as we speak. But if you think it'll keep me and others out of the hotel, you're wrong. It won't."

"Now it sounds as if you're threatening me. What's the problem with providing our guests a sense of privacy?"

"Nothing, if you have nothing to hide. Thomas thinks his ex-wife might be here or somewhere in the area."

"And you believed him?"

"You don't?" Brock said, surprised.

"I wouldn't trust a word that man said," I replied, watching with satisfaction as the usual self-assured look on Brock's face slipped a little.

"Well, I do," said Brock.

I walked past the men working on the gate and turned to face him. "See you later."

"You can count on it," he said before turning back to the water.

I watched him go, worried Brock wouldn't give up on the idea of watching the hotel in hopes of seeing Lindsay.

Inside, I stopped in the kitchen to grab a cup of coffee. Things were back to normal from the party, though not all the staff looked as chipper as they usually did. Their party had been, no doubt, a success. Rhonda and I were happy to allow our people to relax and celebrate another good season at the hotel. Twice a year, they had the chance to do so, with senior management stepping in to give everyone time to join in.

I knew Rhonda would be late and went to Bernie's office to check in with him.

"How are things?" I asked as I met him in the front hall.

"Interesting," Bernie answered cryptically. "Let's talk in my office."

We went into it, and he closed the door behind him. "A few minutes ago, I got a call from someone asking if the guesthouse accommodations were available. I explained that the house was booked for the next several months, that it was popular for weddings and honeymooners."

I wondered what was so strange about that.

"The thing is, I recognized Brock Goodwin's voice," said Bernie. "I tried to have him give me more information so I could call him if we had a cancellation. But he hung up on me. What's going on with him now?"

I filled him in on my recent conversation with Brock. "He's not going to give up on the idea of exchanging favors even after I told him Thomas was headed back to D. C. It's why we have to have our staff keep an eye out for him. If it were anyone else, I'd guess they'd give up fairly quickly. But with Brock, I wouldn't count on it. He's desperate for an influential D. C. contact."

"I'll bring it up in the staff meeting that he's someone to be watched," said Bernie.

"Anything else going on that I should know about?" I asked. "Was Darla able to change her reservations successfully?"

Bernie nodded with satisfaction. "I approved the change a short while ago."

"I'll be in my office. Rhonda will be in later. I'm working on some ideas for wedding promotions. Over the next few months, we'll be busy with that crowd. Rhonda and I are trying to get some national bride magazines to cover a couple of them, along with the social magazines here in South Florida and some life-style bloggers. Unfortunately, we'll have to be careful how we handle the guesthouse rentals. I've promised Tina Marks space there after her baby comes, and she's ready to test our New Mothers Program."

"But you'll keep Lindsay there for the time being?" Bernie asked.

"Yes. At this point, she's our priority. When she's ready to leave, we'll open the guesthouse for rentals again. We can't wait too long because of the bookings we have coming up."

"After seeing her ex-husband and his behavior myself, I agree with you. We need to help her out. And it's not as if the rental on the house is not being paid," said Bernie.

"Right. We'll talk later. Thanks."

I left him and went into the office, my thoughts already diverted to the project ahead. The Beach House Hotel had been listed as one of the best places for a small, destination wedding in the past, but we needed to find new ways to maintain that reputation. While a pain for the staff, they were good moneymakers for us.

I was on the phone when Rhonda came into the office, plopped down in a desk chair, and faced me with a woebegone expression.

As soon as I could, I ended the call. "What's the matter?"

"Will and I went to Angela's to have coffee with Katherine and Arthur, as Angela requested, before they take off later this morning." Her eyes welled with tears. "Annie, it was a fuckin' mess! You know how sweet Will is, how patient. Arthur was so condescending, so rude that Will, who rarely swears, told

Arthur he was an A-hole, that he knew more about good financial management than Arthur ever would, which is why people all over the area hired him and Reggie."

"And?"

"And Arthur told Reggie if he didn't wake up and return to New York, he would never be allowed in either of their houses again."

I clapped a hand to my mouth.

"That's not all! Katherine freaked and told Arthur to shut up, which made him so mad he walked out of the kitchen and wouldn't come out of his room, even to say goodbye."

"Poor Angela! Poor Reggie!"

"I know. Right?" said Rhonda. "They both were crying when Will took Reggie outside so they could talk. When they returned, Reggie was quiet but firm when he told Katherine he wasn't about to change his mind and he would get a limo to take them both to the airport."

"My word! What a morning!"

"It was horrible. I felt sorry for Katherine and told her I'd do what I could at this end to make it possible for her to see the kids again. Even if she had to book a room at the hotel."

Rhonda gave me a wobbly smile. "Katherine thanked me and gave me a hug. How do ya like them apples?"

"Pretty surprising," I said.

"I told Angela that Rita and I would help her out for the next few weeks whenever she wanted us, that it was time for her to recover and enjoy this new baby and still have time for Evan. He needs his mother right now."

"I'll help too," I said, knowing how devastating the morning had been to both Angela and Reggie, who were one of the sweetest young couples I knew.

As Rhonda would say, families were freakin' complicated.

CHAPTER EIGHTEEN

That afternoon, on a whim, I decided to stop by Angela's house with food from the kitchen for an easy dinner. It would be my first visit without Katherine in the picture, and I was anxious to see how Angela was holding up after a tumultuous morning.

I parked my car in the driveway and made my way to the front, listening for signs of trouble. All was quiet. I knocked gently on the door, and after a few seconds, it opened and Reggie stood there.

"Hi, Reggie! I just wanted to drop a few things off for dinner. I hoped to see Angela."

"She's in the living room nursing the baby. I'll take the package, and you can go to her."

As I walked toward her, Angela turned and smiled at me. "Ann! I'm so glad you stopped by. Come sit with me."

I studied her. Angela was dainty compared to her mother, more like her father. Her dark hair pulled back into a ponytail offset a pretty face with delicate features and brown eyes that usually sparkled with life. Now, they showed the strain of the last couple of weeks.

"I heard about this morning. I'm so sorry. Your mother told me all about it," I said, taking a seat beside her.

"I'm so proud of her," Angela said. "Katherine broke down weeping, and my mother actually reached out and pulled her into a hug."

"Ah, I wondered about that. Rhonda said Katherine hugged her."

"No, it was Mom reaching out to Katherine even after all the horrible things she had said. Before she left, Katherine told me she wanted to get to know Mom better." She made a face. "That's a giant step for Katherine."

I heard the sounds of laughter from the kitchen. "How's Reggie? According to Rhonda, his father said some pretty terrible things."

Angela gave me a worried look. "His parents don't understand their behavior is what kept us from deciding to move north. Now, Reggie has a relationship with Will that will never be broken. He's become the father Reggie has always wanted."

"Nice for Will."

"And very good for my husband," said Angela, lifting the baby to her shoulder and burping her.

"She's so beautiful," I said. Sally's pretty pink cheeks were adorable as a yawn escaped her butterfly mouth. Fluffy brown hair sat on top of her head, like that of a duckling.

"I think so too," said Angela. "Want to hold her? She's falling asleep."

I took the warm bundle in my arms and looked down at Sally's sweet face, trying to imagine what it would be like to hold a baby that belonged to Liz.

"I'm sorry about Liz. She called to tell me she isn't pregnant."

"It'll happen in its own good time," I said, pushing away the disappointment I felt for her. We all had to keep upbeat.

"When's Nell coming to town?" asked Angela. "Liz thought it was soon. I'd love to see her."

"She's going to call tonight with her plans. We're expecting her this weekend, but I'm hoping she can stay a couple of extra days."

"Nell's staying with you?" asked Angela.

I hesitated. "I'm not sure. She'll have her choice. Either way, we'll watch the baby so she can get a good night's sleep."

Evan came running out of the kitchen, holding a cookie in his hand. When he saw me, he came to a quick stop.

"It's okay, Evan. This is Auntie Ann. Remember her?" coached Angela.

He studied me and then ran to his mother.

She drew him up into her lap. He stared at me holding the baby and tapped gently on Sally's head. "Baby. That's my baby."

"Yes," I said, wondering at the change in him.

"Different, huh?" Angela said. "I know Katherine tried, but we all suffered under her heavy hand. This little guy most of all."

When Sally started to cry, Evan scrambled out of Angela's lap. "Stop, baby! Stop!" he crooned, patting her again.

Angela looked at me with tears in her eyes. "He loves her."

"Yes, he does." I handed the baby to Angela. "I'm glad to see things are so much better. If I can help in any way, please feel free to call me."

"Thanks." Angela got to her feet and, holding the baby, gave me an awkward hug. "Love you."

"Love you too." I adored her in part because she was Rhonda's child and felt like my own.

I drove home thinking of Vaughn's daughter, Nell. She was another young woman I truly loved. She'd been accepting of me and had even encouraged the relationship between Vaughn and me from the beginning. Though she and Clint would probably never leave the D.C. area and move to Florida, they made an effort to visit as often as they could. And before the baby came, Nell often visited her father in New York.

Now that Bailey, their daughter, was over two months old, Clint and Nell were driving to Florida to spend some time with us while Nell took advantage of the New Mothers Program at the hotel. Besides offering healthy, low-cal meals to those in the program, the spa was offering free massages, facials, and nail services. Troy, who managed the spa, also had designed a low-key exercise plan for those who wanted to get back in shape after giving birth. Unlike the unrealistic pictures of Hollywood stars following the birth of their child, photos of our attendees would look more normal. Rhonda and I insisted the program be more about pampering a new mother than trying to make her look as if she hadn't just had a baby.

Nell was one of our first participants and had agreed to test the program and give us honest criticism of it. In time, Angela would do the same.

As I drove into the driveway, I noticed Debra's SUV parked to the side. *What now?*

Trudy greeted me at the door and raced back outside, where Vaughn was sitting with Lindsay, Debra, and Whit. Robbie was playing with his cars beside them.

"There you are!" said Vaughn getting to his feet. "I was getting ready to call you. We were thinking of an evening cruise. Are you game?"

I looked at the eager expressions on all their faces. "Sounds like a plan."

"Yay, Mommy!" cried Robbie, running to me.

I swung him up in my arms for a quick hug and let him down again.

"I'll go change my clothes," said Lindsay and headed indoors.

"Me, too," I said. But before I could leave, Debra caught my arm.

"Whit and I thought it might be good to talk to you," she

said. Her gaze met mine. "Lindsay would like to stay in the guesthouse as long as possible. Whit and I will stay with her. Considering what has happened with the breach by Thomas, we want to assure you that we'll continue to be on high alert."

"We do suggest, however, that you add a gate across the drive leading to the house," said Whit. "It would prevent an automobile from getting too close. I understand your neighbor and others may be watching for a sign of her."

"No problem. Unfortunately, it's true that others may be watching," I said, irritated by Brock all over again. "I'm not sure if he's the only one Thomas spoke to, and I can't bring up the subject."

"Of course not," said Debra, glancing at Whit. "Together, we can work things out."

He put an arm around Debra's shoulder. "We're a good team. We've worked together in the past."

The loving looks they exchanged told me Rhonda just might win the bet after all.

Aboard the *Zephyr*, we sipped margaritas or beer as we made our way out into open water. The conversation remained pleasant and stayed away from Lindsay's situation. Whit talked about some of the places he'd visited in the past without giving specifics about his former job. Debra spoke about her life in Washington and how she was looking forward to the time when she could leave.

"Where would you go?" I asked her.

"Someplace warm," she said. "I was thinking of Miami." She glanced at Whit.

Whit smiled at her, then explained, "I've got a house in Coral Gables. I've been telling her she can get all kinds of work there."

"So, it would be a good *work*place for you," I said, unable to stop teasing them. It was so obvious they were in love.

Debra's cheeks grew red, but she laughed with good nature.

Lindsay looked at me and grinned.

When Vaughn set the anchor and then dropped and furled the sails so we could eat, Lindsay and I set out dinner—chicken salad, French bread, and a cheese and fruit plate from a local delicatessen.

Soon, the conversation turned to Vaughn's job in New York.

"It's one of those crazy things where my character keeps going on. As long as they want me to be the mayor of the town, I'll continue, though I'm also looking at movie scripts. If the right one comes along, I'll do that too."

"I admit I'd never watched the show until we came here," said Lindsay. "But I enjoy it. And Darla Delaney is great in the role of the new school teacher in town. It somehow works."

"I wasn't sure we could pull it off, but Darla is a good actress," said Vaughn.

"And you're a good actor," I said, smiling at him.

"And you're a good mommy!" said Robbie, making us laugh.

Playing along, I added, "And you're a good son!"

"I know," Robbie said. "I got another gold star today."

"You did? For what?" I asked, pleased to see the pride on his face.

"For telling Katy I was sorry I hit her."

"Whoa! You hit her? Why would you do that?"

"Because she hit me first. Brett says it's because she likes me. But I don't think so."

Hiding my amusement, I remained calm. "Hitting is never the answer. Isn't that so?"

"I know. That's why I didn't do it again," said Robbie.

I glanced at Vaughn.

"We've talked about it," he said, and I let the matter drop. Robbie was usually a peacemaker, not a fighter.

"I'm glad to see you discuss hitting with your son," said Whit quietly. "I've worked with so much violence that I worry about all of it in the games kids play today."

"Me, too," I said, "which is why we keep an eye on things for Robbie."

"I like sailing," chirped Robbie proudly.

"And you do a nice job with it," I said. Though he couldn't handle the boat alone at his young age, he knew much of the terminology and the basics of sailing.

"My son, Ty, and I used to do a lot of sailing together when he was young. He still loves it today. It's why I've been so happy to teach Robbie."

"Would you ever consider helping me out?" said Whit. "I've done a lot of sailing, but I've never owned my own boat. This time with you is making me think about buying one. I could use your input."

"I'd be happy to help," said Vaughn. "And while you're here, we can do some sailing together whenever you can get away. I think you'll agree this Pearson is one to consider."

"I'd like that a lot," said Whit. Grinning, he saluted Vaughn. "Happy to be your mate!"

Vaughn laughed. "Anytime."

That night as Vaughn and I lounged on the steps of the pool under the moonlight, I lay back in his arms. I loved these quiet times together when few words were spoken as we gazed up at the stars, and I felt the comfort of him so close to me.

"Makes me wonder about so many things when I study the nighttime skies," I murmured.

"I wonder how I could've been so lucky to find you," Vaughn said, drawing me closer.

"After Ellie died, I never thought I'd find a woman as wonderful, but, Ann, you're everything I've always hoped for and more."

I turned and faced him. "I love you, Vaughn, and always will."

"Let's go to bed," he whispered. "I want to prove to you how much I care."

We climbed out of the pool and tiptoed inside, hoping not to disturb Trudy sleeping with Robbie.

Some nights it was enough to cuddle. But this wasn't one of them.

The next morning, I packed a lunch for Robbie and made sure he had a good breakfast before Vaughn drove him to school.

I'd already talked to Rhonda and Bernie about adding a simple, unobtrusive gate on the road to the house. A second phone call with Bernie confirmed he had scheduled the work for today, and Lindsay would be better protected on hotel property.

A call came through to me from Amelia.

"Good morning!" I said. "I'm sitting here on my lanai facing a lovely day."

"Good. I just wanted you to know Thomas is here in D. C. The president has assured me that he'll be ordered back into rehab or will, instead, continue treatment in Vermont at their home. Gotta go but wanted to be in touch. Again, thanks for all you're doing for Lindsay."

"Knowing he's there makes me feel a whole lot better. Thanks for calling me."

We hung up, and then I called Lindsay.

"I suppose you heard the news about Thomas being back in D.C. and under the president's dictates."

"Yes," Lindsay said. "Amelia told me the president is furious with his brother and is determined to see that something like his recent trip to Florida never happens again." Her voice broke. "I'm sorry I had to drag Amelia, you, and Rhonda into my problems. Amelia told me she and the president got into an argument over Thomas being able to break away. Helping abused women is one of her top causes, you know."

"I also know how much she loves you. I'm sure you'd be as protective toward her as she is toward you."

Lindsay sniffed. "I would, but it's all so sad."

"Are you going to talk to Barbara Holmes about this new development?" I asked, thinking it would be a good idea.

"I've already set up an appointment for later this afternoon," she responded. "Thank you for all you and Rhonda are doing to help. Amelia and I both appreciate it."

"You're more than welcome," I said. "You can relax now. Debra and Whit promised me they'd keep you safe." I couldn't help smiling. "By the way, you were right. They're in love."

"I know," said Lindsay. "They're adorable together. I would love to repay them for all they are doing for me by helping them out with a wedding at The Beach House Hotel. Do you think we could arrange it?"

"Of course. Let me know if they're interested and when, and we'll go from there. It would be a lovely gesture on your part."

"I'd like to keep as many details secret as I can, but, of course, they have to agree to the idea," said Lindsay.

"A surprise wedding? I like the idea," I said, already thinking of some cute touches. "Maybe something casual on the beach?"

"Yes!" said Lindsay, sounding excited.

It made me happy to hear her so enthused. Focusing on this would help her through more rough moments of breaking away from her past.

CHAPTER NINETEEN

I was in the middle of reviewing an ad campaign Bernie had arranged when I received a call from Nell.

"Hello, darling! How are you? Are you ready to come to Florida?" I asked, excited about the prospect.

"Yes, that's why I'm calling," she said. "To avoid flying with Bailey, we're driving. We'll leave Wednesday, make a stop in Georgia to stay with friends, and plan to be there sometime Friday. Sound good?"

"Sounds wonderful. Your father is home for a few days while an issue at work is being addressed, but then he'll be gone for quite a while to make up for the lost time. One of his co-stars is having an issue with sexual harassment."

"Oh? Darla Delaney, by any chance?"

"Actually, yes, though I don't normally talk about it."

"She's gorgeous," gushed Nell.

"You might have a chance to meet her. She's staying at the hotel through next weekend, though once again, I wouldn't normally tell anyone that."

"I understand, but I'd love that. It's nice to know who Dad is working with."

"Yes," I agreed. "Drive carefully. We can't wait to see you. Robbie will be thrilled. He loves you, you know."

Nell laughed. "And I love him too."

I hung up feeling good about how all the kids got along. I quickly called Liz to tell her of Nell's arrival.

"How are you, honey?" I asked, knowing how disappointed she was.

"Good," said Liz, sounding more like herself. "I've decided to repaint our bedroom. We've wanted to do it for some time, and I think a sunny yellow will brighten the room."

"Sounds like you're feeling better. I'm glad. Nell called. She, Clint, and the baby will arrive on Friday."

"I know. She already called me," said Liz. "I talked to her earlier this week, so she knows about ... me."

"Oh, good. It's nice that she's a good friend as well as your sister."

"I'm so glad I finally have a sister," she said. "How are things at the hotel? When I talked to Vaughn earlier, he mentioned someone had been staying at the house."

"When you have a moment, we need to talk about it. Perhaps we could meet for lunch. Are you free today?"

"Hold on, and I'll see if Chad can cover the store for me."

A few moments later, she returned. "Yes! Let's meet at André's. Say one o'clock?"

"Sounds perfect. See you then." I couldn't stop smiling. Having my daughter live in the same area, available for lunch, was something I treasured.

I drove onto Main Street, found a parking spot, and walked to André's. It was a small French restaurant with outdoor seating in a little alleyway next to a dress shop I loved and a silversmith who did fantastic work.

Liz was already there sitting outside when I arrived. She smiled and waved me over to her. I observed her lovely face with pride. Her features were very much like pictures of my mother. They, her sparkling blue eyes, and long, natural-blond hair were beautiful. More than that, she was a kind, loving person. When and if the time came, she'd make a marvelous mother.

"I grabbed this spot in the corner so we could have privacy," Liz said. "And if you don't mind, I've ordered a glass of a lovely California chardonnay for each of us. I thought we'd celebrate having the chance to have lunch together. It's always such a treat."

"I don't mind at all. Later today, I'm meeting Lorraine Grace off property to discuss a secret wedding, and then Rhonda and I are going to meet."

"Are you and Rhonda doing your margarita meetings again?" Liz said, smiling.

"I'm trying to set them up," I said, placing my purse on an empty chair. "It's a great way to discuss future plans and keep up-to-date on what's happening."

"Speaking of that, a secret wedding and an unnamed guest? What's going on?"

I leaned closer. "The guest who stayed with us for a night is the same one I told you about earlier."

"Oh ... now I get it. Does this have something to do with the man who had to be escorted from the party? Chad and I left before that happened, but I heard all about it from his mother."

"Yes, it does. I'm not mentioning names for obvious reasons," I said, glancing around to see if anybody was within hearing distance. The place was crowded, and even though the noise level was high with conversations, I couldn't take the chance of being overheard. "Sometime, Rhonda and I will give you and Angela the entire story, but for now, I'm sure you know enough to figure it out."

"So where does a secret wedding come in?" she asked, looking puzzled.

"That person is helping to plan one for the two people living with her. As a thank you. Isn't that sweet?"

"Very special. I often look at the photo album of my

ceremony taken at the hotel. It was such a beautiful location for it."

"That it is," I said with satisfaction, remembering my wedding there. "She and I are thinking a casual beach setting."

"Sounds perfect for this time of year," said Liz. "Now that school is almost out, just a few weeks to go, what are you going to do with Robbie all summer?"

"He and Brett are going to day camp together. And then Elena will take over in the afternoons. Even though it's slower at the hotel, we're still busy with group meetings and weddings. And it's a good time for people who want to take advantage of our gourmet or spa packages."

"Nell said she's going to critique the New Mothers' Program for you." Liz couldn't hide a wistful note in her voice.

"It'll be so helpful. We need inside information on how it's working before we do a bigger ad campaign for it."

"Sometimes work at the store is quiet, and you know me, I can easily get bored. So, I've been working on some gift ideas for brides and new mothers." She paused, hesitant. "May I show you?"

"Of course! How exciting!"

Liz opened her purse and pulled out a plastic bag filled with jewelry. She laid the pieces on the table.

I studied the contents. Thin, narrow bracelets held charms and beads of various kinds. For the brides, several bracelets held palm trees, a flamingo, a variety of flowers, initials, along with a pendant with the date strung between crystals and other beads. The new-mother bracelets were done in mostly pinks or blues with tropical charms. There were also some strictly for babies with initials, birth dates, and birthstones.

"They're fabulous," I gushed. "Not like so many others I've seen."

"They won't be cheap because I use only the best of

materials that I get online and from a few local artists."

"If they're top quality, that shouldn't be an issue. The new-mother ones can be something we make part of the program. Let me talk to Rhonda about it."

"Really? You like them that much?" Liz said, her face filling with excitement. "The others can be done for brides and their wedding parties with a choice of beads, colors, charms, whatever they want. The new-mother ones would be pretty standard except for initials and photo charms to show off their baby."

"I think it's a lovely idea. They'd all be special order, so you wouldn't waste inventory," I said. "Though you'd want to have plenty available as I think these will be a big hit."

"If they don't want bracelets, I can make simple necklaces out of sterling silver," said Liz. "I just want something to do while minding the store when it isn't busy."

"I understand. It's hard to be tied to a store six days a week. But remember, when you and Angela come into the hotel business, it's 24/7."

Liz held up her hand. "I know, I know."

"As I said, I'll talk to Rhonda about these pieces, and we'll get back to you. Maybe we'll start with a few bracelets for the New Mothers Program. We can ask Nell what she thinks about it when she's here."

"Thanks," said Liz. She gathered the jewelry, returned it to the plastic bag, and handed it over to me just as our glasses of wine arrived.

"Sorry to be so late," said the waiter apologetically as he placed the glasses in front of us and handed us menus. "I'll be back in a minute to take your orders."

After he left, I lifted my glass and clicked it against Liz's. "Here's to us! Health and happiness!"

"And good things ahead of us!" said Liz.

I watched her take a sip of wine, wishing I had the power to grant her happiness.

Later, as we finished our grilled shrimp salads, I noticed Liz tense and turned to see Brock Goodwin approaching. I patted my mouth with my napkin and waited for him to speak.

"Good afternoon, lovely ladies. I hate to interrupt your lunch, but I was doing my daily walk and noticed you were having some work done at the hotel. A new gate on the road to the guesthouse."

I shook a finger at him. "There's no way we need your permission to do something like that."

"No, no, that's not what I meant. I was just wondering why. Are you hiding something or someone, perhaps?"

I felt my pulse race. "Just giving our honeymooners a little more privacy. With wedding season coming up, family groups and honeymooners will want that space to be off-limits to other guests. It's one of the many reasons guests enjoy our hotel."

Liz looked up at him. "Excuse me for asking, but why would you care what goes on at the hotel? It's not your concern. A friend of mine recently moved into your neighborhood, and she says it's awful that the board is so focused on petty issues."

Brock's eyes bulged. "She obviously doesn't understand what makes our neighborhood so unique. I and my board protect it from becoming cheapened."

"The difference between one flower and another should be of no one's concern," Liz persisted.

"Ah, I know now who your friend is." Brock shook his head. "She was most uncooperative about us wanting her to plant different flowers to match the theme of the building."

"It was a petty complaint. Others in the building were fine with it. I just don't get why you have to be so nosy," said Liz, her cheeks flushed with anger. "You've made her very unhappy when it should have been an exciting time for her."

"You young people have no idea about respect for your elders," said Brock. He glared at her and turned to me.

I ignored his look and lifted my wine glass for a sip when what I wanted to do was just to throw it at him.

He left, and Liz said, "I'm sorry, Mom. I hope it didn't cause more trouble for you. But you know my friend, Chris. She was so excited to buy a condo by the water but ended up in tears when she received nasty letters from the board. She asked me if I knew who Brock Goodwin was. I gave her the story of how he's harassed you and Rhonda and told her he was a total dick who should be ignored."

"He's a most miserable person and one who might be dangerous," I said, uneasy about his snooping.

That afternoon after meeting with Lorraine Grace at her off-site bridal shoppe, I called Rhonda and told her I was on my way.

"I'm ordering the margaritas now and will meet you at our favorite spot," she said.

During the renovation of the hotel, we'd kept one balcony next to the Presidential Suite available through the maid's closet and utility room. No guest would ever know how to reach it. Some afternoons we'd sit together there and have anything from ice water to margaritas while we shared reflections on where we'd been and where we were going. In the hotel business, plans were sullied by circumstances out of anyone's control. We were no different. Weather patterns, illness, and other factors, including Brock and his cronies, played a part in retaining as much flexibility as possible.

Today, I couldn't wait to fill her in on a lot of things. But as I walked onto the balcony, the first thing I did was hand her a ten-dollar bill. "There, now you don't have to say, 'I told you so.'"

She grinned. "But that's always the best part of being right. Does this have anything to do with the lovebirds at the guesthouse?"

"Yes, it does," I said, setting down my purse, lifting my drink, and taking a careful sip.

I settled in my chair facing her and grinned. "Debra and Whit went sailing with Vaughn, Lindsay, Robbie, and me yesterday, and I have to admit they were adorable together."

"See? I told you so," said Rhonda, chuckling.

"I know, I know. But the best part is that Lindsay wants to host a wedding for them right here at the hotel. We're thinking about a beach setting. As soon as she clears it with them and sets up a date, we can work on it. I've already spoken to Lorraine about it."

"Wow! I didn't know I was that good at this matchmaking thing," said Rhonda.

I couldn't help rolling my eyes. "They were already a match!"

"So, it seems," she said. "It's great to get such happy news while we're going through a difficult time with Lindsay's safety. I don't trust Thomas, and I certainly don't trust Brock."

"Neither do I. I can't imagine how Lindsay feels. She was shaken to hear how close Thomas was to her safe location."

"Is she doing better?" Rhonda asked.

"Yes, she scheduled another session with Barbara Holmes, and I think being part of a wedding is a great diversion for her. An affirmation that some marriages can work."

"How's Liz?" Rhonda asked. "Angela told me she's working hard to get over her disappointment."

"As a matter of fact, I have something to show you." I pulled out the bag of bracelets and laid them out on the table between us. "She's been working on a couple of ideas for both bridal parties and the New Mothers Program."

I explained Liz's ideas and watched as Rhonda picked up various pieces. Smiling, she looked at me. "I love these ideas. Especially the pink flamingoes. You know how much I like them."

"Indeed, I do," I answered sweetly. When we'd first thought of themes and decorations, she and I had fought over the idea of flamingoes on the front lawn.

"Liz has good taste, like you, Annie," Rhonda said. "I think we should offer each wedding party the chance to have these made to order, and I like your idea of giving the bride and each participant a free one as a parting gift."

I let out the breath I didn't realize I'd been holding. "Thank you! I think our guests will love the idea, and more importantly, it will allow Liz to do something creative and to earn money of her own."

"Bless Liz's heart; I know how difficult it can be to wait for good news on the baby front. I would've had more kids, but with Sal, it never worked out." She grinned. "Who knew Will would be such a rooster."

"Two kids in less than two years was a surprise to all of us," I said.

"Most of all to me." Rhonda raised her glass. "Here's to all the kids and those to come!"

I clicked my glass against hers, hoping to have good news from Liz in the near future.

Rhonda leaned forward. "While the gate was being put up on the road to the guesthouse, guess who appeared?"

"Brock Goodwin? He all but accosted Liz and me at André's today. Liz told him off."

"She did?"

"Yes. A friend of hers has had a terrible time with the

Neighborhood Association board all because of different colored flowers."

"You've got to be shittin' me!" said Rhonda, her face flushing with anger. "What are we going to do about Brock?"

"Well, I've been thinking about it, and when the time comes, I have a plan," I answered. I explained what I had in mind, and she laughed.

CHAPTER TWENTY

All week, I'd anxiously looked forward to Friday and now stood in the driveway with Vaughn awaiting Nell's arrival. They'd called from the entry gate to say they were here. Looking at the eagerness on Vaughn's face, my heart squeezed with love for him. He was such a loving Dad.

Clint pulled their oversized SUV into the driveway. Immediately after the car stopped, Nell was out of the passenger seat and into Vaughn's arms. Then she turned to me. It always surprised me how much she looked like Liz.

I hugged her. "So glad you're here!"

"Not more than I am," Nell said, beaming at me.

I rubbed my hands together with glee. "Now, let's see that adorable daughter of yours."

Clint came from behind the car holding the baby in his arms. "Here she is!" He handed her to me, a broad smile crossing his handsome face, pride in his voice.

In the warmth of the Florida sun, the baby wore a little pink sundress that I'd sent to her. Her hazel eyes studied me solemnly; then, a sweet smile stretched across her adorable face.

My heart filled with love. "Hi, baby Bailey!" I crooned. "Want to say hi to Grandpa?"

I moved closer to Vaughn so he could get a good look at his first grandchild.

"Hi, there!" said Vaughn softly. She smiled at him, this time displaying a dimple in her right cheek.

"Oh-h-h ... she's so precious!" I said, ignoring the whine

coming from Trudy.

Vaughn picked up Trudy and allowed her to see the baby. Trudy barked and wagged her tail.

Bailey's face crumpled, about to cry, and then she settled her gaze on Trudy with interest.

"I think they'll be friends," said Nell. "Someday, we'll get a dachshund of our own. But I need a little time first." A bright smile lit her face. "I can't wait to start the program tomorrow."

"I think you'll enjoy it," I said and turned to Clint.

He gave me a hug hello. "Wish you had a program for new dads. Bailey's finally sleeping longer, but it's been tough. Poor Nell has the brunt of it with the feedings and bulk of the care of her."

"Well, we're going to do our best to let all of you get a good rest," I said. I'd always liked Clint and his consideration for Nell.

"Where's Robbie?" Nell said.

"At school. Liz is going to pick him up early and bring him home so they both can see you. Chad will cover the store until it closes."

"How are they?" Nell asked, concern crossing her face. "I talked to Liz."

"She's using her downtime at the store to make some jewelry for hotel guests. I'll show it to you later. I think you're going to like her ideas."

"Oh, good. I'm glad she's keeping busy," said Nell.

"We don't have to stand in the driveway talking," said Vaughn. "Come on in."

"I'll unload the car," said Clint.

"And I'll help," said Vaughn.

When I led Nell to their guest room suite, she stopped and clasped her hands. "Oh, my! I didn't realize you'd set up a nursery for Bailey. How wonderful!"

I jiggled Bailey in my arms. "Nothing's too good for our grandbabies, starting with her."

Nell's eyes filled. "It's so sweet. You're always so loving, Ann. I'm disappointed Mom isn't here to meet Bailey, but I'm thrilled you are. After giving birth, you want to talk about it, you know? And there's so much I can learn from you."

"I'm no expert, but I'm willing to help any way I can."

"Good. Because I'm thinking of working part-time from home. My boss wants me back full-time, but I told him no. However, part-time might be a good solution."

"That's a very personal decision," I said. "I would, however, suggest you wait a few months. The changes in babies during the first year, especially, are constant, and you don't want to miss out on any of them."

"Thanks. That's what I was thinking." Nell squeezed my shoulder. "I'm so glad Dad found you."

"It was more that *The Sins of the Children* found Rhonda and me," I said, pleased.

"How's this new starlet doing? Dad sounded concerned when I last talked to him."

"Darla is wonderful, and so is her partner."

Nell blinked in surprise. "Really?"

"Yes, but understandable for career purposes, she's keeping that quiet."

"I'm hoping I get the chance to see her at the hotel," Nell said and turned as the men came in with suitcases and a lot of baby gear.

"Who do you want to see?" Vaughn asked.

"Darla, your new love on *television*," Nell said, grinning.

"That's right. No rumors of trysts. Neither one of us wants that," said Vaughn.

"I like her already," Nell said. "After that horrible woman, Lily Dorio, Darla sounds wonderful."

"She is," Vaughn and I said together, bringing a laugh to all of us.

I looked down at Bailey. She'd fallen asleep.

Nell took her from my arms. "Let's put her in the crib, and we can talk on the lanai."

As we headed out the door, Trudy curled up beneath the crib.

That afternoon when Liz and Robbie arrived, I watched them exchange hugs with Nell and Clint and filled with joy at the warmth between them. Second marriages didn't always work with the kids, and I was grateful for mine.

"Where's the baby?" Robbie asked, rubbing Trudy's ears.

"Right here," said Nell, patting the covered mound at her chest. "She's eating right now."

"Can I see?" he asked.

Nell lifted the blanket. Robbie watched a minute and then turned to me with a questioning look.

"That's how some babies get their milk," I said. "Remember the pictures of baby animals in the book we have?"

"Yes," he said solemnly, staring at my chest.

"Ready for your juice and cookies?" said Vaughn winking at me.

"Okay," Robbie said and hurried toward the kitchen. I knew, though, that more conversations about nursing babies would arise in the future.

"Thanks," I said to Nell. "Robbie's never seen a nursing baby before. I liked how you handled it."

"Nursing babies is as old as time," she said smiling.

Sitting beside her, Liz said, "I intend to nurse my babies too."

"Good idea," I said, my heart breaking for Liz. I wanted to

say something but knew I should be quiet and not add angst to the situation. "If you two don't mind, I have a little boy to tend to."

Trudy sat at Nell's feet, and, amused, I saw she was debating whether to follow me into the kitchen or stay on guard for the baby. With a last look at the baby, she trotted after me.

That evening, Vaughn grilled up steaks while I made my special spinach salad, to which I added fresh strawberries and then tossed it all in a poppyseed dressing. My German potato salad, made this morning, was Chad's and Clint's favorite and something I always tried to have for them.

At the dinner table, we caught up on what was going on in Washington, D. C. with Nell's and Clint's work. They both worked with lobbying groups. As usual, lots of interesting tidbits about various politicians came up.

"What can you tell me about Thomas Thaxton?" I asked, hoping to hear that he was "back in town."

"He's a slime ball. I met him once at a meeting I attended," Nell said. "I didn't like him at all. Pretty scary."

"Is he back in town or in Vermont, do you know?"

"I heard he left the rehab in California and is now in Vermont," Clint said. "Something about being dangerous to his ex-wife Lindsay."

I glanced at Vaughn and Liz and turned my attention to Clint and Nell. "As long as this information goes no further, I have something to tell you." At their nods of acceptance, I continued. "Lindsay Thaxton is staying here at the hotel in the private guesthouse on the property."

"Oh! Is that why Amelia Swanson was here? To help her sister?" said Nell.

I explained the entire situation to them. "Now that Thomas has left the property, we still have to keep an eye on her. We don't know how many people he asked, besides Brock Goodwin, to keep watching the hotel for signs of her. If someone were to release information to Thomas, I don't doubt for a minute he'd come here and try to grab her. The outcome wouldn't be good. I've never met anyone so cold, so dangerous."

"If Whit and Debra, her security people, weren't staying with her, I'd be upset," said Vaughn. "I hate to leave Ann when something might break open about this situation."

"Rhonda and I agreed we'd stay strong. We—our society—can't look the other way when we see abuse of women. Men too."

"I'd consider it a very high honor to have Amelia Swanson's confidence in both of you and the hotel. She's someone who doesn't put up with any bullshit," said Clint. "I've met her, and she's a very imposing figure."

"I suppose it matters what the situation is, but she was wonderful to talk to when she was here. We all must keep our eyes open when we're at the hotel. Even you, Nell, when you're part of the New Mother's Program."

"Speaking of that," said Liz to Nell. "I've got something to show you after dinner." She looked at me and grinned.

"You're going to love it," I said, hoping I was right. Liz was in a fragile condition.

Later, after Liz and Chad went home and Nell and Clint had retired to their wing for the night, I sat on the couch in our lanai next to Vaughn, sipping ice water and chatting with him. One of the strengths of our marriage, I believed, was sharing information and thoughts at the end of each day.

"Nell looks so tired," said Vaughn. "I remember what it was like for Ellie when she had Nell. So many memories."

"I'm glad they're such happy ones. You and Ellie were great parents," I said. At first, I'd been sure I could never measure up to Vaughn's memory of his first wife, who'd died of cancer—especially after my ex had torn away all my self-confidence. Now, I enjoyed hearing about his memories of her and Vaughn's children, who I loved like my own.

"I didn't want to bring it up earlier, but Darla and I had a brief conversation about our need to meet regarding her position on the show. I told her I'd speak to her tomorrow."

"Why don't we invite Darla and Meredith to dinner tomorrow? They might like being part of our extended family, and I know Nell would love to meet her."

"Are you willing to do that? I know how much you disliked being around Lily ..." His voice trailed away.

I looked at him squarely. "Darla seems like a very different kind of person. As long as you're going to be working together and playing lovers on the show, we should all get to know one another. I'll have the hotel cater the meal to make it easy for everyone."

Vaughn's face lit with pleasure. "Have I told you lately how much I love you?"

"Well, not since this morning," I said, playing along.

He pulled me onto his lap and wrapped his arms around me. "I love you more each day, each morning, and each night."

I pulled away from him. "Wait a minute! Haven't I heard you use that line on the show?"

He looked surprised. "Did I? Well, I mean it now."

I settled against his chest. There were times when it was hard to see Vaughn on television acting and sounding as if he were in love with someone else.

Vaughn lifted my chin. "I love you and only you."

"I know," I said happily.

His lips came down on mine, and any momentary thoughts of unease disappeared in the heat of his kiss.

The next morning, I got up early and tiptoed into the kitchen, hoping not to disturb anyone. I stopped in surprise at the sight of Nell at the kitchen table pumping milk.

"I thought I'd get enough bottles set so I can have the whole day to myself," she said.

"Good. You can come home anytime to nurse the baby, but I'm hoping you can take part in our New Mothers Program for an entire day without needing to do that. A lot of our mothers interested in the program are waiting until their babies are older, but I like the idea of your doing it now so we can test that aspect too."

"I'm so happy to be here," said Nell. Her eyes filled. "I've been weepy, trying to get my hormones settled. And, God! I'm so tired."

I rushed over to her and hugged her. "I'm here to help you however I can. Rhonda's covering for me at the hotel. Stay as long as you wish. We'll get you rested again."

"Thanks," said Nell.

"Are you comfortable with me taking care of the baby while you're gone?" Her answer was essential to me. Without her support, I might end up like Katherine and Angela in a quiet destructive war.

"Yes, of course. Clint will be around, too. But I know he's looking forward to spending time on the boat with Vaughn."

"I don't want either of you to worry about my taking care of the baby. I'm thrilled to be able to spend time with her," I said. "Show me exactly what you want, and I'll do it. I know things have changed. When Liz was small, we kept babies on their tummies. Now we're told to have them sleep on their backs."

Nell gave me a sheepish look. "I've typed up a list of instructions. It's three pages long."

I gaped at her, and suddenly we were both laughing.

"I'll read every page," I promised. "But you might want to rethink a few things. A baby's needs at this age are pretty basic. They eat, sleep, and poop with time in between for short interactions with people."

"You're right, but books make it seem like every second a mother spends with her baby will make the difference between raising a child who's ordinary and one who's a champion at anything she wants." Nell sighed. "It all seems so impossible."

"So-called experts place such unnecessary burdens on young mothers today. Keep it simple with lots of love. I can already see how bright Bailey is, how she responds. By the way, Angela wants to see you while you're here."

"How's she doing?" Nell asked.

"Pretty well now that her mother-in-law has left," I said and told her the story of Angela's struggles with Katherine.

"Thank goodness, Clint's mother was good with the baby. She was a big help, though, to be honest, she drove me crazy with her constant chatter."

I looked up as Clint walked into the kitchen. "I need coffee."

"Is the baby still sleeping?" Nell asked, putting away the breast pump.

"Yes, I bet you even have time for a quick shower," Clint said.

"Okay, I'd better run," said Nell, gathering her equipment and leaving the room.

Clint sat down. "Thank you, Ann, for all you're doing. Nell doesn't say much about it, but she struggles with not having her mother here. But she loves you and couldn't wait to get here."

"Vaughn and I are both happy you're here," I said. "How have you handled the new baby?"

"We both are blown away by how beautiful she is, how perfect. But it hasn't always been easy," he admitted. "Sometimes I feel as if I don't need to be around."

"I love your honesty," I said to Clint. "I always have." It was a piece of information I'd remember.

Robbie and Trudy padded into the room. As Trudy went out the doggie door, Robbie climbed up into the empty chair beside me and scooted close for a hug.

"Good morning! Are you ready for something to eat?"

Robbie nodded sleepily.

I got up from the table. Then, after Vaughn entered the room, my day began in earnest.

Later, as I held the baby in my arms while saying goodbye to Nell, who was crying, I hoped a day of pampering would help her turn the corner into a more relaxed routine of mothering Bailey.

Bailey didn't seem to notice the car leaving because she was so entranced by the sight of a blue heron who was walking on his stilt-like legs crossing the side lawn. Hoping the rest of the day would be as easy, I took her inside for a few minutes of playtime before putting her down for a nap. According to the schedule Nell had written, she should sleep for an hour and a half until mid-morning, when her first feeding would take place.

As I'd told Nell, Bailey was an alert baby. When I laid her on a blanket on the floor, she kicked happily for a few minutes. Then she began to cry.

Bedtime, I thought, carrying her into the guest room to the crib.

I laid her down and rubbed her tummy for a few minutes, hoping her eyes would close. She continued to fuss and cry as I talked softly to her. Finally, her eyes began to close.

I tiptoed away ... and stopped when she started to cry.

Nell's instructions said to stay with her until she fell asleep.

I tiptoed back to the crib.

After a couple more times of doing this, I quietly left the room and let her cry for a few minutes. I knew she was exhausted, and so was I. I checked my watch. Nell had been gone exactly twenty minutes.

In the kitchen, I poured myself another cup of coffee and called Rhonda.

"Hi! How's it going?" she asked.

I laughed. "It's going to be a long day, but Bailey is adorable. I love her so much. Like you've told me, grandchildren are special gifts."

"Yeah. I'm taking care of Sally tomorrow. Thanks for covering for me then," said Rhonda.

"I've told Nell about Lindsay and our trouble with Brock."

"Good. Then we can put Operation Bastard into play," said Rhonda chuckling. I'd called it Operation Brock, but Rhonda had changed the name, giving it a more descriptive term.

Vaughn and Clint came inside.

"We're ready to go sailing," said Vaughn. "Robbie decided to go next door to play with Brett instead of going with us."

I raised my eyebrows.

"I think he also wants to spend time with the baby," said Vaughn. "I spoke to Darla, and she and Meredith are coming for cocktails and dinner at five. She and I will talk then."

"Do you guys have everything you need?" I asked Vaughn and Clint.

"We're all set to go," Clint assured me. "Don't worry, the skies look clear."

Vaughn kissed me. "See you this afternoon. I'm guessing around four."

I waved them off, thinking I'd use the free time to set the long dining room table for tonight's dinner.

I'd just gotten out placemats when I heard the baby cry. I checked my watch. She was supposed to sleep another hour.

When the crying grew louder, I went into her nursery.

The crib sheet was a mess, and the smell of her dirty diaper was as horrible. I realized there was no point in changing her without giving her a bath. She'd also need clean sheets. I paused, not sure where to begin.

Her crying grew worse as I ran warm water into the sink. When the temperature was right, I lifted her out of the crib, stripped off her clothes, and placed them into the tub before washing and rinsing her body off with the organic soap Nell had brought. Wrapping Bailey in a towel, I carried her to the middle of the king-sized guest bed and lay her down while I stripped the sheets and mattress pad off the crib and searched for clean clothes for her.

Singing a lullaby, I dried and diapered her and put on a little pink, ruffled T-shirt. The rest could wait.

I placed her in her infant seat, and while she screamed, I rinsed off her clothes, sheet, and mattress pad in the bathtub, wondering how I could get them to the laundry room while watching the baby.

Forgetting the dirty clothes, I carried her into the kitchen to heat a bottle of milk. But by the time I got the milk out of the refrigerator, I saw she was falling asleep. I carried her back to the guest suite, looked through the suitcase Nell had packed for Bailey and found another crib sheet.

Silently thanking her for her thoughtfulness, I slipped the

sheet on the mattress and then settled Bailey onto it, waiting until I was sure she was asleep.

Then I got the wet clothes from the tub, took them to the laundry room, got them started in the wash cycle, and hurried back to the bathroom to scrub the tub.

Not long afterward, I was in the kitchen reading over Nell's instructions when I heard Bailey cry. Had it been only thirty-five minutes?

My cell rang. *Nell.* I stepped into the garage so she wouldn't hear the baby crying. "Hello?"

"Hi, Ann. How are things going?" Nell asked.

"Fine," I said brightly. I knew if I said otherwise, she'd come home.

"Oh, good! I'm having such a nice morning. But, Ann, I remembered our conversation from the other night. Just now, on my way over here to the spa, I saw Brock Goodwin over by the new roadblock to the house. When he noticed me, he ducked into the nearby bushes."

"Thank you. If you can, keep an eye on him. I've got to go." I clicked off the call and quickly phoned Debra. "Operation Bastard is a go. He's in the bushes by the gate."

"Got it," she said and hung up.

A few minutes later, while I rocked Bailey in my arms, Whit called. "It's been done."

"Good. Step one."

My cell rang again. *Nell.*

"Ann! You won't believe it! While I was watching, a large man, a security guard, I think, came out of the guesthouse, dragged Brock from the bushes, flipped him on his back, and yelled at him. I couldn't hear everything, but I know he called Brock a 'pissant pervert who shouldn't be spying on honeymoon couples.' From the way Brock lit out of there, I think your troubles with him may be behind you."

"Thanks, but I doubt it. We're not stopping with a simple warning. We're going to make Brock think he's never going to get rid of Whit."

While I'd talked on the phone, Bailey kept her eyes on me, soothed by the sound of my voice. Now, hungry, she began to cry ...

... and I started the process over again.

CHAPTER TWENTY-ONE

By the time Vaughn and Clint returned from their sail, I was exhausted. Not just from taking care of the baby, but from watching Robbie in the pool, Robbie and Brett playing on the lawn, and giving them both a late lunch after waiting to feed the baby, all while trying to listen to Bailey, feed her, soothe her, and play with her. My thoughts flew to Angela. I had a greater understanding of how busy the weeks ahead were going to be for her.

When Clint went to the hotel to pick up Nell, Vaughn put his arm around me. "How are you doing, Grandma? You look a little tired."

"I can't believe how hard it is to go back to infancy. Robbie was two when we got him. That was difficult enough."

"We'll make it an early night, then we can go to bed," Vaughn said.

"Please don't mention to Nell how exhausted I am. I want her to have all the freedom she wants while she's here, though I have to cover for Rhonda tomorrow."

"I promise." He kissed me. "Here are the kids now."

Nell walked into the kitchen wearing a happy smile. Her blond hair had been styled, her skin glowed, and her fingernails were coated with a light-pink polish.

She threw her arms around me. "Thank you so much. I feel wonderful. Tomorrow should be even better. The crew at the spa will work with me on exercises to relax me and reduce stress. Where's Bailey?"

"She's taking a nap," I said.

"But she's not supposed to be napping now!" Nell said. At the silence in the room, she continued. "I'm sorry. That was such an awful way to thank you. We'll adjust her schedule."

"We're going with the flow. Remember?" said Clint, wrapping an arm around her.

"You're right. I've been so crazy these past few weeks. That's another thing we're working on tomorrow in the hotel's program."

Darla and Meredith pulled into the driveway.

When Vaughn went out to greet them, Nell gazed out the window. "I'm so glad I went to the program today. Look at Darla. She's beautiful ... and so trim."

Clint gave Nell a steady stare. "You're just fine, Nell. Don't even go there."

I slipped out of the room, giving them space, and went to greet Darla and her partner.

"Good evening," I said cheerily. At the sight of a familiar, bottle-green Jaguar roaring toward us, my smile morphed into a frown. *How did he get through the security gate? Probably lied.*

Brock Goodwin climbed out of the car and walked toward me with a stiff gait. "I've already talked to my lawyer," he said, "but felt it was only neighborly to warn you that I'll be filing a lawsuit against you and Rhonda personally as well as the hotel for being assaulted on your hotel property."

"What are you talking about?" I asked. "I heard you were trespassing in a private area of the hotel, and the bridegroom warned you off. Isn't that what happened?"

"Well, yes, but he didn't have to pull some fancy Kung Fu maneuver on me. I ended up flat on my back."

"Just stay away from private areas, and you shouldn't have any need to file a frivolous lawsuit that will expose you, the president of the Neighborhood Association, for trespassing,"

I said, fighting an urge to laugh at the image of Brock lying on the ground. "Now, if you'll excuse me, I have guests to tend to. And once again, you're trespassing. That's twice in one day." I turned away and then, unsettled, turned back to make sure he was leaving.

Brock easily slid into his low-slung car, assuring me the only real injury was to his ego. And that, as we all knew, needed a little adjustment.

As Brock drove away, Meredith said, "He's such a creep."

"Why don't we go inside and relax?" said Vaughn. "My daughter, Nell, and her husband, Clint, and their baby girl are visiting. Nell, especially, is anxious to meet the two of you."

Darla placed a hand on his arm. "Before we go inside, there's something I need to tell you. In exchange for my not suing Simon for sexual harassment, the producers are allowing me to announce my engagement to Meredith."

"Wonderful," I said, giving each of them a quick hug.

Darla took Meredith's hand. "I've told them we're all friends, and they agree that's how it's going to be played offscreen. Thank you for speaking up, Ann. I might not have had the nerve to face them without your encouragement."

"I agree with Ann. I think it's best all around," said Vaughn, wrapping an arm around me. "Foolish PR games can backfire."

Pleased, I followed Vaughn and the others inside.

On the lanai, Nell was holding the baby, and Clint was playing a game with Robbie. Clint got to his feet, and Nell moved forward to greet our guests.

"I just love the role you're playing on the show with my father," Nell told Darla.

"Thanks, I like it too. We're becoming friends." She took hold of Meredith's hand. "This is Meredith Wilkinson. We've just decided to get married."

"Congratulations!" Nell said. "Have you thought of having your wedding at The Beach House Hotel? It's the perfect place."

Darla and Meredith glanced at one another.

"We've already thought of it," said Darla. "Lorraine Grace, the wedding consultant, is helping us figure out the timing for a small one."

"That's so exciting! Please let me know how Rhonda and I can help," I said. Thinking of Rhonda, I smiled to myself. Somehow, she'd find a way to claim that with her matchmaking ability, she'd helped make it happen.

Liz and Chad arrived. After introductions were made and Liz had Bailey in her arms, we all took seats on the lanai. It was a beautiful afternoon with bright blue skies and a soft breeze cooling the temperature, which was in the high 70s. The conversation was pleasant as we all got to know one another. Looking at them, I filled with love, liking the idea of being a big, happy family with our two new additions. Having grown up an only child, it pleased me to see how ours had grown.

After dinner and after Nell had made sure Bailey was set for a while, she and Clint decided to join Liz and Chad and our guests who were going out to a small local bar off the beaten track, which would allow Darla and Meredith privacy.

"I promise we won't be gone long," said Nell. "I have to get up early in the morning."

"Go and have a good time. That's one reason you're here," I said, knowing I'd have to start the day early too.

Though Liz, Darla, and Meredith had insisted on doing most of the cleaning up, I did a few last-minute things in the kitchen.

Vaughn came into the room after putting Robbie to bed and wrapped his arms around me. "Ready for bed? It's later than I thought."

"More than ready," I said, sighing and wiping my hands with a paper towel.

We went to our bedroom and got ready for bed, each with our familiar routine.

Moments later, sliding beneath the silky sheets, I felt every part of my body relax.

Beside me, Vaughn drew me to him. "You're the cutest Grandma I've ever seen. Sexy too."

I kissed him. "Don't get any ideas. You can try. Just don't wake me."

He laughed. "That bad?"

"There's a reason they give babies to the young. I feel every bit my age."

"But you're not that old," Vaughn protested.

"I didn't used to think so either," I said, snuggling up against him and closing my eyes.

The next morning, Rhonda surprised me with an early visit. "Good morning. I couldn't wait any longer to see Bailey," she said, coming through the back entrance.

"Come in," I said, glad to see her. "She's sleeping now, but she should be up in a little while. Want a cup of coffee while we wait for her?"

"Sure, thanks. I needed to get out of the house and want to get caught up on things. You mentioned a visit from Brock and a bunch of other stuff. Give me details."

I grinned. "I've been saving up a few for you." There was nothing I liked better than sitting with my partner catching up on the news. Even though we saw each other almost every day, our lives were full.

"Do you think Brock's lawsuit will go through?" Rhonda asked, looking worried.

"No, I think his lawyer will tell him he was trespassing on private property, and there isn't a real case. The only injury was to his pride. Brock was in the wrong, and he knew it. Furthermore, I think the security cameras on the house will clearly show Brock was breaking the law, sneaking around in an area where he had no business being."

"And hiding in the bushes!" said Rhonda. "That's a big fat giveaway he was in the wrong." She grinned. "What's the latest with Darla and Meredith? I'm pretty sure there's something serious there. I can see a wedding coming up because of us."

"What do you mean?" I asked, hiding my amusement.

"Well, the hotel can do some magical things for some of our guests. Look what happened to Debra and Whit. They come to the Beach House Hotel, rekindled the flame, and decided to get married."

"Well, you're right again. Darla and Meredith have decided to get married and have a small wedding at the hotel."

Rhonda slapped the table gleefully. "I knew it. Maybe we should do an advertising campaign for couples who think they might want to get married."

"Mmm, maybe," I said, "but we'd have to be very careful how we'd word it. We'd have to be subtle."

"Subtle, shmutle," said Rhonda. "Something like: 'Want to turn that spark into a forest fire? Come to The Beach House Hotel for a chance to make it happen.'"

"God! You make it sound like a whorehouse," I said, laughing.

"We could add no pimps allowed," teased Rhonda.

I grinned, thinking back to my childhood. I would never have imagined the way my life had changed from the dutiful, restrained existence I'd lived for so many years.

At the sound of Bailey's cries though the speaker Nell had left on the kitchen counter for me, both Rhonda and I got to my feet.

"Can't wait to see her," Rhonda said, trotting beside me. "And it's so sweet to think Bailey will be friends with Sally."

"Love it! Bailey and Sally." A pang of disappointment for Liz traveled through me.

When we got to the crib, Bailey was awake and staring at a lemony stripe of sunshine entering the room between slats in the fabric window blinds.

"Oh, my!" gushed Rhonda. "Your first grandchild! She's beautiful!"

I couldn't hide the smile that crossed my face and filled my heart. "She's a good baby, but I honestly don't know how you did it with Willow and Drew so close in age."

"I had wonderful help," said Rhonda honestly. "Without Rita, we couldn't function. I've always been grateful to her."

I changed Bailey's diaper and handed her over to Rhonda's waiting hands.

Rhonda hummed a song to Bailey as we walked back to the kitchen. "Thank goodness things have calmed down at Angela's house. And guess what? I got a nice card from Katherine thanking me for my support and my offer to have her stay with Will and me anytime. I don't think she'd ever follow through with that, but it seems like maybe we've come to an understanding. What do you think?"

"Maybe." As I got the bottle of milk ready for Bailey, I turned to her. "I think it was sweet of you to make the first move. Angela told me it was you who did the hugging, not Katherine."

Rhonda shrugged her shoulders. "I guess I did."

"Angela was proud of you, and so am I. It was a kind thing

to do. But what about Arthur?"

Rhonda took the bottle I handed her and sat in a kitchen chair to feed the baby. "Angela told me Reggie tried to call him, but when it wasn't picked up right away, he let it go."

"Maybe it's for the best. Arthur was furious when we were there."

"Yeah, it's too bad he put such pressure on Reggie to do what he asked. Do you think we're putting too much pressure on our girls to take over the hotel for us?" Rhonda asked.

"It won't be for some time, and every time we mention it, they seem excited," I said. "But I suppose we should go easy with that idea for a while."

"Yeah, it's you and me for several more years," said Rhonda. "The hotel is like our special baby. We can never let anyone else try to destroy it again."

"Agreed. But don't worry, we'll make it through until the girls are ready to take over."

"Together and with a few margaritas along the way," said Rhonda grinning.

I laughed. Being her partner meant a lot of detail work for me, some frustrations with the casual way she handled things, and a great deal of satisfaction working with one of the nicest people I knew. We'd always been a good team.

Rhonda burped the baby and handed her back to me. "Can't stay a minute longer. Willow has ballet lessons. It's so cute watching toddlers dance around a room. Willow loves it! She's even decided to follow instructions."

We laughed together. Willow was head-strong like her mother. But I had no doubt that if Willow decided to be a ballerina, she'd do her best, twirling like a whirlwind.

Later, Vaughn returned from doing errands with Robbie in

tow. It pleased me that they spent so much time together. Both Vaughn and I enjoyed the second chance of raising a child as loveable as Robbie.

"While I was out, I got a call from New York," Vaughn said, setting a package down on the kitchen counter. "While Darla is here in Sabal, the producers want to have a glimpse of us with our family, including Darla and Meredith. They asked if they could do a photoshoot here in Florida. I gave them tentative approval with some restrictions on where they could film us."

"When do they want this to happen?" I asked, thinking of Lindsay hiding out at the hotel and wanting the privacy of my home.

"Tomorrow. They'd fly the crew down today, shoot tomorrow, and then Darla and I would have to return to New York for more shows."

"What about Lindsay's safety? With a film crew set loose at the hotel, something could happen to expose her. We can't take the chance of that happening."

"Okay, then, it'll have to take place here," said Vaughn.

My first instinct was to call Elena for help in preparing the house. But then I thought it was better for fans to see Vaughn as a real family man, even if it meant baby equipment was part of the scenery.

"Okay. Let's warn the others that photo shoots will take place. I want everyone in the photos," I said. "Too bad Ty and June can't be here."

"I'll hand the photographers photos of them and explain. Thanks, hon," said Vaughn kissing me on the lips. "I'll be glad to get this PR situation behind us. I know how you hate publicity about our personal lives."

"Yes, but for once, this is honest. And that I can live with."

Nell came home early that morning from her program at the hotel to feed Bailey. Both Bailey and I were happy to see her. Bailey had been crying for a steady twenty minutes while I tried to get in touch with Nell to tell her we were out of milk.

After she fed the baby and put her down, Nell came out to the kitchen. "Thanks for everything. I think this warm, salty air is good for Bailey. I swear I can see her grow. She's eating like crazy."

"She's a healthy, happy baby, and we love having you here. By the way, a crew is going to be here tomorrow to film us for a new PR campaign they're doing about your dad and Darla."

Nell frowned. "How do you feel about that?"

"Actually, very good. It's to show Vaughn as a family man and friend, not a lover, to Darla. Meredith will be included in the pictures. My only regret is that Ty and June can't be here, but we'll provide photos of them."

"What about the mess we're making here? Do we need to clean up?" said Nell, indicating the cluttered kitchen counter.

"No, this campaign is going to be real. On another matter, Angela called and is wondering when she can bring her baby over to meet Bailey."

"I'd love to see her," Nell said happily. "I'll call her now and ask her over in a half-hour. Is that okay with you?"

"Two of my favorite young women getting together? Absolutely. The babies are going to be so cute together."

"These workout clothes need a change. I'd better freshen up."

After she left, I called Darla to make sure she was okay with the photoshoot.

"Hi, Ann, I'm so glad you called," she said. "I was about to call you with some exciting news. After Vaughn told me about the photoshoot tomorrow, Meredith and I have decided to get married this evening. I've talked to Lorraine Grace, and we're going to have the private ceremony in the gazebo in the side garden."

"Oh, my! It's happening so fast. What can I do to help?"

"We both want you and Vaughn to stand up with us. Will you do it?"

"I'd be happy to do that, and I'm sure Vaughn would too. What kind of ceremony is it going to be?"

"We're each wearing white sundresses. Thank goodness we found 'Styles,' the clothing stores Liz told us about. They were wonderful." She cleared her throat. "We thought you'd wear a simple sundress, and if Vaughn doesn't mind, he should wear slacks and a tropical sport shirt. We're keeping it informal."

"What about dinner following the ceremony?" Rhonda and I couldn't afford to have the celebration at the hotel fail to be up to our usual high standards. It would mar our growing reputation as THE place to have a small, intimate wedding.

"We thought we'd keep it simple and just eat as a group at the hotel."

"Leave all those details to me, and we'll make it special."

"That would be wonderful," gushed Darla.

As soon as I hung up with Darla, I called Rhonda. We agreed to meet at the hotel with Lorraine. This wedding would be talked about tomorrow, and we wanted it to be everything both women and the hotel wanted.

CHAPTER TWENTY-TWO

Rhonda and I stood with Lorraine in the hotel's library. Lorraine was our wedding coordinator and was a very talented event planner. Another, larger ceremony was taking place out on the beach that evening, but we could accommodate both.

"We know you're busy with the Altamonte party," I said, "but we need some quick ideas about transforming this room into a lovely place for a reception and dinner."

"I'd suggest you speak to Emily at Tropical Fleurs. She usually has some extra flowers ordered. In talking with Darla and Meredith earlier, they were open to the idea of a basket of tropical flowers on the altar. Does that help?"

I glanced at Rhonda. "That'll give us a chance to use all kinds of colors."

As we talked, I grew more excited about the event. It seemed so easy, so natural, like the participants themselves.

After Lorraine left to take care of details for the other group, Rhonda grinned at me. "This reminds me of how it used to be with you and me doing everything. It's nice to come back to this now and then. Our lives seemed so much simpler before we grew so busy."

"In many ways they were," I admitted.

We talked about appropriate music and the menu. I called Chad to help with the sound system, and we both went to the kitchen to talk to Jean-Luc, who didn't like surprises like this.

When we told him that we'd need a special dinner for ten people at eight-o'clock, he clucked his tongue. "The restaurant is booked tonight, and I have the wedding for forty people, but for you, I'll do it. However, it can't be anything too difficult."

"Anything you cook is delicious," I quickly said. It would be a disaster if he weren't willing to do this for us. I already knew from talking to them earlier that, though they watched their weights, neither Darla nor Meredith had special diets.

After discussing the pros and cons of several selections, we decided on individual Salmon Wellingtons with a spinach-and-lemon topping inside the puff pastry shell, drizzled with a light lemon-and-caper *beurre blanc*. A mélange of vegetables would accompany it along with Meyer Lemon Rice Pilaf and a simple green salad with a French vinaigrette dressing. And for dessert, we chose a small, double-layered vanilla cake with white buttercream icing decorated with fresh flowers and accompanied by scoops of various fruit sorbets to add color and flavor.

Jean-Luc approved it all, using some of the other event's food items to make our dinner.

Satisfied that it would be unique, Rhonda and I left the kitchen and hurried back to the library to meet with Emily from the flower shop.

She greeted us with a smile, an armful of flowers, and a couple of small baskets. With two round tables of five, we needed two small centerpieces and a basket of wildflowers for the dais to match what Darla and Meredith had selected for the service.

"Instead of buying another basket, have someone carry in the flowers from the short service. Those placed on the dais will be a lovely touch. Then the two centerpieces will be all you'll need from me," said Emily.

"Thank you so much!" I said, pleased. "I should warn you we have another small, private wedding coming up soon. I just don't know the date yet. I imagine it will be a weekday because our weekends are full."

"Anything for the two of you," said Emily, smiling. "You've helped me so much in the past."

"It always makes me feel good to have so many weddings here," said Rhonda. "It's like bringing my old house to life in a way I've always imagined."

"It's amazing to think of all the work that you two have done to turn it into a beautiful hotel. It's been a wonderful addition to the community," said Emily.

"To most," I said, making a face.

"If you're talking about Brock Goodwin, I've heard many people complain about the iron-fisted way he's running his Neighborhood Association. He may not realize it, but he's sending a lot of business your way because of the complaints he made over other events in the neighborhood."

Rhonda and I looked at one another and grinned.

"Serves the bastard right," muttered Rhonda.

"I think so, too," said Emily as she continued putting together centerpieces with the baskets and flowers that she'd brought with her.

"I'd better get home and get ready. It'll be 7:30 before I know it, and I've got a lot to do."

Rhonda followed me out of the room. "I'll see you later. I have to make sure Rita is free to babysit."

"Elena and Troy are going to watch Robbie and the baby," I said, sighing with relief. "She just messaged me they could do it."

We headed our separate ways, and I headed home, hoping Vaughn and Clint hadn't sailed very far with Robbie. I needed them back and dressed in time for the ceremony.

When I arrived home, Angela and Nell were on the patio

holding their sleeping babies in their arms. I took a moment to sit with them. The babies looked adorable together, each with a little pink bow in what strands of hair could be gathered.

"Sorry to interrupt, but I need to tell you, Nell, about the wedding you're invited to." I gave her the details.

"Nell told me you're all going to have your pictures taken together. The wedding will make it clear that it's like one big family," said Angela.

"I think that was the intent," I said. "And while we three are together, Nell, please tell me how the New Mothers Program has worked for you. Angela, you're going to do it also, aren't you?"

Smiling, Angela nodded. "But I'm going to wait a while."

"I would encourage your special guests to wait until the first few months have passed. Because I'm still nursing, it's been a bit of an issue," said Nell. "By the time their baby is three to six months, a lot of mothers, like me, will be desperate for some downtime, not only to feel healthy but to look good. The hotel's program is wonderful, though, and I want to come back and do it again when it'll be easier for me."

"Good to know," I said, making a mental note to tell Rhonda.

"I have a feeling the second time around is going to be a very different process of getting back to close to normal," said Angela, patting her stomach.

"As long as you don't push too hard too soon," I said. "You're dainty."

"I know. I take after my father," Angela said, smiling. She drew a finger across Sally's soft cheek with tenderness. "I'm so proud that this little one has his name."

"Angela told me all about the trouble between Rhonda and Katherine," said Nell. "I'm glad I don't have that with Clint's mom." She gave me a quick smile. "And certainly not with you."

"That's good because I'm about to sound bossy. I think you should plan on getting Bailey scheduled so you can be at the ceremony at 7:30," I said, giving her a teasing grin.

Nell gave me a playful salute.

"And I have to get home," said Angela. "Reggie and I are having a dinner catered to the house after we get both kids down for the night." Color flushed her cheeks. "We haven't had a special moment like that in forever. I just hope I can stay awake for it."

I laughed, remembering my remark to Vaughn.

After Angela left with a kiss goodbye from me, I tried calling Vaughn on his cell. Last time there'd been a wedding—his own—he'd been caught on a sailboat without a way to get back to shore.

"Hey, babe," Vaughn said. "What's up?"

"You are about to be part of a wedding party. You guys better bring the boat in," I said.

"Whoa? Wedding party? Whose?"

I told him about Darla and Meredith's decision. "I think it's sweet that they want us to stand up for them. As Angela said, that makes it seem like we're a real family."

"Okay, we're on our way in. See you in a little while," said Vaughn, sounding pleased about the turn of events.

Maybe this would be a good move, I thought. Tina Marks had been a special family member at Vaughn's and my wedding earlier. We could always add more.

As I was getting dressed, Liz and Chad arrived at the house. I could hear their voices in the kitchen, and then a knock sounded at my bedroom door.

"Mom? Are you almost ready? Can I borrow the shell necklace I gave you?" said Liz opening the door.

"Sure. C'mon in. I'm just finishing up." I slid diamond earrings into my ear lobes and searched through my jewelry for the necklace Liz had requested. It was one of my favorites.

"You look very nice," I told Liz. "And this necklace is perfect with your dress." She wore a pink, sleeveless sheath the color of hibiscus.

"Thanks. I told Darla and Meredith about Styles dress store and decided to go myself," Liz said. Her blond hair was shiny, her blue eyes sparkled. "This is all such a lovely surprise."

I returned her smile, happy to see Liz back to normal. She'd be fine. Take it one month at a time, I told myself. Some would be easier than others.

I wore a simple yellow sundress scattered with tropical flowers as Darla had suggested. And the green Hawaiian shirt Vaughn had picked out was perfect with his tan slacks.

Nell and Clint met us in the kitchen looking as tropical as the rest of us in similar, bright-colored clothes. Elena stood by with the baby in her arms and Robbie next to her.

"Thank you so much, Elena, for stepping in and helping us out," I said. Like Rhonda with Rita, I wondered what I'd ever do without Elena's help.

"After all you've done for Troy and me, I'm happy to do it," she responded. We'd helped them secure a loan for their house and paid part of the down payment.

"Can I come?" said Robbie, giving me a woeful look.

I kissed his sun-tanned cheek. "No, I'm sorry, but this is for grownups. Tomorrow is going to be a busy day with everyone here at the house. You'll have a chance to be part of the group then."

Robbie's face puckered, then smoothed out when Elena added, "Besides, I need you here to help me, and Troy is stopping by." Robbie and Troy were close.

Happy that we had settled things so quickly, I followed the others out the door.

At the hotel, I went up to the Presidential Suite to check on Darla and Meredith.

Darla opened the door looking as adorable as her character on the show in a simple white sundress with a small edging of lace at the collar. Meredith stood behind her, dressed similarly and smiling at me. A sprig of bougainvillea was in her long blond hair.

"You both look beautiful," I said. "Are you ready?"

Darla glanced at Meredith. "As ready as we'll ever be. Everyone should gather in the gazebo. Lorraine just called to say the Justice of the Peace is already there."

"Okay, I'll see you downstairs," I said.

"We'll only take a minute before joining you," said Meredith.

The warm evening, the twinkling lights wrapped around the railing of the gazebo, and the basket of fresh flowers on the small altar were perfect accompaniments to the occasion.

As Darla and Meredith walked toward us hand in hand, it was touching to see the expressions of hope and joy on their faces.

The ceremony was very short but sweet, with each woman reciting vows she'd written. As usual, Rhonda was dabbing at her eyes by the time they got through. I'd been floating in and out of the present, remembering my own wedding.

Now, watching them mingle with us at the reception in the library and seeing how gentle Vaughn was with Darla, I felt as if we truly had expanded our family.

Rhonda came up to me. "For a last-minute event, both Lorraine and Jean-Luc performed with flying colors." She indicated the room with a wave of her hand. "This looks beautiful, and the menu is perfect."

"I'm going to write up a summary as I usually do for special events here at the hotel. It'll help us to plan small events like this in the future."

"Thanks. It's a good thing you like to do stuff like that, Annie," Rhonda said, flinging an arm across my shoulders.

I couldn't help rolling my eyes. I'd learned early on in our partnership that the small details would be mine to resolve.

"What are you two up to now?" said Will, smiling as he approached us. Tall and thin with regular features, blue eyes, and gray hair, Will was one of my favorite people. Rhonda's effervescent personality was a good match for Will's quieter ways. I remember how shy he'd been when he first met Rhonda. It was instant love for both of them.

"We're just congratulating ourselves on having Jean-Luc and Lorraine as part of the team."

Will's eyes shone. "That's something you should be proud of. They're both excellent. But then, the way you convince every staff member that they're part of the hotel is very important. I'm proud of you both." He kissed Rhonda. "I've been told we need to get to our seats." He held out his elbow, and she took it.

Vaughn walked over to me. "Darla can't stop raving about how nice everything is. Thanks, Ann."

"It's important for them to have a satisfying entry into our family," I said, pleased. "Besides, the hotel has a reputation to maintain."

We took seats at our assigned table, and I took a moment to observe the staff surreptitiously.

Annette was overseeing an early portion of this dinner but would leave us to help the other group. At a signal from her, waiters and waitresses entered the room together with our first course, a chilled, white-asparagus soup.

Sitting next to Darla at one of the two tables, I watched as she studied the printed souvenir menu at her place then tucked it into her purse.

"I'm so happy we decided to have our wedding here. I can't imagine anything better. Thank you," she said, facing me. Her eyes filled. "You and Vaughn have been so kind to us both. As I said earlier, my parents have turned their backs on me. Meredith's parents are a little better but aren't that happy about our being together."

"Time heals many things," I said. "I hope everyone in both your families comes to accept the two of you. If not, you have friends who do."

"No one could be better friends than you and Vaughn. I wish you two were my parents." Darla dabbed at her eyes with her napkin.

I reached over and patted her hand. "Sweetie, that's about to happen. As far as your fans are concerned, you'll be known as part of our family. And as for me, I feel as if you already are."

Darla's lips trembled. Her eyes glazed with emotion. Unable to speak, she simply nodded.

From across the table, Vaughn caught my gaze and gave me a warm look of approval.

As the meal continued, each course was as delicious as Rhonda and I had hoped. And when at last the wedding cake was brought in, we all applauded. The idea of serving the cake with assorted sorbets worked beautifully and was one I'd remember for other celebrations.

As soon as everyone had finished and prepared to leave,

Vaughn and I said our goodbyes to Darla and Meredith and made our departure. The film crew was coming early.

CHAPTER TWENTY-THREE

The next morning, I worked quickly to restore some order to the house before the filming crew came. But, as I decided earlier, we would leave toys and baby equipment in place like any other household. We'd been blessed with a sunny day, so the photographers would take many shots outdoors. Vaughn and Darla would be interviewed separately and then together, talking about the show and their roles in it. The big family portrait was scheduled for ten o'clock.

Vaughn and I decided to meet the crew outside to make sure the rules Vaughn had specified would be honored—no interior shots except in the kitchen or living room. The lanai and pool were fine, as well as the lawn and the boat. We'd all agreed dress was casual.

The photographer was accompanied by an assistant and a woman named Janie Jacobs, the publicist the producers had hired. Short and stocky and in what I guessed was her mid-fifties, Janie had steel-gray eyes that penetrated with their sharpness. No one, I supposed, got much past her.

After a quick tour of the places they could film, Janie asked the cameraman to set up on the lanai. "We'll start the interviews with you, Vaughn, and hope Darla will arrive soon. I find it best to talk to people at the start of the day when they're fresh and rested."

Vaughn nodded agreeably, took a seat, and allowed a microphone to be attached unobtrusively to his shirt beneath his chin. I stood in the background watching as he assumed a natural pose in front of the cameras while they tested for lighting. It always interested me to see him on camera.

Vaughn saw me and winked.

"Ready? Three, two, one!" the cameraman said.

Janie, sitting beside Vaughn, straightened in her chair and smiled into camera. "I'm Janie Jacobs, and I'm here to talk with Vaughn Sanders, the star of *The Sins of the Children,* one of the longest-running soap operas in the business, due in large part to Vaughn and the character he plays—the mayor of the famous town of troubles. Good morning, Vaughn! It's nice to be here in Sabal, Florida, at your beautiful home."

"Good morning, Janie," he said, giving her the sexy smile that caused a thousand sighs whenever he appeared on the screen. "My wife, Ann, and I are pleased to have you here to meet our family."

"It's so appropriate," Janie said. "You've evolved into the patriarch of the television show, and that's why we're doing this interview. In the past, you've been linked with co-stars like Lily Dorio. But as you've aged, you're no longer the bad boy of the past but more of a fatherly figure. Darla comes under that definition both on and off the show. Isn't that true?"

I could read the anger in Vaughn though no one else would notice anything but the lowering of his voice. "Just to be clear, I never had a relationship with Lily Dorio. That was part of a publicity scheme that backfired. As far as Darla is concerned, Ann and I have happily welcomed other people into our family—people like Tina Marks—and now Darla and her partner Meredith. We're lucky enough to have friends we can include like this."

"Did you know Darla before she started working with you?" asked Janie, pressing close, her eyes gleaming with mischief.

Vaughn stiffened slightly. "No, I didn't. But after working

with her, I admire her acting ability." He faced the camera, "I also like the fact she remembers her lines so quickly. It makes a big difference when you have a real professional working with you."

I loved the zing of truth Vaughn threw Lily's way.

"How did you and Darla become friends so quickly then?" Janie persisted.

"Through my wife, Ann." Vaughn waved me over.

I hesitated, and then because I didn't want to embarrass him by not obliging, I walked over and stood behind him.

He clasped my hand. "This is the person I come home to, the person who is the anchor of the family, the person who welcomes others into it."

"Hello, Ann. Nice to meet you," said Janie. "I understand you and your business partner own The Beach House Hotel. Is that correct?"

"Yes. It's something we're very proud of." I did my best not to be inhibited by the camera though I didn't like being in the public eye.

"The vice president was recently at the hotel. Do you get a lot of guests like that at the hotel?" Janie asked.

"Each guest is special to us and deserves privacy," I said, praying she wouldn't mention Lindsay or Thomas Thaxton. "Excuse me. I'll let you get back to your interview with Vaughn."

I walked away and continued to watch from the sidelines.

I winced every time Janie mentioned how old Vaughn was, how many years he'd been on the show, how he'd once been the sexy soap opera star that became the fantasy lover women dreamed about. She made it sound as if he was old and useless. I wanted to tell her what a virile man he still was, but, of course, I couldn't.

When Janie brought up the topic of sailing, Vaughn perked

up. The conversation was easy from then on.

Darla appeared, and sensing more exciting news, Janie ended the interview with Vaughn.

While Janie took a short break, Vaughn and I approached Darla.

"Remember, you don't have to answer any questions that make you uncomfortable," said Vaughn. "Janie is persistent."

"And not always nice," I added, squeezing Vaughn's hand.

"This, hopefully, will take the heat off any harassment at work and negativity about your relationship with Meredith," Vaughn said. "I'll be right here watching."

Darla gave him a shaky smile. "Thanks. That means a lot."

I left them and went to find Nell and Clint. Liz had left a message on my cell that she and Chad were on their way. Bailey was awake, fed, and dressed in an adorable pink jumpsuit with bunny appliqués. Nell looked great in white pants and a turquoise top. Clint had on a golf shirt like Vaughn's but in blue, not green.

When Liz stepped into the kitchen, my breath caught. She, too, was wearing a turquoise top, and for a minute, she looked so much like Nell it was stunning. Chad was wearing a golf shirt and tan slacks, as had been decided.

Feeling teary at the rush of love I felt, I gave Liz a hug. "Nell and Clint and the baby are already in the living room. You can join them there."

I looked up as Meredith came through the kitchen door. "I'm here. I didn't want to be here earlier because I didn't want to be interviewed with Darla."

"No, problem. I understand. Vaughn is keeping a protective eye on her. How are you?"

"Great. Thanks again for all your help yesterday. It was such a special day for us."

"I'm glad. Now come be part of the group."

We were all waiting in the living room when Vaughn and Darla joined us.

As we gathered, the photographer fussed with his camera while his assistant worked with the lighting. Vaughn and I were told to stand in the middle with the others gathered around us.

"We're missing my son, Ty, and his wife, June, along with Tina Marks," Vaughn said. "Please be sure to make that clear."

"I've already made a note of it," said Janie. "Let's take a few shots here; then I want a shot of just the women, then a shot of Vaughn, and one with him and Ann and Robbie on the boat. Oh, and one of Vaughn with Nell, Clint, and the baby. Our audience will love that. The sexy grandfather and his family."

I glanced at Vaughn. His face had tightened at the idea of the sexy grandfather angle. If I wasn't mistaken, his ego was a little bruised. In a matter of hours, he'd gone from sexy soap star to grandpa.

We all were tired when the crew left after the lunch of sandwiches and cookies that I'd arranged with Consuela to make and deliver.

"How do you think it went?" Darla asked me.

"I think Janie got some good information. Enough that you shouldn't be troubled at work with the deal you made with the producers."

"How can I ever thank you and Vaughn for stepping in to help me?" she said.

"It's the least we could do. No one should have to put up with harassment at work. I just hope this makes things easier for everyone."

"Me, too." She gave me a quick kiss on the cheek. "You're the best. I hope to see you in New York soon. Meredith and I are leaving tonight. Vaughn said he's flying to New York tomorrow morning."

"Safe travels," I said to her, hating the thought of Vaughn leaving.

Nell and Clint decided to meet Liz and Chad for dinner. Knowing it would be their last evening here and some time before they returned, I eagerly agreed to watch Bailey. It might have been my imagination, but in the previous few days, Bailey seemed so much bigger, so much more alert than when she'd first arrived. Maybe, I thought, I'd be able to make a trip to D. C. to visit them before too much time passed.

Later, sitting at the dinner table with the two of us, Robbie played with his food, then set his fork down and looked at us with tears in his eyes.

"Why does everyone have to leave?" he said.

"Dad has to go to work, and Nell and Clint and the baby were here only for a visit," I said. "But remember, you have Liz and Chad here, along with Trudy and me, to keep you company.

"And Brett and Elena and Troy, too," he said, looking a little brighter.

"Yes, you do. It's hard to see loved ones come and go, but you always have lots of people around who care about you." I didn't mention how much I'd miss everyone, especially Vaughn. Without him around, my days seemed dull no matter how bright the sun shone outside.

After dinner, I changed Bailey and fed her, loving the feel of a baby in my arms. Maybe my disappointment over Liz not having a baby was because I'd wanted so many of my own.

Vaughn came out to the lanai and joined me on one of the couches there. "She sure looks a lot like Nell did when she was a baby," he said, smiling down at Bailey as she lay on my legs, kicking playfully.

"It's interesting to see how genetics work. Robbie is such a combination of his father, mother, and Liz. And with Bailey, I see some of Clint, too. Enough that when I mentioned it to him, he puffed up like a proud papa."

"How do you feel about being married to a grandpa?" Vaughn said, giving me an uncertain look, which wasn't at all like him.

I cocked an eyebrow. "Do you mean a grandpa instead of a sexy television star like Janie implied?"

"Yeah, I guess her words hit me pretty hard," he said.

I leaned over and kissed him on the mouth. "Thankfully, she doesn't know you that well. A little later, you can show this grandma all your tricks."

He brightened. "Really?"

"Oh yes," I said. "As soon as the kids are down, I'm going to bed and dragging you off with me."

"Deal," he said, wrapping an arm around me. "God, I'd heard Janie was tough, but I didn't know what angle she was going to play. I admit it stung."

"No worries, big boy! You can prove how wrong she is."

Vaughn drew me closer. "I love you, Ann."

"I love you too, Vaughn. I always will."

Robbie came into the room. "Are you kissing again?"

Vaughn and I pulled apart.

"Later," Vaughn said, getting to his feet.

Vaughn and I stood together in Robbie's room, making sure he was tucked in, and Trudy was settled beside him. Robbie's arms were flung wide as he slept on his back.

"He's growing so much. I was pleased by how polite he was to Janie," I said.

"He's a great boy," said Vaughn. He turned and faced me.

"I believe you made me a promise. Now that both kids are asleep, let's go to bed."

"I'm glad you decided to fly to New York tomorrow instead of tonight," I said as we left Robbie's room and walked to the master suite.

He squeezed my hand. "As I told Janie, family comes first."

We quickly got ready for bed, knowing we wouldn't have much privacy before Nell and Clint would return.

As I climbed in beside Vaughn, I thought back to when we first met six years ago. Like every other woman under ninety-five, I'd fallen for him. Now, six years later, I loved him even more. He was a good man. Tonight, I wanted him to understand that age made no difference in how I felt about him.

And later, he proved to me how physically fit he was for a man who was about to be recognized as an older patriarch.

CHAPTER TWENTY-FOUR

Very early the next morning, Nell and Clint left as soon as Bailey had been fed, hoping to make the road trip a little easier. We all were sad to see them go. Even Trudy. After they'd gone, she wandered from the guest suite to the kitchen and back again as if she could rediscover the baby she loved to protect.

For the last time in a while, Vaughn dropped off Robbie at school, and then it was time for him to leave. Knowing he might not be back for some time, he was as quiet as I was on the way to the airport. Glumly, I pulled up to the drop-off curb at the airport and waited while Vaughn got out of the car and grabbed his luggage.

He leaned into the car and kissed me. "Love you, Ann. I'll let you know when you can expect me home. Take care of yourself. I don't like leaving you when things with Lindsay at the hotel are so unsettled."

"Debra and Whit are good at their jobs. As long as Brock stays out of the picture, I'm not going to worry about it."

"Move along!" said a patrolman, indicating for me to drive away. Vaughn gave me another quick kiss and headed into the terminal.

At the hotel, I stopped in the kitchen for a cup of coffee and a cinnamon roll, attempting to assuage my sadness at feeling alone again.

Rhonda was in the office when I got there. "How was the

photoshoot?"

I told her about the day. "I never thought of Vaughn as being worried about his age, but I must say Janie made it seem as if he was much older than he is."

"Vaughn shouldn't be worried about it. Not with so many women falling for him on television. Even if they change his role, old roosters have the right to crow," said Rhonda.

I laughed. "That is something I'll never say to him. Where do you come up with all these sayings?"

"Who knows? I thought it was appropriate." She grew serious. "I've been over our schedule and Daily Reports and have noticed that our Sunday Brunch numbers are low. Any guesses as to why?"

"Besides having the snowbirds gone? I can't imagine. We'll have to look into it. We just put an ad in the local newspaper. Maybe we'd better call Terri Thomas at the Sabal *Daily News* and see if she'd be willing to do an article for us."

"I bet she will for free food," said Rhonda. "I've seen the way she gobbles up our cinnamon rolls."

"Having her here is fine as long as she doesn't interfere with anything related to Lindsay. You know how nosy she is," I said, more than a little concerned.

"Thinking of Lindsay, how's she doing on wedding plans for Debra and Whit? Have they settled on a day? We have some Thursdays that could use a little boost," said Rhonda. "Let's talk to them about setting it up for two weeks from now." She grinned. "Now that we're such experts on short-notice weddings, we can easily handle this. It's a small one."

"That was the plan. Let's go see."

My spirits lifted as we headed to the guesthouse. Debra and Whit's story was a sweet one.

Debra met us at the door. "Good morning! What brings you here?"

"A wedding," said Rhonda bluntly. "Has Lindsay talked to you about one?"

A bright smile filled Debra's face. "If you're talking about one for Whit and me, then yes. We've been discussing it. Come on in."

Lindsay appeared. "Hi! Did I hear 'a wedding' mentioned?"

"We'd like to talk to all of you about dates," I said. "Our weekends are booked, but we have other times that would be perfect."

"Whit is out doing errands," said Debra. "But let's talk. Now that we've decided to do it, I don't want much time to pass. It's going to be just us with Lindsay and a couple of other people."

"Whether it's big or small, we want it perfect for you," I said.

"Right," agreed Rhonda.

Debra led us to the living room and offered us seats on the couch. Lindsay sat in a chair nearby, holding a notepad and pen.

"I've been making notes about different ideas," said Lindsay to Debra. "It's been so much fun planning a happy occasion. The two of you are perfect together."

"Thanks," said Debra. "Whit and I dated a couple of years ago, and then our jobs caused us to step away from one another. But neither of us forgot what we'd shared. Now that we're together again, we want to make it official."

"And I'm helping them do it," said Lindsay. "I've made notes so far on what they want. Whit doesn't care about the details as long as it happens. The sooner, the better."

A blush crept up Debra's cheeks. "We're both excited about it."

"Okay, first things first. Let's pick a date," I said.

"Thursday evenings are a good time of the week because

then you have the whole weekend to celebrate," said Rhonda.

"And it's easier on the staff. Especially with this late notice," I added.

"I like that." Debra looked at the calendar Lindsay handed her, and they quickly agreed on two weeks from the upcoming Thursday.

"That'll give Debra time to find a dress," said Lindsay.

"You have some options," I said. "You'd mentioned a beach wedding, or a garden wedding is also available."

"Whit and I definitely want a beach wedding in the late afternoon," said Debra.

"And I would like to host a meal afterward for them," said Lindsay.

"Sounds great," said Rhonda. "If you need help with flowers or anything else with the ceremony, Lorraine Grace will help you."

"And, Lindsay, you can work with Jean-Luc on the meal," I said, watching a smile cross her face.

"We just celebrated a small wedding reception in the library at the hotel, and that worked out well. Lorraine has notes on that too," said Rhonda.

Debra grinned. "Now I'm getting excited. Thanks so much! Lindsay has insisted on helping us. I can't tell you what that means to us."

"It's the least I can do for protecting me," said Lindsay. "You make me feel so safe. And after the hell I've been through, it's wonderful."

"Okay," I said, getting to my feet. "We'll tell Lorraine to expect a call from you. Simply call the hotel and ask for wedding services. She'll put you in touch with everyone you need."

"And we'll talk to Bernie about staffing," said Rhonda, rising from the couch.

"Rhonda and I and the entire hotel staff are at your service," I said. "This wedding is very special to us."

"Thanks," said Lindsay. "You're two more of my angels."

Rhonda and I glanced at one another. We were no angels, just two people wanting to keep a promise to the vice president of the United States.

We met with Terri Thomas a couple of days later. An older, oversized woman with hair dyed red and beady eyes that reminded me of a snake before it sprung, Terri was a formidable woman intent on spreading the news—both good and bad. But she was essential when we wanted to get the word out about the hotel. In return for bits of information, she was rewarded by being allowed to order anything she wanted to eat. And she always chose brunch time so she could have both lunch and our famous cinnamon rolls.

I sat quietly with her in the dining room as she bit into her second cinnamon roll.

Rhonda spoke. "You know how well known we are in the community for our Sunday Brunches. We need to bring in more people. Do you have any suggestions?"

Terri finished swallowing and nodded. "Let's talk about some of your famous guests. You just had the vice president of the United States here. That's big news in this town."

"Terri, you know we can't do that," I said. "Each guest is assured of privacy when they stay at our hotel."

"Hold on. Brock Goodwin tells me that I should keep my eye on things, that there might be some other famous people staying here."

I felt the hairs on the back of my neck rise.

Before I could say anything, Rhonda said, "Brock Goodwin is a major asshole. You can't believe anything he says."

Terri puffed up with indignation. "Well, for your information, I know that Thomas Thaxton was here and left abruptly. Brock confirmed it."

I could see frustration building inside Rhonda and quickly said, "Let's try a different angle. Let's talk about the food and the chef behind it." The minute the words left my mouth, I wished I could take them back. Would anyone, including Jean-Luc himself, inadvertently mention Lindsay?

I saw the look of dismay on Rhonda's face and knew she was worried about it too.

"We could give you some of our recipes to use. For anything but the cinnamon rolls," Rhonda said.

"I'll do both, the interview and the recipes," said Terri with a look of satisfaction I dreaded.

Rhonda and I exchanged worried glances but didn't want Terri to notice our distress. Thankfully, she was reaching for another roll.

As soon as the meeting with Terri was over, I hurried into the kitchen to talk to Jean-Luc.

He was sitting at his desk but stood when I approached. "What is it?"

I told him about the upcoming interview with Terri and warned him to be careful about any talk of Lindsay from either his staff or himself.

Jean-Luc frowned. "I don't like it. I remember that woman. She is a ... *serpent dans l'herbe!*

"I know. I think of her as a snake in the grass, too," I said. "That's why I'm so sorry I thought of the idea to use you to promote our Sunday Brunches."

He spread his arms and shrugged. "Ah, well, I'll do the best I can with that woman, and I'll warn my staff that my private life is my own."

"Thank you. I know you enjoy Lindsay's company, but we

all have to be careful about keeping her safe."

"She's safe with me at my house," said Jean-Luc. "Whit and Debra approve."

"Yes, they told me so." I touched Jean-Luc's arm. "I'm happy that the two of you spend time together."

"Me too." Jean-Luc smiled. "I find her very easy to be with after losing Sabine."

"She's lovely," I said, and his eyes lit with happiness.

I left him and went to talk to Bernie. Rhonda and I handled a lot of the publicity for the hotel, but we needed to keep him informed.

"I understand your worry about Terri Thomas," Bernie said. "Especially because she's been talking to Brock Goodwin. Funny, though, I haven't seen him around lately."

"You will," I said. "He can't resist coming here to see what's happening."

Just before it was time to leave to go home, Rhonda looked up from her computer, where she was investigating gift ideas for weddings. "I haven't found anything exactly like Liz's bracelet idea and think we should go ahead and place an order right away for more samples. Lorraine just sent me a message saying the Carpenter wedding party in June is interested in Liz's work.

"Wonderful! Liz will be thrilled." I was exhausted by the ups and downs of the day. "I don't know about you, but I'm ready for a margarita before I head home. Elena called to say that she and Troy are taking Robbie shopping with them."

"Margaritas here at The Beach House Hotel? Sounds perfect. I'll call Will and tell him I'll be a little late, that we have a short business meeting to get through."

I laughed. Will knew exactly what that meant and approved the need for us to spend some downtime together.

As we walked into the bar to place our orders, I noticed Brock seated at the bar and was tempted to turn back, but he'd already seen us. "Hello, Ann! Rhonda! What's new?"

"Nothin'," said Rhonda sullenly, bringing a frown to his face.

Wanting to make peace, I smiled pleasantly. "Busy as usual. You?"

"I think I may have a big deal in China. I'm working on it," he said. "But you know how these things can take time. Can I buy you a drink?"

"Sure, Brock, go ahead and pay for something we can get on our own. How kind of you," said Rhonda with enough sarcasm to end any conversation.

I shot her a warning look. "No, thank you. We've already placed our order."

The bartender looked at me. "The usual?"

"Thanks. We'll sit over there." Before Rhonda could say anything else, I took hold of her arm and led her away to a table in the corner of the room.

"What are you doing?" Rhonda whispered. "I wanted to make him leave."

"Operation Bastard ... Remember?" I whispered back, punching in a message to Debra.

The bartender served us our drinks, and I sat back waiting for the next step in Operation Bastard to begin.

Sure enough, Whit strolled into the room wearing shorts and a T-shirt that showed off his bulging biceps. He stopped and stared at Brock. "Hey! What are you doing here?" he said to Brock. "I thought I told you to stay away."

Brock straightened. "This is a public space. You can't make me leave here. You're just a guest, like me. Besides, I know the owners of the property."

Whit walked over, leaned against the bar with one elbow,

and faced Brock. "You spied on my bride and me. I didn't like you then, and I don't like you now."

The bartender glanced at me.

Brock got to his feet. "Look, I don't want a fight. I'll leave, but I'm reporting you to the police for harassing me. Got it?" He flipped a few bills onto the counter and stalked over to Rhonda and me.

"I hope you heard that. I'm going to report that man to the police for harassing me. I was minding my own business. Neither of you stood up for me. I'm going to remember that. And if you think I don't know something fishy is going on here, you're crazy."

"I have no idea what the disagreement is between the two of you," I lied. "The man might've been rude to you, but he didn't touch you. I don't think that's reportable."

"If I didn't know better, I'd think you were in cahoots with him," said Brock.

"Why would we do that?" Rhonda asked, sounding as if she really meant it.

"We want all our guests to be comfortable," I said.

Brock stared at me, then turned on his heel and stomped away.

Whit left the bar a few minutes later, carrying two margaritas with him. No doubt for Debra and Lindsay.

"Whit would scare me too," said Rhonda. "Did you get a load of those biceps, the way he flexed his muscles?"

"Yes. It made me feel good about Lindsay being protected by him," I said. "Now, tell me about your latest visit with Angela and the baby."

Rhonda grinned. "Sally is so smart. I swear she's going to talk early. Like Willow."

I laughed. "She's less than a month old."

"I know, I know, but I'm her grandmother," said Rhonda.

CHAPTER TWENTY-FIVE

A t home, the house seemed too empty. Trudy followed me around as I wandered from one room to the next, remembering how good it felt to have the others around. With Robbie spending time with two of his favorite people, I had the house to myself.

I poured myself a glass of pinot noir, fixed a plate of nibbles, and took them out by the pool. One margarita was all I usually had, preferring an excellent red wine instead. I sat on the edge of the pool and dipped my legs into the water, enjoying the coolness against the warm air. There was something about the salty fresh air and warmth of the sun that made my body happy. While I was growing up in Boston, my grandmother had kept her house cool, and for so many reasons, I'd never felt warm there.

My thoughts wandered back to the present. Weddings and babies were such a big part of my life right now.

As if by magic, my cell rang, and I discovered Tina Marks at the other end.

"Tina! How are you? How's that baby boy of yours?"

"Little Victor is wonderful. I'm so glad I named him after my brother. It brings me a lot of joy to see this happy baby after knowing how difficult Victor's own life was." She paused. "And I think he somehow knows."

Tina's mentally challenged brother, Victor, had died in a house fire that had occurred because of her mother's careless smoking. It was something Tina would never forget, blaming herself for not being there to protect him.

"It's sweet that you're carrying on his name. I know how much he meant to you," I said. "Any idea when you're planning to come for a stay? Nell was just here with her baby, and she's going to come back in a couple of months when staying in the New Mothers Program will be easier."

"That makes sense. That's why I'm calling. I wanted to come to you sometime soon, but I've been given an interesting script. It's about a woman whose husband stalks her. If I get the role in the movie, I won't be able to come to Florida until late summer or early fall. Will that work for you?"

"Yes, of course. I can't wait to see you and the baby. How's Nicholas?" Nicholas Swain, her husband, was a well-known Hollywood director.

"He's wonderful. He's directing the film and specifically wants me to be in the movie. It's going to be very interesting working with him because he makes me believe I can do anything."

I laughed. "Tina, I know what a strong, talented person you are."

She giggled. "But he's magical. I swear I never knew love could be so wonderful." Her voice changed. "Heaven knows I didn't have much of it growing up."

"Well, everyone in the family loves you and can't wait for you to come." It was strange how some guests became so close. Tina was one of the special ones.

I chatted a few minutes more with her and clicked off the call.

Trudy did a happy dance on her short legs when Robbie joined me outside.

Elena followed him. "As usual, Robbie was great with us. How are you doing now that Vaughn is gone?"

"I was feeling a little sorry for myself until I got a call from a friend. And now you're here."

"If you're offering a cup of coffee, I'd take one," said Elena.

"That sounds good. Let's go into the kitchen, and while Robbie plays, we can talk."

As I made two cups of coffee, I asked, "Is everything all right?"

She shrugged and accepted a cup from me. "Troy wants to expand his business. In addition to handling the spa at the hotel, he wants to open another spa farther up the coast. I don't think it's a good idea and want to know what you think of it."

"Troy hasn't mentioned it to Rhonda or me. Does he know you're talking to me?" I asked, unsettled by the idea.

Elena gave me a sheepish look. "No, but I'm talking to you woman-to-woman."

"If you're asking about the need for you to step into his business to help him, I would suggest speaking to Liz. She's had to do that for Chad."

"How's it going?" Elena asked.

"The business has its ups and downs. At the moment, Liz is trying for a baby. That's what's consuming her. That and the new jewelry business she's setting up." I told Elena about the idea of custom jewelry for new mothers and bridal groups.

"I love that," said Elena. "Maybe she could include a symbol for the spa. That would help Troy's business."

"Suggest it to her," I said. "As for the other topic, tell Troy to feel free to come to Rhonda and me anytime."

"Okay, thanks. I respect your decision not to discuss it with me."

That night as I talked to Vaughn in bed, I told him about my conversation with Elena.

"Are you worried Troy will devote too much of his attention to any outside project?" he asked.

"It crossed my mind," I admitted, "but he's young and should have the opportunity to grow his business. I'll talk it over with Rhonda to see how she feels about it before approaching Troy."

"Business is never static, you know," Vaughn said.

"That's the truth," I said. "In the hotel business, the fluctuations are constant. We're hoping to increase our Sunday brunch business with Terri Thomas's article in the newspaper. She's revisiting the property tomorrow morning with a photographer and will interview Jean-Luc."

"He agreed to an interview?" Vaughn said.

"Good man that he is, he's doing it for us. And, no, he doesn't like the idea, and it's all my fault for suggesting it. Especially when Lindsay is here at the hotel. He's afraid a connection will be made between the two of them by someone speaking out about it."

"I understand his worry. As I said in the beginning, it's a huge responsibility you and Rhonda have taken on. I'm glad that Debra and Whit are there with Lindsay."

"Yes, me too."

Vaughn's voice lowered to a sexy whisper. "I've been thinking about you."

"You have?" I said, playing along. These harmless little games could be a lot of fun.

By the time I'd described the fictional nightgown I was wearing, we were both laughing.

"Ah, Ann," he said. "I miss you. Have a good sleep. I'll talk to you tomorrow night. And, if I can, I'll call Robbie at dinner time. I miss him too."

"And Trudy?" I asked, stroking her ears. When Vaughn was away, she sometimes divided her time between Robbie and me.

"And Trudy," he admitted. "Love you all."

"We love you too," I said, clicking off the call. I realized I'd forgotten to ask him about seeing Simon, the producer.

The next morning Terri Thomas arrived promptly at ten with a photographer. The breakfast rush had died down, and because Jean-Luc didn't normally come in until eleven, he was available for the interview, which we'd scheduled to take place in his office.

Rhonda and I stood by nervously, hoping that his distaste of the woman remained well hidden. Terri's job as a reporter on the social scene meant many people paid attention to her, and she'd grown to believe she wielded a lot of sway in the community. As much as I didn't care for her, I, like Rhonda, treated her very well. This interview, usually not allowed by Jean-Luc, was a prime example.

To Jean-Luc's credit, he handled the interview with aplomb, injecting French charm into it, delighting Terri. As the interview was ending, I felt my earlier tension leave.

"One last question," Terri said. "A single, handsome man like you is a catch for any woman in the area. However, I understand you have a mystery girlfriend. Care to give me the inside scoop on who the lovely lady is?"

Jean-Luc stiffened. *"Absolument non!"*

Terri raised her hands in defense. "Okay, okay. I get it. Your private life is your own." She paused. "At least for now! These things eventually come out. So, whoever she is, she's one lucky woman snagging a man like you who cooks!"

Jean-Luc was visibly upset as he said good-bye to Terri and left the kitchen.

"Sorry," said Terri watching him leave. "I hit a real sore spot. But he should be warned people are talking."

My body turned ice-cold. "What people?"

She gave Rhonda and me a coy look. "A little birdie?"

"A big fuckin' turkey called Brock Goodwin, I'm guessin'," Rhonda said.

Terri put a finger to her lips. "Sh-h-h. I didn't tell you a thing."

Rhonda handed Terri the two recipes we'd typed up for her. "You'd better tell that snoop to lay low around here. Got it?"

Terri's cheeks flushed. "What are you two trying to hide, anyway?"

"Nothing," I said. "As many in the neighborhood know, Brock is always trying to cause trouble with the hotel and us. It goes back to the beginning when neighbors took our side in a couple of disputes."

"Yeah, he thinks he's lord of his kingdom or something like that," said Terri. "But I have to admit that he's a good source of information."

"If we have something we think you need to know, we'll be in touch," I said, placing a reassuring hand on her arm. Terri was nosy, but she wasn't cruel.

Consuela came over to us holding a paper bag. "Here are the sweet rolls for Ms. Thomas to take home with her."

Terri's face lit. "Thank you! I can't have too many of them."

Rhonda said, "I'll walk you out to your car."

I said goodbye to Terri and sank onto a chair in the kitchen feeling sick.

A few days later, Rhonda and I sat in the living room of the guesthouse with Lindsay, Debra, and Whit to discuss final plans for the wedding, which was to be held next week. Lorraine had booked a large one for the same day and was relieved Debra and Whit's would be small enough not to require her presence.

While we were talking, Lorraine called. "Hi, Ann. The minister who's handling the ceremony for Debra and Whit is here to see me about another wedding party, but I thought they might like to meet him. As part of his service, he usually spends at least a short amount of time with the bride and groom beforehand."

"Sounds good," I said. "Why don't I have them meet him in your office right now. They can walk over and be there in a few minutes."

"That would be wonderful. I think it's important," Lorraine said.

I clicked off the call, turned to Debra and Whit, and told them of Lorraine's request.

Whit studied Debra and shrugged. "We'd be gone only a short time." He looked at us. "You'll stay right here, won't you? Lindsay, are you okay with the idea of Deb and me leaving you for a few minutes?"

Lindsay laughed. "Go, you two! It's part of planning for the wedding. Besides, I'm going to take a nap. I didn't sleep well last night. Rhonda and Ann can leave if they want." She looked at us.

"We're staying right here," said Rhonda.

"I agree. It'll be for only a few minutes, but I'll feel better if we stay," I said.

"I don't want to be rude ..." Lindsay said.

"Sweetie, go take your nap. It'll give Ann and me a chance to sit in the sun," said Rhonda smiling at her.

"Okay, then. Thanks." Lindsay left the room.

Rhonda waved me out of the living room. "C'mon, I wasn't kidding. Let's use this time to relax. I stayed with Angela's kids for a while last night, and I'm still exhausted."

I followed her out to the patio and took a seat on the lounge next to Rhonda's.

Stretched out, I closed my eyes, taking a moment to relax.

I felt something rather than heard it—a rustle in the

landscaping. Furious to think that Brock, a reporter, or someone else was snooping, I rose and shook Rhonda gently.

"Wha ...

I covered her mouth with my hand. "Sh-h-h. Come with me."

As silently as we could, we tiptoed to the lanai screen door and opened it.

I studied the bushes at the edge of the lawn. No movement. Rhonda frowned at me.

I motioned her forward with me.

As we got closer to the thick oleander hedge, the leaves in one area fluttered.

"Okay, whoever you are, come out of there," I said.

"If it's you, Brock Goodwin, I'm going to forget I'm a lady and rip your balls off," said Rhonda.

A man dressed in black sprung out of the bushes toward us, knocking me against Rhonda.

We both went down in a heap.

"What are *you* doing here?" said Rhonda, sitting up and breathing heavily.

He pointed a gun at her and then at me. "Shut up! Both of you! I'm here to get my wife."

I stared in shock at Thomas Thaxton. He'd looked terrible before. He looked worse now—thinner and wild-eyed. God knew what drugs he was on, but he was flying high, which meant we were in more than a little bit of trouble.

He grabbed my arm and yanked me to my feet. "Now, where is she? I know she's staying in this house."

"I don't know who told you that, but he's lying. She's not here," I said, praying Lindsay wouldn't appear.

Rhonda stood. "Look. Just drop the gun, and we'll get some help for you."

He pointed the gun at her. "Shut up, or I'll kill you."

"You don't want to do that," Rhonda said, her voice shaking. "I'm a mother and a grandmother."

While they exchanged words, I tried to gauge how hard and where I'd have to hit him. Quickly, before I chickened out, I jumped.

Two shots rang out!

I watched in horror as Rhonda fell to the ground.

"Rhonda!" I cried, throwing myself at her.

She lay still. Sobbing, I checked her body.

Confused by the sounds behind me, I turned to see Whit kneeling beside Thomas. Blood was oozing from Thomas's chest. Debra stood a few feet away, holding onto Lindsay, who'd raced outside and was doubled over, crying.

I turned back to Rhonda and shook her hard. "Rhonda! Rhonda! Talk to me!"

She sat up. "What happened? I remember seeing Thomas, and then everything turned black."

Whit knelt by her. "You fainted. It happens sometimes."

"Oh my God!" Rhonda said. "Don't tell anyone!"

Whit put a hand on her forehead and checked her eyes. "You're going to be just fine." He turned. "Unfortunately, we have someone who isn't. Deb is calling the police now. And we'll need to get security over here to keep everyone away."

"Okay. I'll call them. What else do you want us to do?" I asked.

"Just rest here. The police will have questions," Whit said.

I called security and then lowered myself next to Rhonda and hugged her. "You scared me! What would I ever do without you?" Adrenaline left me in a rush, making me feel as weak as a baby. Then the tears came.

We clung to each other, crying.

When we finally pulled apart, Rhonda said, "Annie, I had a near-death experience."

I looked at her with surprise. "How can you have a near-death experience when you weren't even hurt?"

"All I know is I'm going to try to be better, act more like a lady, no swearing, and all that stuff," she said. "Maybe lose some weight."

I gave her a steady look. "I don't know what happened to you, but I and everyone else I know loves you just the way you are, Rhonda. You're beautiful inside and out. You're outspoken but honest, kind, and loving."

She wrapped her arms around me. "Oh, Annie, it was such a lucky day for me when you first came to Florida with Liz."

"Even if I looked very beige," I said, teasing her.

"Yeah, even then. But we got you brightened up," she said, half-laughing, half-crying.

"And much, much more than that," I said, giving her another hug as the yard filled with police officers and security guards.

Debra came over to us. "Why don't the two of you come inside with me? You don't need to see the crime scene."

"Nothing bad is going to happen to Whit, is it?" I asked, getting to my feet.

"He was just doing his job. He'll have to fill out a lot of paperwork and follow other procedures, but he should be fine. It's a good thing Thomas was a lousy shot, and Whit didn't get hurt."

"How's Lindsay?" I asked, getting to my feet.

"As upset as we all are by the close call," said Debra. "I've put in a phone call to Amelia. And we'll try to keep the press away until we get things sorted out. Lindsay will go stay at Jean-Luc's house for the time being."

"Oh, my God! Does he know what's happened?" Rhonda said.

"He's on his way," Debra answered as she led us inside.

CHAPTER TWENTY-SIX

Inside the house, Lindsay was stretched out on her bed weeping. I went in and sat down beside her. "I hope you don't mind my being here with you," I said softly. "I just want to make sure you're all right."

She rolled over and gazed up at me. "No, Ann, I'm glad you're here. I want to thank you. You and Rhonda saved my life."

"Whit is the one who saved not only you but us," I said honestly.

"But you were already on the lawn to protect me," Lindsay protested. "All four of you should get the credit. Debra came right into the house and stood guard, not leaving my side."

Jean-Luc rushed into the room. "*Chérie?*"

"Jean-Luc!" Lindsay cried, scrambling to her feet. She allowed herself to be swept into his arms.

I left the room to give them privacy and went over to the couch to sit next to Rhonda. "Are you all right?" I asked her.

"Still shook up, but I'll be fine," she said. "I called Bernie. He's keeping everyone calm at the hotel. Most people didn't hear the shots, but they're confused by all the police cars."

I stood and looked outside. The body had yet to be removed. I turned back and faced Debra. "What is the president going to say about all this?"

"He's not going to be happy, that's for sure," said Debra. "But if Thomas had killed Lindsay, the situation would be much worse. No matter, he'll put a spin on it, so his image isn't tarnished."

"The bastard. He'll go for a cover-up," said Rhonda.

"I'm afraid so," said Debra. "That's how a lot of these things go down."

"It's so unfair," I said, thinking of the weeks of stress keeping Lindsay safe, to say nothing of what it had cost Amelia both in worry and expense.

"The press will be arriving soon," said Debra. "We need to get Lindsay and Jean-Luc away from here. I'll walk them along the back path to the hotel and help Jean-Luc get Lindsay into his car and then go with them until they're safely beyond the hotel. Then I'll come back and talk to Bernie about security from the press." She turned to me. "Please let Whit know what I'm doing."

"Sure. I'll do it now."

I left the house and stood outside behind the yellow tape the police had placed around the area where the body lay.

Whit saw me and came over. "What's up?"

I told him what Debra was doing and watched as security kept people from coming down the driveway to the house.

"Good thing Deb has taken Lindsay away. Now we can honestly say she's not at the house." He frowned. "I wonder if Brock Goodwin was somehow involved."

"He knew something was going on. I wouldn't put it past him to give Thomas a call as he'd promised. He had nothing to lose by doing so and everything to gain," I said.

"I'm sure he'll deny it," said Whit shaking his head. "I suspect we'll never know for sure."

"As obnoxious as Brock is, I don't believe he'd ever want to be part of a murder."

"Yeah, maybe you're right. Guys like that are so self-centered and so eager for power and money they don't think beyond it." Whit indicated the press of people standing at the gate. "If I'm not mistaken, there he is now."

I looked at the crowd standing behind the gate. Sure enough, there was Brock with none other than Terri Thomas. A shiver crawled down my back. I knew Brock had something to do with it. I studied his face, but he looked as stunned as the other onlookers.

I returned to the house dispirited.

Inside, Rhonda was talking to Will in a quiet but urgent voice. I knew how rattled she was and walked into the kitchen.

My cell rang. *Liz.*

"Mom? Are you all right? I heard there's been a shooting at the hotel." Her voice was high with worry.

"Rhonda and I are both fine," I said, beginning to shake as the words came out. "We were accosted by Thomas Thaxton. Whit shot him and saved our lives."

"Oh, my God! You could've been killed? Oh, Mom! That's so awful! Is Lindsay safe?"

"Yes, she was inside the house while Rhonda and I were in the backyard. I'd heard someone in the bushes, and we thought it might be Brock Goodwin. Turns out it was Thomas."

"I thought he was with his family," said Liz, her voice shaky.

"I guess he didn't give up on the idea that Lindsay was staying here at the hotel. It's going to be pretty busy here for a while, so I'd better go," I said.

"Does Vaughn know what happened?" Liz said.

"No, but I'll call him now. Thanks, sweetheart."

"I love you, Mom!" said Liz, sounding as if she'd begun to weep.

"I love you too, Liz," I said, clicking off the call and phoning Vaughn.

When Vaughn's voicemail message came on, I left a message that Rhonda and I were all right, but he should call me when he could.

Rhonda came into the kitchen, her eyes red from crying. "I just got off the call with Will. He's going to talk to Angela. I think we should meet with Bernie to discuss holding a press conference, letting everyone know the hotel is fine and unaffected by the shooting."

"You're right. I wonder if we should call Amelia to see how she wants to handle things," I said as my cell rang. *Amelia.* I put her on speakerphone so Rhonda could hear.

"Ann, I just got off the phone with Debra, so I know pretty much what happened. It's important that we all handle this carefully with the press. I'm flying down there tonight. In the meantime, why don't we just say that there's been a terrible accident, and we'll release details tomorrow. Will you agree to that?"

"You're on speaker so that Rhonda could hear." I turned to Rhonda for her approval. "Yes, we both will agree to that. We were about to confer with Bernie on how to handle it, so we'll tell him this is how you want it. We're trying to keep the press at bay, but they're already here. However, our security is keeping them away from the scene."

"Excellent. I'll be in touch with the president, of course, before I come down. Will you have room for me at the guesthouse?"

"Yes, we'll have the maids prepare Lindsay's bedroom for you. She's staying with Jean-Luc as you no doubt know."

"I do know that." Her voice softened. "How is my sister doing?"

"She, like the rest of us, is pretty shaken by how close Thomas was to harming her. But being with Jean-Luc has always been good for her, and it's good for her now. And best to be away from the crime scene," I said.

Amelia let out a sad puff of air. "What had started as

something sweet and wonderful changed so quickly. Neither Lindsay nor I knew that having his brother as president would produce such long-hidden jealousy, such a dive into drugs and alcohol and violence."

"Well, it's over," I said. "Now, we all can begin to heal."

"I can't thank the two of you enough for all you've done to keep my sister safe," Amelia said, her voice cracking. "I have a feeling the president will want to thank you too. We'll set up a meeting for tomorrow. I'll talk to Bernie later with some plans for a brief news conference."

"That sounds good," I said, relieved that Amelia would handle a lot of that responsibility.

A knock sounded at the door.

Rhonda answered it and stepped back as a policeman entered the house. "Okay, if I talk to you about what happened?" He held up a tape recorder. "It's a very straightforward investigation, but we want all the facts lined up as quickly as possible."

Rhonda and I sat on the couch facing the policeman as he asked us about what we saw and heard.

When one of us made a statement, he looked to the other for confirmation or denial. What had seemed a lifetime was merely a matter of minutes, so there wasn't much to describe.

Satisfied, he rose. "I think we have everything we need. If you can think of anything else that was said or you saw, please let us know.

After he left, Rhonda and I hugged each other, rattled after experiencing those moments all over again.

"Thank God, Whit appeared when he did," I said, remembering how sick I'd felt hearing gunshots and seeing Rhonda fall to the ground.

"Of all the things that have happened to us here at the hotel, this was the scariest," said Rhonda.

"You don't actually want to make all those changes that you talked about, do you?" I asked.

"You mean to become more like you, no swearing and all?" Rhonda shrugged. "Will says just be myself. That's who he married; that's who he loves."

"See? I told you," I laughed as she gave me a big, bosomy hug.

I'd just come out of Bernie's office where Rhonda and I had met with him to discuss how to handle the press when Vaughn called.

"Ann? What's this I hear about a shooting at the hotel? It's all over the news. What happened? You said you weren't hurt but were you involved?"

"Yes. Hold on! Let me get to my office."

I hurried away from Bernie and Rhonda to hide my tears. Just hearing Vaughn's voice had brought home how different things would be if Whit hadn't arrived to save us.

After I finished telling Vaughn the story, he let out a long, slow breath. "Ann, you and Rhonda are very kind, but I don't want you to do something like this again. Taking in someone who needs to hide isn't a good decision for the hotel."

"It was something we wouldn't ordinarily do, but even if the vice president of the United States wasn't involved, how could we turn away a woman who needed our help? And speaking of helping someone, how is it going with Darla and Simon?"

"Funny you should ask. Simon is nowhere to be found, and suddenly Darla's scenes are just fine."

"I'm proud of how you stepped up to help her. How is it being the old man figure now?"

"That's another story. I'm not quite ready to take on that

role in the show."

"How are your fans reacting to the story of Darla and Meredith being part of our family?"

"The producers tell me it was a class act, and everyone loves it."

"Good. I'm glad to have that behind us. You'll be able to come home for the wedding as scheduled, won't you? Next Thursday it will go forward as planned."

"I'll be there. The more the merrier, huh?"

"There'll always be room in our family for more. I have a feeling Lindsay and Jean-Luc will be next, but who knows?"

Vaughn's voice softened. "It was such a lucky day when I met you."

CHAPTER TWENTY-SEVEN

After the harrowing experience with Thomas and the scrambling we had to do to keep a lid on the facts boiling beneath the surface, I was more than happy to accept Amelia's invitation for Rhonda and me to join her for margaritas on the Tuesday afternoon before the wedding.

As we walked into the bar, I saw Amelia sitting alone in the corner, her Secret Service agent nearby, and decided this would be a good time for her to visit our special hiding place. I placed an order for the margaritas and turned to Rhonda.

"I think we should ask Amelia to join us in our secret spot."

"Good idea," said Rhonda. "After all the publicity of the past few days, I like the idea of quiet time. You get the drinks; I'll get Amelia."

The bartender fixed me a tray with the drinks and a bowl of nuts and said, "I'll carry it up for you."

I smiled my thanks and led the way to the storage room, unlocked the door, and waved him through to the balcony, where he set down the tray. "Enjoy."

He left as Rhonda and Amelia arrived. After her guard checked the area and left, we arranged chairs and then took seats around the table.

Rhonda handed out the drinks and lifted hers in a toast. "Here's to life!"

"Yes," said Amelia smiling and looking better than when she'd arrived the night of the shooting.

We clinked glasses and let out a chorus of appreciative sighs. The ability to relax out of sight was precious.

Amelia spent some time looking out over the property. It was one of those days that people in Maine might call a "high sparkler" with clear, blue skies and bright sunshine that cast a lemony glow making it seem as if the earth was relaxing too.

"You have such a lovely place," Amelia murmured. "I hope the weather holds for the wedding. Debra and Whit deserve the best."

"Whit was terribly worried you'd be mad about their leaving Lindsay with us for a few minutes to meet the minister who is to marry them."

"Lindsay spoke to me and told me they were not to be blamed in any way," said Amelia. "No one had any reason to suspect Thomas would appear. How he managed to get on the plane without being flagged is beyond me."

"Lindsay didn't even want Ann and me to stay with her," said Rhonda.

"Well, it's a good thing you did." Amelia reached into her pocketbook and brought out two envelopes. "The president sent these to me for you."

"The president is writing to us?" Rhonda said, grinning. "Hot damn! Who'd a thunk it?"

Amelia laughed. "In my opinion, you need more than a letter, but he's trying to keep everything private."

"I'm going to save mine to read when Vaughn gets home later tonight," I said.

"I'm going to open mine now," said Rhonda. She ripped open the envelope and brought out a sheet of thick, creamy paper.

"Go ahead and read it," I said. "I'm sure mine says the same thing, but I want Vaughn to have the pleasure of opening it."

"Okay," said Rhonda. "Here goes:"

Dear Ms. Grayson,
It is with the sincerest of gratitude that I write to

thank you for the role you played in keeping my beloved sister-in-law, Lindsay, safe from her very ill husband. My family and I will be forever grateful to you for protecting her.

If you ever come to Washington, D. C., I would like to welcome you to the White House to give you my personal regards.

Sincerely,

Edward Thaxton

President of the United States

Rhonda grinned. "Short but sweet. Wait til Will sees this. He's going to be so proud. 'Course he didn't vote for him, but who cares? My parents would never believe all that's happened to me. Too bad they're not here to see it."

"I bet they wouldn't be that surprised," said Amelia. "I understand you come from a good, hard-working family."

"How'd you know?"

Amelia placed a hand on Rhonda's arm. "I know more about you than you could guess. Tell me, how did it feel to win the lottery?"

Rhonda laughed. "After I stopped hyperventilating? Sal said for me to go ahead and buy a ticket, that he wanted nothing to do with it. But I knew I'd win. Not sure how, but I had a feeling I would. Served him right when I put the money in my name. As it turned out, it's what made it possible for me to do this hotel with Ann. I had the money, but she had the business experience."

Amelia raised her glass. "Here's to the two of you! You've made it a success."

"We worked hard to make it happen," I reminded her.

She laughed. "That, too. I'd like to put the two of you on my board of directors for the non-profit organization I started for women recovering from spousal abuse. Think about it and let me know."

"I'd love it," I said, "but I don't think it should be for just spousal abuse. Abuse in the workplace too."

"I agree," said Amelia. "That's next on the list. We women have to stick together. Men are being abused too, but for the moment, we're dealing with women."

"Count me in," said Rhonda.

"Thank you. Shall we toast that too?" Amelia lifted her glass, and we raised ours.

As I did, I thought about the guests who come and go in a hotel and how interesting it was that it could bring people together.

That night I lay in bed waiting for Vaughn to arrive. He'd caught a late flight so he could be present for the wedding celebration. I was wearing the blue nightgown he loved to see me out of, and I'd placed the letter from the President on his pillow.

Sometime later, I felt someone shaking my shoulder and let out a scream.

"Hey, Ann, it's me," came a voice I knew.

I opened my eyes and blinked my bad dream away. A dream where Thomas shot me and forced me to watch Rhonda die.

Vaughn sat on the edge of the bed and pulled me into his arms. "What was that all about?" he asked softly. "The shooting?"

I pressed closer to him. "It's been a difficult time. I'm glad you're here."

"Me, too. I hate the thought of anything bad ever happening to you." He kissed me on the cheek, and when I relaxed, his lips met mine.

My eyes stung with gratefulness. He made me feel safe and loved.

After we broke apart, I lay in bed and watched while he undressed and got ready for bed. As he went to climb into bed, he noticed the envelope sitting on his pillow.

"What's this?"

"Go ahead and open it. I know what it says."

Vaughn picked up the envelope. "Pretty impressive when you get a letter from the president of the United States." He read it and set it on the nightstand. "I'm proud of what you and Rhonda did to help Lindsay, but it could've ended badly. Too bad politics sometimes comes before common sense. Thomas is someone who needed a lot more help than being hidden in Vermont. I thought dealing with mental health issues was one of the president's interests."

"Not if it meant exposing his own family," I said. "I knew when I first met Thomas that his problems were severe."

Vaughn climbed into bed and drew me up against him, easily fitting me to his form. "The world is a crazy place. Let's enjoy the next few days. We all could use a happy occasion."

With my thoughts centered on a wedding and Vaughn's arms around me, I fell into a deep sleep.

Rosy fingers of dawn were spreading in the sky when I heard Robbie's cry, "Daddy's home!"

Giggling happily, he and Trudy crawled into bed with us. Pulling him close, Vaughn looked at me. "Looks like we're a family again."

I filled with happiness. This was a good way to try to forget the past few days and start the celebration.

###

Rhonda and I drove together to Flowers, a boutique restaurant downtown known for ladies luncheons and afternoon teas. Amelia was hosting a luncheon for Debra with only Lindsay, Rhonda, and me as guests. Coming from a broken background, Debra had wanted to keep the wedding low-key, and we all respected that. Whit's brother had flown in for the ceremony, but no one else had been invited. Tonight, the reception would take place in the small dining room we used for VIP guests. The ceremony would be in a private area on the beach in front of the hotel. The nearby sunset-viewing platform and bar would be temporarily closed for the event. The Secret Service agents assigned to Amelia had agreed that would be best.

When I stepped inside the restaurant, I paused, taking it all in. In a word, the décor was adorable, definitely catering to women. The walls were painted a pale pink. Pink linen tablecloths covered tables, china with delicate floral designs matched the flowers sitting in vases atop the tables, and teacups sat at every place.

Amelia and Lindsay were already seated at a table with Debra. Not too far away sat two male customers who I realized were Secret Service agents protecting Amelia.

Smiling, Amelia got to her feet. "Here come the warriors."

Rhonda and I looked at one another and laughed. She'd been going through some post-trauma episodes the same as I'd experienced.

The luncheon was a quiet, sweet affair. Amelia had ordered tea sandwiches, salads, and plenty of wine. As we talked, I discovered that Debra had been a softball star in high school and joined the Marines after graduation. She'd met Whit when they served in the CIA for a brief time, and as Debra said, they had a hot time together, separating when Debra left to go into the security business with a friend.

"It wasn't until we were working together again that we both knew it was a mistake ever to have broken up," said Debra, her cheeks blushing prettily.

"I knew the two of you were right for each other the first time I saw you together," said Lindsay, lifting her wine glass in a toast. "Here's to the two of you."

We all raised our glasses.

Amelia turned to Rhonda and me. "I've heard bits and pieces about how the two of you met each other and your husbands. It seems like a lot of serendipity."

"I would never have met Vaughn if the producers hadn't decided to film his soap opera at the hotel."

"We needed them to come to the hotel because we were struggling to get the hotel going," said Rhonda.

"I love stories like that," said Lindsay. "Jean-Luc says the two of you are wonderful not only as people to work for but as friends."

"Speaking of that," said Rhonda. "What's going on with the two of you? I see how you look at each other."

'He's been wonderful to me," said Lindsay, "but it'll be some time before I'm ready to be more than friends."

I glanced at Rhonda and Amelia, and we silently agreed that though Lindsay wasn't ready to tell us about it, she and Jean-Luc were already past that initial stage.

After lunch, Amelia said, "Thank you, Ann and Rhonda, for coming. Now, we're going to take Debra to see Malinda at Hair Designs."

"I'm going to surprise Whit," said Debra grinning. While Debra wasn't beautiful, she was lovely in a healthy, girl-next-door way.

"Have fun," I said, hugging her goodbye. "Vaughn and I'll see you on the beach at five-thirty."

"Enjoy all that pampering," said Rhonda, wrapping her

arms around Debra.

We left the restaurant and climbed into Rhonda's red Cadillac convertible, the car she loved to drive.

As she dropped me off at my house, she turned to me. "How are you doing with everything? I've been having some nightmares."

"Me, too," I said. Gazing at my best friend, I was so happy things had turned out as well as they had. Whit would always be a hero in my mind. I couldn't wait to help him and Debra celebrate their wedding.

Rhonda gave my hand a squeeze. "See ya later, hon. Glad we have this happy occasion today."

"Strange how things work out," I said, thinking back to the day I stepped off the plane and into a life I'd never suspected.

CHAPTER TWENTY-EIGHT

At exactly 5:30 P.M., Vaughn and I joined the others on the beach, waiting for Debra to arrive with Whit. They'd chosen to forego tradition and come toward us together.

They appeared, and as they moved toward us, my eyes remained glued on Debra. She was wearing a white silk dress with cap sleeves, a V-neckline, and a skirt that flowed from the waistline into long, soft folds to her ankles. Her dark hair was cut and styled in a way that brought out the lovely lines of her cheekbones and made her light-brown eyes look bigger. I let out a sigh of happiness. She simply glowed.

My gaze turned to Whit. Taller than Debra by a few inches, his muscular body made Debra appear fragile beside him. Though I knew Debra's strength, the effect of seeing them like this was touching.

The minister stood beside a small, round, sturdy white table whose legs had been dug into the sand. On top of the table was a vase of white orchids.

Lindsay and Whit's brother, Jim, stood on either side of the minister.

Debra and Whit walked up to the minister and turned to us, their faces filled with broad smiles that captured the moment. Behind them, the sun, hours away from setting, washed the background with a softening light. Blue waves rolled onto the shore and pulled away in a steady rhythm. Seagulls swirled in the sky above, their cries providing music that seemed right.

I listened as Debra and Whit recited vows to one another and couldn't help glancing at Vaughn. He winked at me, and I knew he, too, was remembering our own wedding.

When at last the minister announced, "You may now kiss your bride," we watched with amusement as Whit picked up his bride and twirled her around in his arms as he kissed her. When he lost his balance and almost stumbled, we all reached out to catch them.

He regained his footing and turned to us. "She drives me crazy, you know?"

And that, I thought, were among the sweetest words said that day.

At the hotel in the small dining room, the reception Lindsay was hosting was underway quickly. While we waited for dinner, appetizers and drinks were served.

Everything was as lovely as I'd hoped. More important than the setting was the gathering of family and friends for such a happy event.

I gazed around.

Vaughn was talking easily with Amelia. Jean-Luc and Lindsay were standing apart looking like the love-struck people they were. Will was talking to Debra, who glowed with happiness, and Rhonda, Whit, and Jim were laughing over something that had been said.

A waiter approached, carrying a tray of margaritas. He offered me one, and I took it.

Margaritas at The Beach House Hotel were occasions for celebrating many things, but most of all, the success of the hard work Rhonda and I had done to change her seaside estate into the well-respected, upscale hotel it was today. Two women who beat the odds.

From across the room, Rhonda caught my eye and lifted her glass in a salute to me.

Smiling, I held mine aloft to her, certain that though we had challenges ahead of us with guests constantly arriving and departing, we'd meet them together.

# # #

Thank you for reading *Margaritas at The Beach House Hotel*. If you enjoyed this book, please help other readers discover it by leaving a review on Amazon, BookBub, Goodreads, or your favorite site. It's such a nice thing to do.

The other books in The Beach House Hotel Series,
Breakfast at The Beach House Hotel
Lunch at The Beach House Hotel
Dinner at The Beach House Hotel
Christmas at The Beach House Hotel
Dessert at The Beach House Hotel
are available on all sites.

Coffee at The Beach House Hotel and *High Tea at The Beach House Hotel* will be released in 2023 and 2024, respectively.

Enjoy an excerpt from my book, *The Desert Flowers – Lily*, Book 2 of The Desert Sage Inn Series:

CHAPTER ONE
LILY

In the early morning light on this March day in Palm Desert, California, Lily Weaver jogged in nice, easy steps on the path beside the Desert Sage Inn golf course. Her life, which had seemed so settled, had recently gone through a dramatic shift. Alec Thurston, her former employer and lover, was dying and had asked her to leave her job in New York and come to his home in California to help with the sale of the inn and its transition to the buyers, The Blaise Hotel Group. Here, she'd formed friendships with Rose Macklin and Willow Sanchez, two other women he'd asked to help him as well. Alec called them The Desert Flowers. They had separate jobs to help Alec, a man they each dearly loved.

Rose was working with a consultant for the Blaise Group to ensure that all social media and other PR going forward did nothing to destroy the panache of the upscale inn Alec had worked so hard to create.

Willow was working opposite the two young men in the hotel company's ownership family who were vying for the position of managing the inn after the sale went through.

She herself, as someone who had once been Alec's assistant, was on hand to take careful notes of meetings and to oversee and control the paperwork involved while the hotel company did property inspections, market research, and other due diligence activities. She worked alongside Brian Walden, another consultant hired by the Blaise Group to head their transition team.

As she followed the path by the golf course, she admired both the greens and the desert landscape. Some thought the bland colors of the desert were boring. She loved seeing sandy, rocky areas accented by green cacti and a variety of desert flowers. It made each color seem special. Hummingbirds were in abundance, their tiny bodies airborne by the constant fluttering of their wings, allowing them to hover about the bright flowers among the growth. In the distance, snow-capped mountains glistened in the sun, adding color to the purple-gray hue of their textured surfaces.

Hearing footsteps behind her, she turned to see Brian approaching. They sometimes met in the morning as they were jogging. At one time she'd entertained hopes of his being more than a co-worker. On their one so-called date, they'd ended up meeting a whole group working at the Desert Sage Inn, and he'd made it clear that this gathering was all business. Since then, she'd kept her distance. But despite telling herself not to dream foolishly, those secret hopes still lingered.

As he moved toward her, she observed his thick brown hair, handsome, athletic body and the ease at which he handled his prosthetic lower left leg. Brian was the sort of man she hoped to marry someday —kind, thoughtful, and smart.

"Morning!" Brian said, coming to a stop beside her. "How's it going? I haven't seen you in a while. Keeping busy with Alec?"

"Actually, I've been waiting for you to call a meeting. As lovely as it is to be here, I like to feel as if I'm doing my job."

"Ah, well, things have been put on hold while details are being worked on for the conversion of Desert Sage Inn to be the lead property in the new Corona Collection. I've missed those meetings myself." He smiled at her.

Her heart rate kicked up. That smile was lethal. Telling herself to be professional, she said, "I'm thinking of taking up Bennett Williams' offer for me to apply for a job in his law office. Part-time, of course, until the sale of the inn takes place. I'd still help with that and any other projects Alec might have for me."

"So, you've really decided to move here?" Brian said, his hazel eyes drilling into her.

"Yes," she said. "I've already put my condo in New York State up for sale. I still have to convince my sister to move here, but the rest is underway."

"I'm scouting around for places to live here on at least a part-time basis. At the moment, Austin is still home."

She gazed up at him thinking Texas suited a big guy like him. She could even imagine him in a Stetson.

"I'd better go. Don't worry, I'll let you know when the next big meeting takes place. And if you need any help getting that job with Bennett Williams, call me. He owes me."

"Thanks." She lifted her hand to say goodbye as he jogged away. His steel blade made a distinctive sound as it hit the pavement in syncopation with his other foot. She sighed. The man was dreamy.

Lily watched him for a moment and then headed back to Alec's house where she and the other Flowers were living. Life here was so pleasant. Her childhood had been tough with an absentee father and an alcoholic mother who was distant, even cruel, a lot of the time. She'd been forced to be strong and self-sufficient even when she had the care of her sister, ten years younger and the daughter of a different father. A teacher had given her some guidance, but pride had kept her from asking for more help, which is why as an adult she'd sometimes found it difficult to maintain relationships. Now, at forty-two, she was hoping to find the love she'd missed so much in her life. Alec had been the one to introduce her to a calm, secure, loving lifestyle. She longed to have that again.

She sighed and picked up speed. Enough of fairy tales about finding a prince. It was time to get real.

Back at the house, Lily freshened up and then went to talk to Alec. At one time, she'd hoped he'd ask her to marry him. But Alec had been honest when they started dating, telling her marriage was not part of it. She should've known he'd stay true to his word. He was that kind of man. But their relationship was a gift. He'd taught her to open her heart to love, to find respite from the chaos that had always surrounded her. Prior to that, she'd been cautious about letting a man into her life. God knew, she didn't have the example of a wise woman to follow. She'd never known her own father, and the men her mother had hung out with were unreliable creeps she'd never accept.

As she walked toward Alec's wing of the house, sadness filled her at the thought of him dying. She considered it a real honor that he'd trusted her, along with Rose and Willow, to help him get his hotel safely sold before he died. The Desert Flowers act was like that television show with the man and his three angels, *Charley's Angels,* on a mission to save the inn. Lily loved being part of it.

At the entrance to his private space, Lily knocked gently at the door and cracked it open.

"Alec?"

"Here," came a voice weakened by the cancer that was slowly stealing his life.

Lily stepped into the living area to find him reclining on a lounge chair and smiling up at her. "Lily, my dear. How are you?"

Normally a large, rangy man with thick gray hair and startling blue eyes, a Sam Elliott look-alike, Alec's thin body and weakened state tore at Lily's insides.

She pulled a chair up next to his and took hold of his hand. "I've been wanting to talk to you. I'm left doing almost nothing while meetings have been put aside. Rose and Willow are very busy, but not me. I'm used to doing my share of work and am thinking of taking Bennett Williams' offer for me to come work for him on a part-time basis. With my upcoming move here, it might be wise to have work outside of the project for you. How would you feel about that?

Alec's blue-eyed gazed rested on her. "I think if it suits you, it's something you should do. Believe me, Bennett wouldn't ask you to work for him if he wasn't serious about it. He told me he was very impressed with you. And you couldn't find a nicer guy to work with. Not only is he my lawyer, he's a friend. He now has a young partner working with him. Another great guy."

"The transition period you hired us for is three months. But you know I'd be happy to stay for as long as you wish and do anything I can to help you."

"Yes, I know. Three months seemed like such a long time. Now, I'm trying to make it through these last two months before the sale goes through," said Alec. "Any day beyond that is an unexpected gift."

Tears filled Lily's eyes. "I wish this hadn't happened to you."

His lips curved into a crooked smile. "So, do I. But after I get through all this, I'll be with Conchita and the baby. At least, I hope I will."

Lily nodded. It was a well-known story that Alec's wife and baby had died in a house fire for which he'd always blamed himself. That's one reason he had vowed never to marry again. Some people thought it was twisted thinking, but Lily understood his devotion to them. He'd shown her what love could mean, and though she'd asked for and wanted much more from him, she knew deep down it wasn't ever going to happen. After he ended their relationship, he found her a job with a business associate in Phoenix and helped her move on with her life. But he could never erase the love and gratitude she felt for him.

Juanita appeared. "Hi, Lily. Time for your medicine, Alec."

Lily got to her feet and kissed Alec on the cheek. "Have a nice day. I hope to see you tonight." She moved the chair back into place. "See you later. 'Bye, Juanita."

Juanita gave her a smile and turned back to Alec. Juanita Sanchez was a cousin of Alec's wife, Conchita. She and her husband, Pedro, were Willow's parents and had worked for Alec for years. They were lovely people. Juanita and Pedro were exactly the kind of people Lily wished she'd had as parents.

Back in her room, Lily looked at her reflection in the mirror. She was of medium height with curves in all the right places—curves she'd once done her best to hide. Her shoulder-length, blonde hair was highlighted by both her hairdresser and the desert sun. Freckles, few enough to be of interest, were sprinkled across her nose. She'd always thought she was drab. But Willow and Rose had helped her change—not only with her wardrobe but in believing in her self-worth.

Taking a deep breath, Lily called Bennett Williams' office and asked to speak to him. Her fingers were cold with nerves, and she almost dropped her phone. She was uncomfortable putting herself out there.

"Well, hello," said Bennett after her call went through. "I'm glad to hear from you. I hope you're calling about a job because I've just learned that one of the women in the office is going on maternity leave."

Lily's breath left her in a puff of surprise. Things didn't usually come that easily to her. "As a matter of fact, that's what I wanted to talk to you about. I've decided to stay in Palm Desert following my work for Alec and will need a job. May I make an appointment to meet with you?"

"Absolutely. Send me your resumé, and I'll have my assistant schedule a time for you to come into the office." He paused. "I'm glad you called Lily. As I mentioned to you earlier, I'm impressed with your work."

"Thank you." Lily ended the call and sat down on her bed, struggling to accept what had just happened. The arrangements had fallen into place so quickly it almost seemed as if it had been preordained. That, or maybe her luck had changed. Either way, she was going to update her resumé and send it along as soon as possible.

Two days later, Lily dressed carefully for her interview with Bennett and his staff. In New York, the law firm for whom she worked had insisted on conservative clothes. Here in the desert, Lily agreed with Rose and Willow that brighter colors were acceptable.

Her black skirt, white-on-white print blouse, and hibiscus-colored soft jacket looked both professional and light-hearted. Studying herself in the mirror, Lily smiled at the changes living here had made to her appearance. The tan on her skin and the lack of stress lines on her face made her appear younger than her age and healthier than she'd ever been.

When Lily walked out to the kitchen to face the inspection Willow and Rose were sure to give her, she felt confident.

"Wow! Look at you!" said Willow, smiling at her.

"You look terrific," Rose immediately agreed. "Good luck with the interview."

Lily smiled. "Thanks. For once, I'm not a nervous wreck. Bennett made it seem as if it were a mere formality. I'm hoping so, anyway."

"He'd be lucky to have you on his staff. How many texts and calls have you received from your old job in New York?" said Rose.

Lily laughed and shook her head. "Too many. They keep promising to raise my salary if I come back. They increase the amount each time they call, but I finally told them I'm staying here no matter what they offer me."

"I'm so glad you are," said Willow. "Sarah is too."

Lily filled with pleasure. While Rose was spending time with Hank Bowers, the consultant the Blaise Group had hired and who was now her fiancé, she, Willow, and Sarah Jensen spent time in the evening together whenever they were all free. Sarah, a part-time assistant manager at the inn, was living at home with her parents and two-year-old son while her husband was serving in the military in Afghanistan. They'd quickly become friends. With this kind of support, Lily felt comfortable about her decision to move here. She hadn't yet chosen a place to live because she needed to sell her condo first. Her sister, Monica, who lived nearby her had promised to make sure the condo was ready for showings. So far, no luck, but Lily felt uncharacteristically optimistic.

Driving through the town, Lily bypassed the usual tourist places on Route 111, turned onto Cook Street and easily found the law office of Williams and Kincaid. She parked the car and entered the modern building trying to stem the nervousness that threatened to break through her shell of calmness.

She took the elevator to the third floor and exited into an attractive reception area. A young man smiled at her from behind a long desk.

"Good morning. May I help you?" he asked.

"I'm here to see Bennett Williams," she answered politely. "Lily Weaver."

He smiled. "Of course. I'll let Mr. Williams know you're here. May I get you something to drink? Water? Coffee?"

"Water would be nice," said Lily. "The weather has turned hot."

"It's going to stay that way for a few days," said the receptionist whose nameplate said *Jonathan Waite*. He left and returned with a small, chilled bottle of water, which he handed to her.

Right then, Bennett appeared in the reception area, filling the room with his presence and his booming, jovial voice. "Ah, Lily. I'm so glad to see you. Come on back to my office. We'll talk there."

Lily followed him down a hallway to a corner office whose

windows looked out at a landscaped garden below. The fronds of nearby palm trees danced in the playful breeze. But it was the beautiful fountain sitting in a small pond that caught her attention. The free-form shape, like high desert boulders that had tumbled together, was the kind of thing she'd been researching for the Blaise Group's two hotels in Arizona—the hotels they hoped to bring into the Corona Collection of Fine Hotels.

"Something peaceful about water flowing, especially in a desert setting," said Bennett standing beside her.

"Yes. Very refreshing."

"Have a seat," said Bennett. "I'll chat with you, then I'll ask my partner to join us. Okay with you?"

"Sure," Lily said. Bennett, with his easy-going manner and lack of airs made her feel comfortable. She knew enough from being in a couple of meetings with him, though, to understand he was a stickler for detail, much like her old boss.

"As you probably are already aware, our firm deals with trusts and estates, probate, and civil litigation. We've been in business here for close to forty years. Our company is hands-on, which is why we maintain a small staff of ten. It's a close-knit group."

"I like the sound of that," said Lily. "Some law firms get so big you lose some of that close feeling."

Bennett looked over her resumé. "You've got an impressive background. I took the liberty of going ahead and getting a reference from the law firm you worked with in New York." He smiled. "They'd do anything to get you back."

"I know," said Lily. "But I've decided to stay here. I've put my condo in New York up for sale."

"Great." Bennett discussed what he was looking for, how he saw someone like her fitting into the office, quizzed her on strengths and weaknesses, and asked the normal new-hire questions.

Finally, he leaned back. "I'm more than satisfied. Let me call my partner and have him come meet you. His name is Craig Kincaid."

Lily nodded politely and waited while Bennett called him on the intercom. A low voice said, "Be right there, Ben."

Lily waited quietly for him to appear, imagining him as much of a cowboy as Bennett, whose brown cowboy boots were worn with age and activity. They and the turquoise and silver bolo tie around Bennett's neck against his crisp white shirt gave him an undeniable Southwestern flair.

A knock at the door signaled Craig's arrival. Lily turned to see a young, broad-shouldered man with caramel colored-hair studying her with a green-eyed gaze that made her catch her breath. Struggling to maintain her composure, Lily thought he was one of the most handsome young men she'd ever seen.

He came right over to her and shook her hand. "Pleased to meet you, Lily. I've heard a lot about you and have already reviewed your resumé."

The three of them sat together and talked for a while. Craig asked some of the same questions Bennett had, but she cheerfully answered them.

Finally, Craig rose and turned to her. "I'm satisfied by everything I've heard. I think you're going to make a nice addition to our staff, Lily."

She shook herself mentally. He looked like one of the heroes on the cover of an historical novel, one that showed a man in a kilt. That thought brought a flush of heat to her cheeks.

"Thank you," she finally managed to say. "I'm looking forward to it."

"You may occasionally be asked to help me out, but I have an assistant who's quite capable of taking care of me."

Bennett chuckled. "Loretta Morales is the boss of not only Craig, but the entire office. In fact, I thought you and Loretta should have a chance to talk. Do you mind?"

"Not at all," said Lily.

"Why don't I show you the way? Her office is next to mine." Craig stood and waited while Lily got to her feet.

"Thanks," said Bennett. "After you're through with Loretta, you and I will go to lunch and make final arrangements."

"That sounds nice," said Lily, hoping Bennett hadn't noticed her reaction to Craig.

Leaving the office, she walked beside Craig down a hallway, studying his easy gait from the corner of her eye.

With her short, comfy body and gray hair pulled back into a bun at the back of her head, Loretta was the image of an old-fashioned grandmother. Her dark eyes sparkled as she got to her feet. Names were exchanged, and Loretta greeted Lily with a quick, firm handshake.

"This woman is the one I can't live without," said Craig, with a teasing smile. "I'd ask her to marry me, but she's already taken."

Loretta's laugh rose from her belly. "No woman would ever put up with your shenanigans. Not me, for sure." Still smiling, she turned to Lily. "This young man has to learn to make up his mind. Every woman in the area is after him, but he still hasn't settled down."

Craig's fair-skinned cheeks turned pink, but he gamely nodded. "I'll know when the right one comes along." He winked at Lily. "Loretta treats me like a son."

Loretta's expression turned serious. "Craig's mother and I were best friends. She died way too young. But I'm here to take over for her."

His face softened with affection. "Yeah, Mom would be pleased. I'll leave you two alone to talk. Then Ben is going to take Lily to lunch."

"Okay," said Loretta. "Sounds like a plan."

As Craig walked into his office, Loretta waved Lily to a chair in front of her desk. "Have a seat, and let's get to know one another a bit. Bennett already had me look over your resumé, but I like to meet people face-to-face, see what they're all about."

"I agree," said Lily. "So far, I like what I see here. How long have you been working in the office?"

"For over twenty years. Ben, Alec Thurston, my husband, Ricardo, and Craig's dad, Ken, play golf together. They became friends back when Bennett was growing his business and my husband was a professional golfer. When Ben knew I was looking for work, he suggested I give his office a try. I've been here ever since. The time's coming, though, when I'll want to retire." She leaned forward. "Tell me a bit about yourself. I hear you're helping Alec out. How's that going?"

"It's a sad time for me. Alec is a friend. I hate the thought of him dying. We dated for a couple of years. I moved to Arizona and then to New York to help out my sister who has a precious three-year-old daughter whom I adore."

"Ah, so you like children?" Loretta said, smiling.

"Very much. I'd still like to try for a child of my own," Lily said, then wondered why on earth she'd say something like this on a job interview. It was just that Loretta made her feel so comfortable.

"I've got three boys, all decent men," said Loretta with obvious pride. "I count Craig as one of them. Ben tells me you've decided to relocate here. May I ask why?"

Lily hesitated, not knowing if this was some sort of trick question. "In the time I've been here, I've been happier than I've been in years. I've learned to enjoy being outdoors, have already made great friends, and I want a better lifestyle." She cleared her throat and recalled the words she'd rehearsed with Rose. "I'm very good at my job and can work anywhere. I choose to do it here."

Loretta nodded. "Smart answer." She got to her feet. "I'm sure we're going to get along just fine. I mostly work for Craig, and you'll be on Ben's team, but it's important for all of us to be able to work together. Welcome to the group."

"Thank you so much," said Lily, feeling as if she'd just joined some kind of exclusive club.

About the Author

A *USA Today* **Best Selling Author**, Judith Keim, is a hybrid author who both has a publisher and self-publishes, Ms. Keim writes heart-warming novels about women who face unexpected challenges, meet them with strength, and find love and happiness along the way. Her best-selling books are based, in part, on many of the places she's lived or visited and on the interesting people she's met, creating believable characters and realistic settings her many loyal readers love. Ms. Keim loves to hear from her readers and appreciates their enthusiasm for her stories.

Ms. Keim enjoyed her childhood and young-adult years in Elmira, New York, and now makes her home in Boise, Idaho, with her husband and their two dachshunds, Winston and Wally, and other members of her family.

While growing up, she was drawn to the idea of writing stories from a young age. Books were always present, being read, ready to go back to the library, or about to be discovered. All in her family shared information from the books in general conversation, giving them a wealth of knowledge and vivid imaginations.

"I hope you've enjoyed this book. If you have, please help other readers discover it by leaving a review on Amazon, Bookbub, Goodreads or the site of your choice. And please check out my other books:

The Hartwell Women Series
The Beach House Hotel Series
The Fat Fridays Group
The Salty Key Inn Series
Seashell Cottage Books
The Chandler Hill Inn Series
The Desert Sage Inn Series
Soul Sisters at Cedar Mountain Lodge
The Sanderling Cove Inn Series
The Lilac Lake Inn Series

"ALL THE BOOKS ARE NOW AVAILABLE IN AUDIO on Audible, iTunes, Findaway, Kobo and Google Play! So fun to have these characters come alive!"

Ms. Keim can be reached at **www.judithkeim.com**

And to like her author page on Facebook and keep up with the news, go to: **https://bit.ly/3acs5Qc**

To receive notices about new books, follow her on Book Bub: **http://bit.ly/2pZBDXq**

And here's a link to where you can sign up for her periodic newsletter! **http://bit.ly/2OQsb7s**

She is also on Twitter @judithkeim, LinkedIn, and Goodreads. Come say hello!

Acknowledgments

In addition to my usual thanks to Peter and Lynn, two of my editors, I wish to extend a very special thank you to my friends in the private group of Women, Words, Wisdom for their continuing support – Ev Bishop, Kelly Coates Gilbert, Tammy L. Grace, Violet Howe, and Tess Thompson. You're the best!

And, as always, I thank my readers for your continued support and encouragement.

Made in United States
North Haven, CT
16 April 2023

35521840R00178